C000263632

WITHOUT HER CONSENT

MCGARVEY BLACK

Copyright © 2020 McGarvey Black

The right of McGarvey Black to be identified as the Author of the Work has been asserted by her in accordance to the Copyright, Designs and Patents Act 1988.

First published in 2020 by Bloodhound Books.

Apart from any use permitted under UK copyright law, this publication may only be reproduced, stored, or transmitted, in any form, or by any means, with prior permission in

writing of the publisher or, in the case of reprographic production, in accordance with the terms of licences issued by the Copyright Licensing Agency.

All characters in this publication are fictitious and any resemblance to real persons, living or dead, is purely coincidental.

www.bloodhoundbooks.com

ALSO BY MCGARVEY BLACK

I Never Left

The First Husband

Without Her Consent is dedicated to my sister, Diane McGarvey, and my mother-in-law, Regina Turkington—always supportive, kind and enthusiastic from the first stroke of my pen.

A lie keeps growing and growing until it's as clear as the nose on your face.

The Blue Fairy, Pinocchio

1

A family of four in a green mini van motored up the Florida Turnpike headed towards Orlando, their final destination —Disney World. In the backseat, two little girls sang songs from *The Little Mermaid* unaware they would never make it to the gates of the Magic Kingdom.

'When are we going to get there?' asked ten-year-old Eliza Stern.

'We've been driving forever,' said her identical twin sister, Emily.

'Thirty minutes,' said their father, laughing at their excited impatience. He and his wife had surprised their daughters with a trip to Disney to celebrate the girls' tenth birthdays.

'There's the sign for Disney,' their mother said as they passed a billboard on the side of the road. 'We're almost there.'

Ahead something moved oddly out of place. Their father squinted at the oncoming traffic and cocked his head as a single flickering light raced closer and grew larger. He had just enough time to comprehend that the errant light was a car with one broken headlight that had jumped the divider. Careening at a high speed directly towards the Stern's mini van, the father tried to swerve out of the torpedoing car's path but it came at them too fast. With one last useless attempt to protect his wife, he threw his right arm up in front of her.

When the out of control car slammed into the Stern's van there was a thunderous crash followed by the sound of shattering glass and a car horn that refused to stop screaming.

Spring 2014 (Eleven Years Later)

Silently climbing the stairs to the third floor of a long-term care medical facility, the intruder's latex-gloved hands pulled open the heavy fire door, providing a view into a long hallway. The corridor was empty—just as planned. Walking softly ten feet down the hall and turning to the left, the intruder entered a dimly lit hospital room. A young woman lay in the bed and appeared to be sleeping. If she made a sound, she would be muffled with a pillow to keep her quiet but not to hurt her. It would be so easy. No one was on the floor. Nobody would hear her, even if she did make a fuss.

With the bedroom door closed, the blankets covering the sleeping woman were carefully removed. Taking a few deep breaths, the intruder slowly peeled back the remaining sheet but the woman didn't stir or acknowledge it in any way. Gently, her hospital gown was lifted and her legs methodically spread apart. She wasn't wearing panties—one less step. Carefully, the unwanted penetration began. When the woman moaned, a bed pillow was placed over her face to quell the noise. The unholy act didn't take long and soon everything was back in its proper place. No one would ever know. It had gone perfectly.

2

EIGHT MONTHS LATER

It had been a busy week for forty-four-year-old Angela Crawford, MD, administrator of Oceanside Manor, an extended-care facility in Oceanside, Florida. At her desk for hours, Angela was painstakingly going over the following year's budget when her phone rang.

'Dr. Crawford, it's Lourdes on 3 West,' said the frantic woman's voice on the phone. 'We have an emergency and there's no doctor on the floor. I need a doctor now. Eliza Stern is in labor!'

'What?' shouted Angela. 'That's impossible. Are you sure you...?'

'I know what labor looks like,' interrupted the seasoned nurse. 'You've got to come. She's crowning and moaning. We need you, now.'

Angela, a trained OB-GYN, was already on her feet. 'I'm on my way,' she replied as she slammed the phone down and sprinted out of her office in her heels. Running down the institutional yellow hallways with white speckled terrazzo floors popular in Florida in the mid-twentieth century when the building was built, Angela dodged gurneys and food carts while sidestepping visitors and staff. Passing a nurses' station filled with stuffed animals, balloons and bowls of candy, she barked orders at the attendant without stopping.

'Find Dr. Horowitz. Send him down to 3 West. STAT!'

With no time to wait for the perennially slow elevators that should have been replaced ten years before, Angela opted for the stairs, taking two at a time. As she raced up a flight in the east wing, she was vaguely aware her heart was pounding and she couldn't feel her feet beneath her, a strange sensation. Arriving on the third-floor landing, she pulled open the heavy metal door and stepped into the hall. Taking a moment to get her bearings, she picked up her pace and jogged towards the 3 West wing.

When she arrived at the nurses' station slightly out of breath, she shouted to the attendant.

'Which room is Eliza Stern in?'

The startled attendant pointed to her right. '312.'

Still breathing hard, Angela bolted down the corridor to a doorway where a small crowd had gathered. Two nurses and an aide were already inside with the patient.

'Thank God you're here, Dr. Crawford. I didn't know what else to do. Everything's happening so fast,' said Nurse Lourdes Castro, wringing her hands.

'Let me get in there,' said Angela, stepping past the other women. 'Someone get me a gown and gloves.' A forty-something male floor nurse ran off as Angela carefully examined the physically distressed woman in the bed.

'It looks like this baby is coming within the next few minutes,' said Angela, shaking her head. The woman in the bed softly moaned again.

'She can feel this. Eliza's in pain,' said Jenny O'Hearn, a young, blond floor nurse. 'It was that same sound that made me come in here and check on her. Can we give her something?'

'Let me think a minute,' said Angela, combing her fingers through her long loose hair to get it out of her face. 'I don't want to give her anything yet. It might complicate things and I don't know exactly what I'm dealing with.' Frustrated, she looked around. 'Where is my gown?' she shouted out to no one in particular.

As if on cue, the breathless male nurse appeared in the doorway with a pair of gloves and a light blue gown. In a few swift moves, Angela kicked off her red high heels sending them scattering across the room in a clatter. She pulled her thick shoulder-length chestnut-colored hair into a ponytail with the stretchy band she had on her wrist for just this type of occasion. Within seconds, the gown and gloves were on and Angela turned her attention back to her patient.

'How the hell did this happen?' Angela muttered as she checked the pregnant woman's pulse. 'Can someone please explain this to me?'

'I have no idea, doctor,' said Nurse Castro. 'Jenny found her.'

Twenty-eight-year-old Jenny O'Hearn stepped forward. 'I was going on my break to the supply room and heard a noise coming from Eliza's room,' Jenny said. 'This part of the hospital is usually so quiet. It was strange to hear that kind of sound coming from one of our patient's rooms. I walked in and saw Eliza was in distress. I checked her pulse and it was elevated so I decided to get a better look at her. When I pulled back her covers, there was a big wet spot on the sheets beneath her. At first, I thought she'd wet the bed but I remembered that would be impossible because Eliza's got a catheter. So, I checked the catheter to see if it was leaking but everything was fine. I examined her from head to toe until I figured out what it was. Her water had broken.'

Eliza made another low moan.

3

DAY 1

Just as she had been medically trained to do, Angela quickly assessed the condition of her patient. 'This baby is coming right now. I need towels,' she shouted as Eliza's soft distress sounds continued.

'Come on, Eliza, you can do this,' said Angela, focused only on her patient, oblivious to the small crowd growing inside and outside of the hospital room.

'Doesn't she have to push?' said an attendant. 'How can she push if she's unconscious?'

'She's doing just fine,' said Angela calmly, not taking her eyes off the woman in the bed. 'The human body is an amazing machine. It knows what to do even when we don't. Here we go, the head is coming out!'

Fifty-eight-year-old Lourdes Castro tucked a few loose strands of her salt and pepper hair behind her ears and made the sign of the cross while Angela skillfully tended to her patient and the baby that was about to enter the world. 'The head is almost out. Once it's completely clear, I'll help her along,' said Angela confidently. Moments later, the baby's head was free and with a little manipulation, Angela cleared the shoulders and seconds after that, the tiny legs slipped easily out. Within fifteen seconds the sound of a crying baby was heard on the third floor, something that had never happened before. Everyone cheered as Angela looked down at the infant in her arms covered in blood and vernix. It had been a long time since she had done a delivery and she had almost forgotten how incredible it felt to bring a life into the world. This baby, in particular, was a miracle.

'It's a boy,' whispered Jenny O'Hearn, tears pooling in her blue eyes.

'What a beautiful baby,' Angela said, smiling and showing the child to the others in the room. 'No matter what the circumstances, life is life and it's always beautiful. Welcome, little one.'

'He's a perfect little boy,' said Nurse Castro, smiling and reaching for the baby. 'Let me have him, doctor, so I can clean him up and weigh him.'

Angela handed the newborn infant to the nurse as a growing audience gathered around the hospital room foreshadowing the firestorm that was coming.

'Take care of that baby,' Angela called out as Nurse Castro left the room with the child. 'Don't let him out of your sight.'

'You did good, Eliza,' whispered Jenny as she leaned over the always sleeping new mother and rubbed the woman's arm. 'I don't know how it happened, but you've got yourself an amazing little boy.'

'This is not a happy occasion, nurse,' said Angela, bristling as she removed her gloves. 'This is going to be a legal and PR nightmare. We need to figure out how this happened and who did this.'

'Are you going to call the police?' asked Jenny.

'Of course,' said Angela. 'Who would do such a thing?'

'Do you want me to make the call?' said Jenny.

'I'll do it. I have to inform the board of directors before I do anything,' said Angela. 'Eliza has no family that I'm aware of so there's no one else we need to notify. From a medical perspective, it appears that mother and baby are fine. Before Oceanside Manor is swarming with police, I have to talk to our lawyers and reach out to the other patients' families so they hear about it directly from us and not the newspapers.'

Nurse Castro returned a moment later carrying the still crying baby now swathed in a white blanket. Angela reached her arms out and Lourdes placed the baby into them.

'He's small — five pounds eight ounces, but seems healthy enough,' said Lourdes, smiling. 'He sure makes a lot of noise. That's a good sign. Means he's strong.'

Angela looked down at one of the baby's tiny hands that had slipped out of the blanket papoose. As the baby squirmed and made funny faces, Angela touched and stroked the fine coating of light red fuzz that covered the child's head. *He's perfect*, she thought, as she looked down at the new life in her arms. When she glanced up, the room full of people was staring at her, waiting for her next direction. Angela sat up straight.

'Call the hospital next door. Ring pediatrics. Tell them it's highly confidential and that we need a doctor over here immediately,' said Angela, barking out orders. 'I want nurses minding this baby 24/7. Is that clear? He is never to be left alone, ever. Not for one second. If you need to use the bathroom, you get someone to cover for you. If he so much as sneezes, I want to know about it. And nobody, and I mean nobody, breathes a word about this to anyone until I say so. Is that clear? Not even your families.'

Jenny O'Hearn's brow raised.

'No one, Nurse O'Hearn,' said Angela, observing Jenny's surprised expression. 'Not your mother, not your father, not your boyfriend. Do you understand?'

Jenny, Lourdes and several nurses and aides all nodded. 'I'm deadly serious. If one word about this gets out before I can manage it properly, we're all screwed. If anything leaks, I'll know it's come from one of you and you will be fired immediately.'

'I'm sure everyone understands the sensitivity of this situation,' said Lourdes. 'No one will say anything until they've been given the green light. I'll make sure of it.'

Angela let out a sigh of relief and handed the newborn to one of the aides. 'Lourdes, you're in charge down here. Get Eliza cleaned up and set up a crib in her room for the baby. I want them kept together.'

'Absolutely, Dr. Crawford,' said Nurse Castro. 'Shouldn't we send the baby over to neonatal at the hospital?'

'Not yet. That's why I asked for a pediatrician to come here and why I want 24/7 nurses with this baby,' said Angela. 'We'll send him over if the pediatrician thinks we need to, but not until I square things with the board. We can't afford any publicity. If we send a newborn over to Oceanside Medical now, we'll lose control of the situation.'

The older nurse nodded.

'Once everything is taken care of here in the room,' said Angela to the two nurses, 'I want to see you both in my office.'

Angela removed her gown, put her shoes on and walked over to the aide holding the newborn and took one last look. 'Let me hold him for one minute,' said Angela, smiling at the baby while the aide carefully passed the child to her.

'You're an amazing little boy, aren't you,' Angela said cooing directly to the baby. 'I've delivered my share of kids. That makes me an expert when it comes to knowing a cute baby when I see one.' She took a long last look at the baby in her arms, and reluctantly passed him back to the waiting aide.

'Lourdes, thirty minutes, in my office,' said Angela as she left the room and headed back downstairs to the administrative floor. So many thoughts and questions rattled around in her head that she couldn't think straight. The only thing she knew for sure was that her life was about to become a living hell.

Being an administrator was supposed to bring balance to my life. No middle of the night phone calls, strictly nine to five. When the board hears about this, they're going to crucify me. She shook her head in an attempt to block all the negative thoughts but it didn't work.

Her assistant, Vera, looked up from her computer when she heard the familiar sound of Angela's heels clicking on the tiled floor as she walked down the hall. 'Everything okay, Angela?' said the grandmother of three, noticing the peculiar expression on Angela's usually composed face.

'No, everything is not okay.'

'Can I help you with anything?'

Angela signaled for Vera to follow her into her office. Once inside, Angela closed the door. 'You're going to find out, anyway,' Angela said. 'But, you've got to commit to complete secrecy on this. Do you understand?'

Vera's eyes grew round as she nodded.

'One of our patients on 3 West just delivered a baby boy.'

'3 West?' Vera gasped. 'But half the people in that wing are on respirators, some with feeding tubes. Everyone on that floor is in a coma.'

'That's correct,' said Angela with a sigh.

'But, then how…'

'Exactly.'

'Oh, my God,' said Vera, placing her hands on her newly flushed cheeks. 'What do you think happened?'

'I-I don't know,' said Angela, rubbing her temples. 'I have such a headache right now, I can't think straight.'

'Do you think someone actually…?'

'I don't know what to think,' snapped Angela. 'This situation is now our singular priority, do you understand? Move everything else off my calendar. Cancel my appointments for the next week. All hell's about to break loose and it's going to get ugly.'

Thirty minutes later, Jenny O'Hearn and Lourdes Castro were seated in Angela's office.

'Start from the beginning,' said Angela.

Jenny took a deep breath. 'Eliza is checked three times a day,' she said.

'Set times?' asked Angela.

'Yes. She's checked in the morning on first rounds and in the evening between seven and nine,' said Jenny. 'She's also usually seen at a random time between eleven and three when she's rolled and changed to prevent bedsores. During that session she might also be washed, it depends on the day.'

'What happens on the morning and evening visits?'

'We check the feeding tubes, vitals, temperature, equipment,' said Jenny. 'We make sure everything is running properly.'

'How is it that nobody noticed the woman was pregnant?' demanded Angela glaring at Lourdes, the floor supervisor.

'We don't examine her abdomen,' said Lourdes. 'I mean, I'd only look at it if there was some kind of a problem. The machines record all her numbers automatically. Aides are the ones who change her and move her around so we don't have any infections.'

'None of the aides noticed she was nine months pregnant?'

'We don't know if she was nine months pregnant,' interrupted Lourdes.

'I've delivered a lot of babies. That baby was close to full term,' said Angela impatiently. 'How is it possible that no one saw any of this?'

'She was on her back, and probably carrying small because of her limited calorie intake. I never looked under her blankets,' said Jenny.

'Maybe you should have,' hissed Angela.

Tears welled up in Jenny's eyes.

'I'm sorry, I didn't mean to snap at you,' said Angela softening. 'This has all been extremely stressful.'

'I understand,' said Jenny. 'It's a terrible situation.'

While tapping her dark pink nails on the desk, Angela grilled the two nurses for over thirty minutes. Neither woman could offer any further information that could explain how Eliza Stern got pregnant or how it had gone undetected for so long.

Minutes after the women left her office, a young pediatrician from their sister hospital next door, Oceanside Medical Center, knocked on Angela's door.

'Did you examine the baby?' Angela asked the young male doctor.

'Yes.'

'And?'

'He seems just fine,' said the pediatrician with a thick Boston accent. 'Everything checks out. High APGAR score. Breathing normal, color normal. Weight, a little small but acceptable. I'd say he's somewhere between thirty-four to thirty-six weeks, give or take. He was sleeping quietly in the arms of one of your nurses when I got there.'

'That's the first good news I've heard today,' said Angela with an audible sigh of relief. 'At least the baby's healthy, that's the most important thing, isn't it?'

'You want to tell me what's going on, Dr. Crawford? Why is there a baby here?' asked the pediatrician.

Angela rolled her eyes, as she filled the pediatrician in on what had happened.

'Oh boy,' said the pediatrician, shaking his head as he walked to the door. 'You've got yourself one wicked situation.'

After he left, Angela had to make the call she had been dreading since the moment she first saw Eliza Stern starting to crown. She had been putting it off, but she had to call the hospital board. About to punch the board president's number into her phone, she changed her mind and decided to do a video call with her boss, Frank Farwell. Dr. Farwell was the actual facility administrator of Oceanside Manor and Angela was filling for him while he was on a year-plus-long sabbatical in Ecuador. She and Frank were not particularly close and he had a nasty habit of talking down to her. Still, he usually had a cool head during a crisis and this was, in her estimation, the mother of all crises. Frank had been running Oceanside Manor for twenty years and Angela desperately needed his advice before she dealt with the all-male hospital board.

4

————

Thousands of miles away in Guayaquil, Ecuador, Frank Farwell's thinning red hair barely covered his middle-aged scalp. He had convinced himself that his follicular magic tricks hid the fact that he was balding. Every morning he made a concerted effort to carefully comb each strand into place, securing them with industrial-strength hairspray. He thought it worked well and no one noticed. They did.

Sitting in his small bare-bones office outfitted with metal furniture in the back corner of one of the largest and most rundown hospitals in the sprawling city, he opened up a brown paper packet that contained his lunch and licked his lips with anticipation. His time in South America, as part of a medical intelligence exchange program had been eye-opening and grati-fying, and was nearly over. His team of American and British doctors and nurses had introduced hospital administration best practices to some of the poorest facilities in South America. His group had made real progress in updating facilities, improving systems and bringing them into the new millennium. The program would ultimately save many lives.

He had just taken a second bite of shawarma, spiced chicken

served in a pita, a Middle Eastern street food popular in Ecuador, when a video call came through on his laptop. Angela Crawford's image popped up on the screen, and made him audibly groan before he accepted it. Communication from Angela was usually bad news. So far, all the calls he had received from her since he left were one annoyance after another. He continued to eat his chicken shawarma while his computer call buzzed until guilt won out and he accepted her call.

'Angela, what a pleasant surprise.' Farwell said, wiping a blob of creamy red sauce from the corner of his mouth. 'You don't mind if I eat my lunch while we chat, do you?'

Dispensing with any niceties, Angela got right to the point and laid out the events that had taken place that day.

'Is this some kind of a joke?' said Frank half-laughing after Angela finished her sordid tale. He glanced around his office for hidden cameras. 'You're punking me from three thousand miles away, right? Where's the camera crew?'

'This isn't a joke, Frank,' said Angela, pursing her lips. 'An hour ago, on 3 West, I delivered Eliza Stern's baby. It was a boy, in case you're interested.'

Frank Farwell, usually never at a loss for words, was uncharacteristically silent. Mouth open, eyes wide, he stared in disbelief at Angela's image on the screen.

'Frank? Are you listening to me?'

The staccato sound of Angela's voice drew him back into the moment. 'Umm...What's the condition of the baby and the mother?' he asked, suddenly all business.

'They're both fine,' said Angela. 'Eliza is resting comfortably, no post-partum problems and the baby, though a little on the small side, is extremely healthy. I had one of the pediatricians from Oceanside Medical examine him. Everything checked out. I've assigned nurses in the room 24/7 to look after both mother and baby.'

'How could something like this happen?' said Frank, getting animated, his voice growing louder.

'I don't know, Frank. If I did, I wouldn't be calling you in South America. I need your help, not your condemnation.'

'I can tell you one thing, you're about to have a massive PR holocaust.'

Angela stared at Frank for several seconds. *Are you going to help me or not, you fat windbag?*

'First thing you need to do is call the hospital board. Get a hold of Bob Beckmann,' said Frank, blowing out a breath of air. 'As the Oceanside Manor board president, he's got a right to know what's going on and needs to be brought into the loop immediately. He's not going to be happy, I can tell you that.'

'Tell me something I don't already know. Beckmann is a misogynistic lunatic,' said Angela. 'He's going to unleash all his vitriol on me.'

'Put on your big girl pants, Angie. You wanted my job so badly. This is what comes with the territory,' said Frank starting to lecture.

Angela looked into his eyes and thought she detected he was gloating. It pissed her off, but she bit her tongue.

'Once the board's been briefed,' Frank continued, 'you'll need to interview every single staff member to get to the bottom of this situation. Scratch what I just said, you have to talk to *anyone* who's set foot in the goddamn building in the past nine or ten months. Also, you'd better check all the other female patients to make sure no one else is pregnant.'

'Oh my God,' gasped Angela, 'I didn't even think of that. You don't think there are others?'

Satisfied that he was still the head honcho running the show, Frank stuffed the remainder of his shawarma in his mouth and chewed. A thin rivulet of creamy red sauce trickled down his chin and he reached up with a napkin and wiped it away.

'You think there could be more women?' asked Angela again. 'Frank, you've got to come back, now.'

'No way,' he said with his mouth full of chicken. 'Why would I want to step into this mess and slime my reputation? Not a chance. Besides, I'm committed here for a few more months. I can't just pick up and leave. We're in the middle of a big hospital overhaul and I'm the project director.'

Angela sighed loudly.

'You can handle this, Angela. You've always been a smart cookie. And frankly, this happened on your watch, not mine. I'm not dipping my toes into this crap. It's your debacle, you clean it up.'

'Eliza Stern's pregnancy could have occurred before you left,' said Angela bitterly. 'Technically, Frank, this could have happened during *your* watch. Based on the size of the baby, Eliza could have been impregnated right around the time you were leaving.'

'You wanted to be top dog, Angela, now you have to deal with what comes with it. What's that saying? "Our greatest glory is not in never falling but rising up every time we fall."'

'I don't need greeting card philosophy right now. I need help. This isn't a normal situation and you know that.'

'That's an understatement. It's a bloody disaster,' said Frank. 'Let's call it, what it is. Rape. Somebody raped that young woman and you need to find out who, how, and when it happened. The why is sadly obvious. There are a lot of sick people in this world, Angela, and apparently one of them was at our facility and got his jollies off. Bottom line—you've had a massive security breach at Oceanside Manor and it's going to reflect badly on our parent hospital, Oceanside Medical. I don't need to tell you that the board will not be pleased. Buckle your seat belt, things are going to get rough.'

Angela let out another loud breath.

'You can do this,' said Frank quasi-reassuringly. 'If it makes you feel any better, in a misery-loves-company sort of way, I won't get off free and clear on this situation either. There will be plenty of aftershock left for me to deal with when I come back,' said Frank, feeling a little sorry for his colleague. 'You realize that this kind of story isn't going to disappear overnight.'

'What do I do first?' asked Angela.

'The police have to be brought in for sure. But, you can do a little end-run before you call them to keep the hospital's PR risk to a minimum,' said Frank. 'My advice would be to see if you can identify who the perpetrator is or at least narrow it down and have the cops make a quick, quiet arrest and put the whole damn thing to bed—fast, before the reporters spin it into a tsunami.'

'Reporters?'

'The press is going to be all over this story which is why the sooner we can wrap it up, the better. The longer this investigation takes, the more the media will make it their headline. It's exactly the kind of story that sells newspapers and bumps up ratings on cable news shows. And, don't even get me started on the tabloids. You don't want that to happen under any circumstances. The board doesn't want that either. Clear?'

When the call was over, a mentally and physically exhausted Angela closed her laptop and texted her husband.

Babe, will be late tonight, got a situation going on at work. Will explain when I see you. Eat without me. Love you. Xo

5

Fifteen minutes later, while on speakerphone, Angela broke the explosive news to notoriously abusive board president, Bob Beckmann, and several other board members. After she finished downloading what little she knew, everyone on the call started talking at once, pointing metaphorical fingers and asking a million questions.

'I don't have any logical explanation for what happened, but I assure you we will get to the bottom of it,' said Angela as coolly as she could muster. 'I promise that we will find out how this happened and who did this.'

'I know how it goddamn happened,' growled Beckmann. 'Some perverted handyman or intern got his rocks off with a defenseless, unconscious woman in a goddamn coma. What kind of person does something like that? It's like having sex with a dead body. What the hell is that called?'

'Narcolepsy,' said the voice of another board member on the group call.

'Right,' said Beckmann, 'narcolepsy. You've got some depraved narcoleptic mental case running around loose in your hospital assaulting patients. What kind of place are you running over there, Angela?'

Another voice interrupted on the speaker. 'Excuse me, Bob, I think you meant to say, necrophilia, not narcolepsy. My understanding is that necrophilia is when you get turned on by dead bodies whereas narcoleptics are people who fall asleep all the time.'

'I don't give a shit whether they're dead, sleeping or standing on their fucking heads,' screamed Beckmann. 'This is a PR nightmare and we need to contain this.'

'Bob, please calm down,' said Angela in quiet measured tones. 'We still don't know anything yet. It just happened. We don't know if it was an employee. It could have been an outside contractor or a delivery man, even the mailman. Hundreds of people come into this facility every year for all sorts of reasons. Tradespeople, clergy, medical students, visitors, family, staff, deliveries. It's endless.'

'Every man who has been inside that building in the last nine months needs to be interrogated and have his DNA checked,' said Beckmann. 'Am I making myself clear?'

'Very clear,' said Angela quietly, 'but by law, people do not have to provide their DNA if they don't want to.'

'Figure it out! The fallout from this could be a financial disaster for the entire Oceanside Medical Center. How do you think the other families with loved ones in our care are going to react? They could shut us down and the lawsuits could be astronomical. They could even hold the board and you personally responsible, Angela. Did you think of that?'

'Me?'

'People sue people for anything in the United States, especially if they think they can make money,' said Beckmann. 'We could all be sued. I've seen it happen before.' Everyone on the speakerphone started talking and protesting at once.

'Quiet!' sounded Beckmann's loud bark from the black box. 'Angela, I will call our corporate attorneys to give them a heads-up before any of this gets out. They'll tell us what we can and can't say. One thing I'm sure of, if we don't handle this exactly right, you and everyone on the Oceanside Manor staff will be out of a job. Oceanside Medical Center isn't going to let this stain their high hospital rating. They'll just move all the patients to one of their other facilities and shut you down.'

Angela took a deep breath and exhaled. She couldn't afford to lose her job, especially now with all the bills piling up at home. 'If I could just have a little more time to go over some of the visitor logs and work schedules, I might be able to pinpoint the likely suspect. Can you give me a week to figure it out?'

'We can't wait that long. We have to call the police, but I'll give you twenty-four hours before we do,' said Beckmann brusquely as he hung up.

It was nearly 10pm and Angela was exhausted. First thing in the morning, she'd begin the massive undertaking of examining all records with the hopes of identifying every man that had set foot in Oceanside Manor in the past year. She started to make a list of things that needed to be checked the following day. Their security cameras wouldn't have footage from nine months earlier. The policy was to only keep footage for thirty days—so the film wouldn't reveal anything. She'd have to review every employee, all visitors, nurses, aides and doctors along with scrutinizing every male employee in maintenance and food services. Every single person would have to be interviewed, no exceptions.

For an hour she worked on her time-sensitive to-do list. When she was finished, she acknowledged to herself that the project was going to require more manpower than just her and her assistant. She'd need extra hands.

She turned to her computer and opened the Oceanside

Manor employee roster and reviewed some of the nurses and aides who she might be able to move onto this project. She wanted someone smart but more importantly, someone who could work fast. Her eyes went to Lourdes Castro's name. *Too senior and she has too much responsibility to pull her off the floor.*

She continued scanning the list of names, looking over each person's background. She opened Jenny O'Hearn's profile. *Jenny is young, energetic, and single. She'd be able to put in the long hours. She already knows about everything that happened with Eliza because she was in the room. If I use Jenny, I wouldn't have to bring another person into the loop. The fewer who know, the better.* As she read Jenny's profile, she noticed an odd notation and clicked on it.

'Would you look at that,' Angela said out loud to herself. *Two years ago, Jenny O'Hearn took three months off. I wonder why?*

Angela wrote Jenny's name down in her notebook and decided the young nurse would be the perfect person for the project. Jenny wasn't essential to the hospital operation, and she was energetic and efficient. She wasn't married and didn't have kids which meant she could work the fifteen-hour days needed for the next couple of weeks. Angela picked up her phone and called the number in Jenny's file.

'Jenny, it's Dr. Crawford, sorry to call you so late,' said Angela over the phone. 'Given what's happened today, the board has asked me to look into this terrible situation. They gave me a little time to try and figure things out before notifying the police. Bottom line, I need your help.'

'I'll help you in any way I can, Dr. Crawford.'

'I mean full time,' said Angela, 'until we can figure out what happened, I want to pull you off the nursing floor and put you on this research project. It's going to be long hours, are you up for it?'

'Absolutely.'

'Come to my office tomorrow morning at eight fifteen and we'll get you started,' said Angela. 'And, Jenny, not a word to anyone. Not a soul.'

6

At 11:30pm that night, worn out and mentally spent, Angela drove down her street lined with palms and nicely maintained Cape Cod homes that had been built in the 1930s by a prolific yet unimaginative Florida developer. She pulled onto her gravel driveway and stumbled through the front door of her house. One lamp in their blue living room had been left on. She did not stop but walked directly through the room into the kitchen, and dropped the three tote bags filled with files on the kitchen counter. She headed directly for the open wine bottle nestled in the fridge door and poured herself a large glass of sauvignon blanc. Out of habit, and maybe to distract herself, she picked up the pile of mail left on the kitchen counter, sifted through it and frowned—all bills, some with overdue notices stamped on the outside.

'Doesn't anyone write letters anymore,' she muttered under her breath and took a gulp of her drink. Only twenty-four hours earlier, she had been stewing about something completely different. January 12th was always a difficult anniversary. Her husband knew that, which is why the day before he had been waiting for her when she came home.

'You're finally home,' he had said, smiling encouragingly as he stood in the kitchen with a plate of Swiss chocolates in one hand and a glass of cabernet in the other—her favorites.

'Wine and chocolate, you always remember,' she said as he handed her the glass.

Every January 12th, on the anniversary of her brother Michael's death, Angela and her husband, David, danced the same macabre waltz. She was only fourteen when her sixteen-year-old brother had died and it had been nearly thirty years, but the shock and pain was still there. After getting through the anniversary, now, one day later, January 13th had brought unimaginable new problems for Angela to cope with.

'Hello, my love,' David said, coming down the stairs in his bathrobe. He pecked her on the cheek and gave her a quick hug. 'You look exhausted. It's nearly midnight. I was about to send out the cavalry. I've kept a dinner plate warm for you.'

'I'm not really hungry. I think I'll just drink my dinner tonight.'

Angela turned her attention back to the mail.

'I've actually had a very good day,' said David, trying to lighten his wife's obviously gloomy mood. 'Want to hear about it?'

Angela forced a smile and nodded, happy for a distraction.

'I had a breakthrough on my third chapter today. You remember how I was stuck for the longest time. This morning, the creative log jam miraculously unclogged and I wrote four whole pages. I'm on a roll, Angie. I think I'm going to go all the way this time.'

Angela forced another smile as she gazed at her husband, so different now from the person she thought she married twenty years ago. The strong memory of her original intense attraction to him had stayed with her all these years and kept her love intact, despite his many disappointments. She still saw that handsome, clever, rising literary star she met when she was in college.

They met on the first day of the fall semester of her senior year. She was in an English class seated next to her best friend, Faye, while listening to her new professor, David Crawford, give a lecture on Edith Wharton's *The House of Mirth*. While he talked, Faye reached over and scribbled something in Angela's notebook.

Dr. C is hot
Tell me about it!
He's old.
Who cares??? He's smokin'.

Angela turned her eyes back to the handsome young teacher. With long wavy reddish-brown hair and a beard, he looked more like a country-and-western singer than an English professor. She checked his hand for a wedding ring and smiled when she saw his fingers were bare. David Crawford was charming and eloquent and had an easy breezy way about him. She noticed his robin's egg blue eyes seemed to sparkle whenever he got excited about something.

At the end of that first class, Angela hung back as the other students left the room. Pretending to organize her notebooks while the others cleared out, she waited until she and her teacher were the only two left in the cavernous lecture hall.

'Professor Crawford, I'm Angela Asmodeo. I wanted to introduce myself. This is actually my first college English class.'

'Hello, Angela Asmodeo. What year are you in?'

'Senior.'

'And this is your first English class?'

'I'm pre-med. Been taking mainly science, math and psychology. English is an elective for me. I saved up all my electives for senior year. So, here I am.'

'You're going to be a doctor. Impressive.'

'I still have to take the MCATs. But that's my goal.'

'What area of medicine do you plan to go into?'

'It's between obstetrics and psychology.'

'Those are very different fields.'

'I'm interested in neuroscience so that's what draws me to psychology but I also like the idea of working with women and bringing a new life into the world. I think it would be amazing to deliver babies. A lot depends on if and what program I get accepted into.'

'I'm honored to have a future physician in my class.'

Angela felt herself smiling from ear to ear as she drank in her teacher's intensely blue eyes.

'I heard from some other kids that you wrote a novel and that the critics gave you really good reviews,' Angela said, trying to keep the conversation going. 'They said you could be the next great American author, the writer for the new millennium.'

David bowed his head and feigned modesty but Angela detected he enjoyed the recognition. 'It was a first effort, my *debut* novel. You're only as good as your last book, Angela, always remember that.'

'What was it called?'

'*Where the Falcons Go*. It's an allegory on the eroding moral compass of civilized societies.'

'It sounds complex. And, where *do* the falcons go?' she said, laughing.

'They don't go anywhere. That's the whole point of the story. The characters can't find their way. They're lost in their own self-imposed exile.'

'That sounds very highbrow but I think I'd like to read it.'

'I'll bring in a copy for you. I was about to do a coffee run, want to join me? I can tell you all about it, if you're interested.'

That's the way it had started. Coffee led to dinner. Dinner became weekends. By the time Angela graduated, David Crawford had asked her to be his wife. The future looked so bright for both of them. She was planning a career in medicine and he was an up-and-coming novelist. Life was sweet and full of surprises. He was intuitive, creative and brilliant. She was practical, pragmatic and sensible. He could be silly and involved in a million projects while she was focused and driven but made sure the bills got paid. They complemented each other and were madly in love. She didn't see his flaws. It was as if she had a blind spot when it came to him. Hard as nails with other people, when it came to David, she always forgave him and made up excuses for his shortcomings.

Angela went on to medical school and sailed through her residency in obstetrics, while David's literary career gradually dried up. His second book was an unmitigated flop and eventually, his agent dropped him. Trying to stem the tide, he stopped teaching to write full time which proved to be a financially and emotionally disastrous decision.

During those early years, they had also tried over and over to have a baby but nothing ever gelled. After six failed IVF treatments, they were left only with incredible disappointment, an empty bank account and plenty of bills. Later, when Angela had further complications, a hysterectomy had been recommended. At that point, David had suggested adoption but Angela wanted no part of it.

'I've delivered too many sick babies from drug addict mothers and women who were drinking all through their pregnancy. When you adopt, David, you don't know what you're getting,' she had said. 'I'm not going to put myself in that position.'

'We could thoroughly vet the birth mother,' David argued.

'Look what happened to my family,' said Angela. 'My parents adopted my brother Michael and me and by the time Michael was fifteen, his schizophrenia had kicked in and he started using drugs. I found him, remember?'

'I know that.'

'My mother's life was hell.'

'You're not your mother.'

'I won't put myself in that situation.'

'Not every adopted kid has problems,' her husband said. 'Look at you. You turned out fine.'

'Did I?'

'You're being overly dramatic, my love. Come here,' he said as he put his arms around his wife to soothe her. They had similar conversations many times over the years and it had always ended the same way.

It was shortly after their last IVF, while looking for a pen in David's old cherry wood writing desk, Angela found a pile of receipts from local casinos in one of the desk drawers.

'I thought you were writing while I was at work?' she demanded when her husband walked into the room.

'I am writing, love. What's making you so unhappy?'

She held up a wad of receipts from the Hard Rock Casino in Hollywood, Florida. There was a long pause as David took a moment to process what the papers in her hand were. When he realized, he blushed.

'Just a little fun, love, that's all. No big deal. Helps take the edge off.'

'The edge off?' said Angela, her voice getting louder. 'I'm trying to keep us afloat financially and you're out blowing our money at a craps table.'

'It's blackjack. Sometimes, I just need a little release after being cooped up here all day staring at a blank page.'

'I get up in the middle of the night and deliver babies and

you're pissing away our money on a card game? I thought you were done with that after those disastrous junkets you took to Vegas where you lost practically everything we had. You know I'm still trying to pay off my medical school loans. Every step forward I take, you pull us back two.'

'You're making too much of it. Besides, I won this week. I'm up a hundred.'

'This week! What about last week or next week?' said a furious Angela as she walked out of the room. After all the years of marriage, she had realized that her once perfect husband had a gambling problem and to make matters worse, he wasn't very good at it. They had quarreled that night and few words were spoken over the next several days. Then, he did something sweet and she forgave him. She always did.

This night, after everything that had happened that day with Eliza Stern and the baby, seeing her smiling husband standing in front of her made her feel better. He still knew how to make her laugh and she couldn't resist him when he laid on the charm.

'What do you think about my news?' said David, filling her wine glass again.

'What?'

'My writing breakthrough.'

'That's great, babe. I'm happy for you,' said a distracted Angela, her mind elsewhere.

'Enough about me. Tell me what was the *situation* at the hospital that kept you so late,' said David. 'What was today's nightmare?'

For the next fifteen minutes Angela told her husband all the details about the baby, Eliza Stern and the terrible behavior of the board on her conference call.

'The woman who had the baby has been a patient at Ocean-side Manor since she was ten-years-old?' said David. 'My writer's brain is going to all sorts of dark places. Do you have any idea how it happened?'

Angela shook her head and sighed.

'What are you going to do?'

'I don't know,' she said, taking another big gulp of wine. 'Honestly, I haven't had time to think. Everything was moving so fast today.'

'Did you call the police?'

'I had to talk with the board first. They don't want any bad publicity and it was so late in the day. I'll call the police tomorrow or the day after at the latest.'

'This has *National Enquirer* written all over it,' said David.

'We need to do our own internal investigating before we bring the police in or the press gets wind of it. Once the cops are involved, it will be out of my hands. The board gave me permission to take a day to look into it quietly before I reach out to the authorities.'

'How are the baby and the mother doing?'

'The baby is just fine,' Angela said, smiling. 'He's gorgeous, actually. I've got registered nurses taking care of him round the clock. In fact, they're fighting over who gets to hold him next. Our staff is used to monitoring lifeless bodies with brain injuries. Having a cherubic baby boy on the floor is like giving them a new puppy. That baby will get plenty of attention, I'm not worried about that. Odds are that child will never be put down.'

'You said the mother has no relatives. What's going to happen to the baby?'

'I don't know.'

'How do you think this happened?'

'I don't know, David,' said Angela, slightly irritated. 'Stop asking me so many questions. If I knew how it happened, we wouldn't be in such a mess.'

'It's totally sick, that's what it is. What kind of person would do something like this? Why would someone get pleasure from having sex with an unconscious woman connected to feeding tubes?' said David. 'You've got to have a serious defect to do something like that.'

'I took a few psych courses in medical school. I don't think it's pleasure, it's more about control. A man having sex with a woman who can't fight back, that's a total power play. I've got one of the psychiatrists from Oceanside Medical coming in tomorrow morning for a consult. I'm hoping to get a profile from him on the type of person who would do something like this.'

'Any way you slice it, it's a terrible story. Obviously, someone raped that poor girl,' said David. 'The press is going to go nuts.'

'I know, and I'm dreading it,' said Angela. 'Until we sort things out, I'm hoping we can just keep the baby safe and sound at Oceanside Manor. I intend to get to the bottom of this starting tomorrow.'

'Why don't you call Frank Farwell and get some advice? He's been doing this a lot longer than you. He might have some insight.'

'Already did. He told me it was my problem and mine to clean up.'

'I always said he was a weasel,' said David. 'Angie, I'm sorry you're in the middle of this thing. It can't be fun.'

'That girl was impregnated anywhere from seven to nine months ago,' said Angela through clenched teeth. 'The fact is, Frank Farwell could still have been in charge of Oceanside Manor when it happened. He was so quick to palm it off onto my watch when it could have happened while he was still here.'

Angela sat at the kitchen counter while David fixed her a plate of cold chicken. Pouring them both another glass of wine, he watched silently while Angela picked at her food but ate little.

'My sister called today,' said David, breaking the silence and changing the subject.

'Oh.'

'You know how she's into that whole genealogy thing.'

'Everyone knows, that's all she ever talks about. I don't know why people get so obsessed over that stuff. Who cares?'

'Remember when they visited us last Easter and told us how she's traced the Crawford family back to twelfth-century Scotland?'

'Not really.'

'She was excited because our family always thought we were English,' said David, looking a bit dejected when his wife showed no interest.

Noticing the look on her husband's face, Angela reached over and rubbed his arm. 'I'm sorry, babe. Thank you for dinner. I'm just tired. I think I'll go to bed,' she said as she put her dish in the dishwasher. 'Coming?'

'My sister sent me some stuff about our Scottish ancestors. I think I'll poke around online for a little while,' said David. 'She thinks there might be a Crawford family connection to the Vikings. If there is, you'll have to start calling me Thor.'

He didn't see the irritation flash across his wife's face because she had already turned to walk away. *If he spent half the time trying to make some money as he does on pointless crap, we might not be in so deep a financial hole.* She said nothing and continued up the stairs.

At work, Angela was an alpha dog but at home she often deferred to her husband. It was a pattern that had been established from the beginning of their student–teacher relationship. Based on the way she efficiently commandeered Oceanside Manor, no one would have ever guessed how acquiescent she was in her own home.

7

DAY 2

W hen Angela arrived at the sixty-year-old Oceanside Manor building the next morning, Jenny was already waiting for her outside of Angela's office. She had told the young nurse to be there at 8:15. It was only 7:45 and it looked like Jenny had been there a while. The young nurse was eager and energetic—exactly the kind of person she needed.

Angela tossed her bags on her desk and waved her hand. 'Come with me,' she said as she sailed past Jenny out into the hallway. 'First, I want to check in on Eliza and the baby. We can talk while we walk.' Angela explained precisely how she would need Jenny's help pulling together the many documents the police would undoubtedly require.

'We haven't been fully automated yet, not like the hospital next door,' said Angela. 'It's a huge job and will require you to dig through reams of files.'

'I'm ready,' replied Jenny.

When they arrived at Eliza's room, Angela checked the unconscious woman's chart. Satisfied that everything was fine with the mother, she turned her attention to the sleeping baby in the nearby crib. Staring down at the child she smiled. The one thing she had always wanted that eluded her was children. At age forty-four, it was evident it was not likely to ever happen.

She picked up the sleeping baby and sat in the rocking chair that had been brought in by some of the staff and rocked him while she barked whispered orders at Jenny, telling her what to compile and where to find it. Young and wanting to please, Jenny took copious notes and nodded her head frequently.

'I want all visitor and vendor lists cross-tabbed. I want to know which vendors were in this building between April and June of last year,' said Angela. 'April through June is the critical window, do you understand?'

'It's going to take a while,' said Jenny. 'But, I'm on it. I keep thinking about this electrician who was here last year who was a little weird. Remember when we had to rewire all the overheads on the third and fourth floors? He and another guy did all the work. He was always creeping around and once I found him in one of the patient's rooms. When I asked him what he was doing, he said he saw the patient's name on the door and thought he knew them.'

'Did he?'

'I don't think so. I told him he wasn't permitted in any patient rooms ever, and he went back to work. I didn't give it another thought, but now I wonder.'

'See if you can remember who he was,' said Angela, looking down at the baby again.

'Will do,' said Jenny, nodding while writing herself a note.

'Also, get me a list of every person who interviewed for a job here. I even want the names of people we didn't hire, even those who just applied. They may have come in person to drop off an application and somehow gotten in,' said Angela. 'We don't always walk people out after an interview. When someone leaves an office, we just assume that they leave the building, but I suppose someone could go to another floor.'

'It's possible.'

'And Jenny, I need all this yesterday,' said Angela. 'My assistant, Vera, will help you. The board gave me a day to see if I could figure out this mess and the clock is ticking. If we can turn over a few suspect's names to the police quickly, and they can make an arrest, then this whole thing can be wrapped up much faster. We have to keep bad publicity to a minimum or all of our jobs will be on the line. Understand?'

Excited to have such an important role, Jenny nodded enthusiastically.

For the rest of the day, the young nurse combed through lists and files culling out all visitors, workmen and staff, and mixing and matching them against dates and times. She set up a spreadsheet allowing the user to change the order based on dates in the hospital, sex, and work affiliation. When she was through she had over four hundred names and more than two hundred of them were men.

At six o'clock that evening she went to find Angela to present her preliminary findings and was told that the administrator had gone up to 3 West. Jenny found Angela in the rocker in Eliza Stern's room with the baby boy in her arms. She handed Angela the document.

'This is very comprehensive,' said Angela out loud to herself as she reviewed the reports. 'Two hundred and eighty-six men. That's a lot of people for us to vet. It's going to take a long time. I think it's better that we put out a statement immediately rather than having it look like we were trying to hide something.'

'This was just my first pass at the list,' said Jenny. 'I have to go through it a few more times to make sure I've got the correct counts but at least it gives you a ballpark number of the universe we'll need to look at.'

Angela nodded wearily and looked down at the sleeping baby in her arms.

'He's really sweet, isn't he?'

'He is,' said Jenny, taking the baby from Angela so she could better sift through the papers while Jenny placed the baby back in his crib next to his silent, sleeping mother, Eliza.

8

After leaving Eliza's room, Angela walked back through the yellow halls to her office for the meeting with the clinical psychiatrist. She hoped the consultation would help her develop a profile of the kind of person who might be responsible. This particular psychiatrist was an expert on deviant psychological behavior.

'What's the emergency? I cancelled my morning appointments because your message said it was urgent,' said the psychiatrist.

'*Urgent* doesn't begin to describe what we're dealing with,' said Angela, shaking her head as she told him the story.

'No one noticed the woman was pregnant?'

'Why does everyone keep asking that? She carried small. I've seen it before. It's not common but some women barely show at all. Between us, I don't think anyone ever looked at her abdominal area. Eliza has been in a coma for so many years. The aides are the ones who move, change and clean her and most of them don't have a high school education. Their job is very specific and they don't venture out of their lane, if you know what I mean.'

'But still...'

'I know it's hard to believe, but we missed it,' said Angela. 'Sometimes I go on the floors myself and check in on patients to stay connected to what's going on in the building. I've checked in on Eliza a few times over the past year and I didn't pick up on it either.'

'What do you want from me?' asked the psychiatrist.

'I have to develop a profile of the kind of person who would do something like this. It might help us identify who it is.'

'It's hard to say definitively without more information,' said the psychiatrist, pulling at his eyebrow. 'A man who would have sex with an unconscious or compromised person would likely be someone who had serious inadequacy issues. But, they might not appear that way to other people. They might present as someone who has a terrific life, has everything one would want —career, family, friends.'

'You mean like the singer, Phil Markley?'

'That's a good example,' said the psychiatrist. 'Markley was famous, had money, power, an incredible career. He had a wife and family. Plenty of women would have willingly slept with him. Yet, he preferred it when they were inebriated or unconscious. It's a fetish, really. Women become objects. In my world we call it a paraphilia. It's when a person's arousal and gratification depend on fantasizing and engaging in sexual behavior that is atypical and extreme. It can revolve around objects like children, animals, feet or a particular act like humiliating someone or exposing oneself. When the women are unconscious or—as in your case—in a coma, they become just an object. Most people with paraphilia can trace this desire back to an early sexual experience. Of course, there's always somnophilia too.'

'What's that?' said Angela with a grimace.

'That's when someone gets sexually aroused from a sleeping person.'

'Good Lord.'

'That's rarer. Lastly, there's necrophilia, which is sexual arousal from dead people.'

'Eww.'

'A woman being asleep or unconscious absolves the perpetrator from his sins,' the psychiatrist continued. 'Men who get aroused by violence or sadistic fantasies don't have to own it when the victim is asleep.'

'Is there any particular profile for the kind of person who would do this? We need to find the man that did this—fast.'

'I'm afraid not,' said the psychiatrist. 'Let's take Phil Markley again, one of America's favorite singers. With Christmas specials on TV every year, he's the last person you'd ever suspect or so you'd think.'

'What do you mean?'

'People with inappropriate predilections oftentimes put themselves in positions where they can access the stimulation,' the psychiatrist continued. 'People who are attracted to children will seek out teaching positions or Scouts or even the clergy. Places where they can easily interact with their intended victims. In this case, if this act was done by someone who gets pleasure from being with a person who is unconscious and immobile, they may have sought out a job at an extended-care facility deliberately. They may have assaulted more than one patient.'

'Do you really think so?' said Angela.

'No matter how you look at it,' said the psychiatrist, 'it's not a pretty picture. My suggestion would be to look for someone who has a past. Going to this extreme—it's probably not his first time at the rodeo. Look for a previous criminal record or a complaint filed somewhere. Check for restraining orders and sexual predators lists. I'd bet money that your guy has done something like this before.'

9

Hours later, with Jenny standing in front of her, Angela looked over the updated employee and visitor spreadsheets the young nurse and Angela's assistant had put together. The administrator looked at her watch and let out a sigh. It was nearly noon and her time was running out. Beckmann was only concerned with his own ass and he'd throw anyone under the bus—including her, if he thought he was in some legal or financial jeopardy.

'You've done a good job so far, Jenny, but I'm afraid, given the tight time restraints, it's not fast enough to bring this investigation to a close. I'm going to notify the police.'

'It *is* a big project,' Jenny said, 'and I've only just scratched the surface.'

'Another day isn't enough time to make a dent in this huge list.'

Angela's phone rang and she groaned when she saw the caller ID said 'Beckmann, Bob.'

'Is everything all right, Dr. Crawford?' asked Jenny.

'It's the president of the board. I've got to take it. Jenny, keep doing what you're doing. I'll stop by to see you later.'

Jenny gathered her papers and left as Angela took a deep breath and answered her ringing phone while forcing a smile onto her face.

'Good afternoon, Bob. How are you?'

'What's going on over there?'

'I'm fine. Thank you for asking.'

'Get off your high horse, Angela. You of all people have no right to be up on one. From the beginning, I knew it was a mistake when Farwell went to South America and put you in charge. You were too green. I told him that. Unless you're prepared to give me a name right this minute, it's our legal responsibility to bring the police in now.'

'My team is doing the best they can with limited resources and time,' said Angela. 'We're a medical staff, not the FBI.'

'Do you have a name?'

'We've compiled a preliminary list of men who were in and around the building last year between April and June. That's our target period based on the baby's size and weight. I've met with a clinical psychiatrist, who gave me a personality profile on the kind of person who might be responsible,' said Angela.

'And?'

'It's going to take more time,' she continued. 'Assuming the perpetrator *is* on one of our lists and he may not be, we'll have to run DNA tests on everyone unless someone confesses, which isn't likely. Legally, I don't think we can force people to provide their DNA. It would have to be completely voluntary. My guess: not everyone is going to agree to give us a sample.'

'If a person is innocent, why wouldn't they provide their DNA?' barked Beckmann. 'If someone doesn't give it, it probably means they're guilty.'

'Not necessarily,' said Angela. 'There could be all sorts of reasons. Even if we did get everyone to give a sample, we still might not get a match. The names we compiled are from people who officially signed into logs. If someone snuck into the building without us knowing it, we wouldn't have them on the list. That's something we need to be prepared for. We may not ever get closure on this.'

'That's not an option,' said Beckmann. 'Call the police now and I'll call our corporate PR team to get them started on a spin for this. I don't want the press to find out about anything before we come out with a statement or they'll think we're hiding something. I had hoped we could resolve this quickly and quietly. From what you're telling me, it's going to be a much bigger deal. Right after you speak to the police, let the lawyers know and make sure you keep them in the loop so we limit our liability. A press release has to be pulled together today so we can feed the media our narrative. They are going to be like piranhas on human flesh.'

'I'll call the police now,' said Angela. 'If I had more time, I might be able to...'

Before she finished her sentence, Angela realized the board president had already hung up.

10

Driving north along the shore on A1A, two highly decorated Oceanside FL police detectives, John McQuillan and his partner, Anita Blalock, looked out of their unmarked car window at the rows of swaying palms that lined the shore road. A popular winter vacation destination, Oceanside's population soared to nearly 70,000 in the winter months when all the snowbirds came down to vacation from the colder northern states. Through the passenger window, the surf splashed rhythmically on the white sandy beaches. On their left, crowded cafes with long waiting lines of hungry tourists were flanked by souvenir and beachwear shops.

McQ, as he was called by friends and colleagues alike, and his partner whose nickname was Blade, as in 'sharp as a' had met several years before while working together on one of John McQuillan's most important cases, the Quinn Roberts murder near Rochester, NY. McQ had searched for the killer for over six years. At the time, Anita Blalock was on the Atlanta police force and had been instrumental in helping McQ arrest the murderer he had pursued for so long. After that, a deep friendship, rooted in mutual professional respect had developed. When the Quinn

Roberts murder trial was over and the killer convicted and locked up for good, McQ decided it was time to pack it in and leave the cold Rochester winters behind.

One day on a lark, he responded to a job opening for a detective with the Oceanside Police in Palm Beach County, Florida. Soon after, he was offered the position and he and his longtime girlfriend, Marie, a court stenographer, packed up and headed south. Six months after he arrived, there was another opening for a detective and McQ reached out to his old friend, Blade. Though a good fifteen years younger than McQ, she was more than ready to leave the chaos of Atlanta behind and try something lower key. After much discussion with her wife, Eve, a physical therapist and vegan cook extraordinaire, the two women rented a U-Haul truck and drove caravan style south to the Sunshine State.

Since then, McQ and Blade had become partners and they couldn't have been happier. At fifty-nine, slightly out of shape and occasionally winded, McQ had been paired with a lot of partners over the years, mostly men. He reckoned that he never had a partner that he enjoyed or respected more than Anita Blalock. Blade was tiny in stature but made up for it in personal ferocity. She was a five-foot-three package of pure muscle developed from a lifetime of diligent workouts and low carbs. Her compact body and ebony complexion were capped off with piles of braids tucked into a neat and tidy bun. When she smiled her perfect white teeth gleamed and gave one the sense that she was in on a joke that you completely missed. Half the time that was true. Blade was as sharp as they come, she missed nothing.

Until recently, Oceanside had grappled with a fairly large drug and vagrant problem. Over the past two years, a concerted effort to turn things around by Mayor Davidson and the chief of police had made a big difference. The cops had successfully reversed the trajectory of the drug and homeless population and the mayor was happy because he got re-elected.

Riding in their dark gray Toyota Camry along the shoreline, McQ and Blade were rerouted by the police dispatcher to head across town to the west side.

'This is coming directly from the chief,' said the voice on the radio. 'Get over to Oceanside Manor right away. Possible rape.'

'Is Oceanside Manor part of the hospital?' McQ asked the dispatcher.

'It's the long-term care annex adjacent to Oceanside Medical Center. It's a separate building for brain injuries.'

'Copy that,' said McQ, signing off on the radio.

'Still glad you came to South Florida?' said McQ, while rolling down his window to put his siren light on the roof. Cars moved out of their way as the sound from the siren pierced the air and their car picked up speed as it headed towards a crosstown street. 'Well, are you?' asked McQ again.

'Haven't decided yet,' said Blade.

'You've been here for six months. What's not to like? You gotta admit it's beautiful here.'

'I might need a couple of years to make up my mind.'

'C'mon, Anita, look at that beach, all that white sand and blue green water.'

Blade looked out of the passenger window at the sparkling blue ocean. Happy tourists carrying chairs and umbrellas scurried along the ocean promenade enjoying the eternal sunshine. Tons of strollers, some containing babies, more containing dogs, created an odd kind of parade that included skaters, walkers, runners and bikers and the occasional Jehovah's Witness.

'What's not to like about Oceanside?' said McQ with a smile. 'Sure beats the cold winters of upstate New York. If I had to live through one more blizzard, or shovel one more walk, I would have killed Marie or more likely, she would have killed me. The cold weather up north didn't agree with either of us anymore. Must be getting old.'

'Uh-huh.'

'Look out your window,' said McQ. 'What do you see? Happy faces. Everyone here is happy.'

'Everyone here is white.'

'You got a problem with white people, Anita,' he said, poking her in the shoulder, making her grin.

'It's just that we had a teensy bit more diversity in Atlanta, that's all I'm saying,' said Blade, laying on her childhood South Carolina drawl as she often did to make a point. 'All I can say is, they ain't having no Kwanzaa celebrations in downtown Oceanside.'

'True. Let's see what you and I can do to shift that paradigm.'

'You're on, my friend.'

The unmarked car sped west down the main thoroughfare, Harbor Avenue, a street filled with restaurants, shops and throngs of partying tourists visibly thrilled to be in the warm weather.

'Look at 'em all,' said McQ, pointing to all the visitors as they sped by them. 'They think they've died and gone to heaven. They're all smiling because they think they're in paradise.'

'They're all smiling cause half of 'em started drinking at breakfast,' said Blade with a smirk.

11

Detectives Blalock and McQuillan walked through the front entrance of Oceanside Manor and gave their names to the receptionist. Moments later they were met by a young woman who said she worked in the public relations department.

'Is this facility affiliated with the hospital next door?' asked McQuillan.

'We are an adjunct to the hospital. Our facility is strictly for brain trauma,' she explained. 'We provide palliative care and the best possible quality of life for our patients but if they are in here, they will not recover. Our job is to keep them comfortable.'

'Why are most of them in here?' asked Blade.

'We have a variety of traumatic brain injuries, coma and even some cases of severe dementia,' said the PR lady as she led the two detectives to Angela Crawford's office in the administrative wing.

'This is a depressing place,' whispered Blade to her partner as they followed the young woman through the dismal yellow halls. 'Nobody here gets better.'

Angela Crawford along with Oceanside Manor's attorney and Head Nurse Lourdes Castro were waiting for them when the detectives arrived. Within a few minutes, the two detectives were briefed on everything that had transpired.

'Let me get this straight. You're saying that the mother of the baby has been a patient here for the past twelve years?' asked McQ.

'More or less,' said Angela.

'And, she's been in a non-responsive coma the entire time?' asked McQ.

'The whole time. Almost twelve years ago Eliza Stern's entire family, which included her mother, father and identical twin sister were in a terrible car accident with a drunken driver on the Florida Turnpike. Everyone else was killed but, miraculously, little Eliza survived but never regained consciousness. She was sent here from Boca Point Regional when no more could be done for her. The family's estate and insurance cover the costs.'

'Any chance she'll wake up?' asked McQ.

'I'm not a neurologist, but from what they tell me, there's no possibility,' said Angela. 'For every additional day someone remains in a coma, the odds of them recovering become less likely. It has to do with generating neuron connections. Once that ability is lost, it's almost impossible to bring them back. From what I recall from Eliza's file, she had some pretty serious head trauma. According to the notes from when she was admitted, even if she had regained consciousness, they didn't have much hope for any meaningful functioning. If she had woken up, she would have had the developmental abilities of a six-month-old or less.'

'How is she now, after giving birth? Any change in her condition?' asked Blade.

'She's the same. There were no complications. Dr. Horowitz, one of our staff physicians, thoroughly examined Eliza,' said Angela. 'No unusual bleeding or residual problems from the birth, other than her milk coming in, which we're addressing with hot compresses.'

'None of the doctors or nurses who attend to Ms. Stern noticed she was pregnant?' asked Blade, squinting her eyes and tilting her head to the side.

'That seems to be everyone's overarching question. Lourdes, that's your floor, why don't you take this question?' Angela asked, turning her attention to the head nurse.

'I'm embarrassed to say it, but no one noticed,' said Lourdes. 'I mainly supervise. I don't do much with the patients other than to check their vitals occasionally, make sure their tubes and medications are in order. It's usually the aides who change their gowns and bedding, give the sponge baths or roll them to prevent bed sores.'

'How often is she seen by a doctor or a nurse?' asked Blade.

'A nurse will typically check the charts and look in on each patient at some point during their shift. Feeding tubes, catheters, heart monitors et cetera, will be evaluated to make sure everything is operating properly,' said Angela.

'What about the doctors? How often do they come around and examine patients?' asked McQ.

'We've got two MDs from Oceanside Medical who care for the patients in that wing—Dr. Steve Horowitz is the primary and George Kantounis fills in when Horowitz isn't available. Both are general practitioners and have patients over at the hospital and here. Dr. Horowitz sees our population about once a week unless we have a medical problem. If a patient has a health issue the doctors are brought in to address it. Overall, the day-to-day with our patients is primarily with the aides. They're our first line of defense.'

'Looks like your first line got ambushed,' said Blade with a raised eyebrow.

'We'll need to talk to all the aides,' said McQ, making a note in his book.

'And the baby, you said it was a boy,' said Blade.

'Yes,' said Angela, breaking into a smile for the first time since the meeting started. 'He's actually a beautiful baby. Quiet, content, cherubic. Maybe it's because he had such a quiet and sedate womb to develop in. They tell me he hardly cries. I've got nurses taking care of him round the clock.'

'Why did you wait so long to call us?' asked McQ.

'It was extremely late when the baby was born, and everyone was exhausted. I needed to alert our board first so it just made sense to wait until the next day,' said Angela. 'The crisis was over at that point so I didn't think it mattered.'

'I see,' said McQ, making a note. 'We're going to need all your records.'

'Detectives, for obvious reasons, this whole awful thing needs to be resolved as fast as possible,' said Angela in an official tone. 'I'm afraid because of the HIPAA laws regarding patient confidentiality, our staff will have to vet the records first, before we turn anything over to you. My staff and I have already started going through everything with the hopes of providing you with as much help and data as possible.'

'How long do you estimate it will take to come up with a comprehensive list?' asked McQ.

'Unfortunately, Oceanside Manor is a small facility and we are woefully behind the times when it comes to automation,' said Angela. 'Believe it or not, a large part of everything we do is still on paper. This year we were supposed to move everything over to digital but the money wasn't there.'

'What about your security cameras? We noticed there were some in the lobby when we entered the building,' said Blade.

'They're only in the lobby at that particular entrance, nowhere else,' said Angela, shaking her head. 'We only save footage for a month. We wouldn't have film going back nine months. Every thirty days it records over itself and the old files are deleted.'

'How about sign-in logs?' asked Blade. 'Does everyone who comes in have to sign in?'

'They're supposed to,' said Angela, biting her lip, 'but sometimes the person at reception is called away for a few minutes or needs to use a restroom so it's possible, every once in a while, someone comes in and doesn't sign in.'

'What about tradespeople or deliveries?' asked McQ. 'Do they have to sign in?'

'Again, they're supposed to,' said Angela. 'I would guess we have a record for about ninety-eight percent of the people who come into our building. Of course, it's always possible that a few may have slipped through the cracks.'

'Now, why is that?' asked Blade.

'You might have a group of relatives who come in and one person signs in for all of them and doesn't put everyone's name down,' said Angela. 'Or an air-conditioning guy who signs in but his assistant doesn't. There's a lot of coming and going around here. A lot of deliveries. We get most people but I'm sure we miss a few.'

'That's going to be a problem,' said Blade. 'Let's hope the two percent you didn't record had nothing to do with this situation.'

'Dr. Crawford,' said McQ, 'we'll need a private room here to conduct interviews. We'll want to see all your logs, video, employee rosters and shift schedules from the past year. We don't know much yet, except for one thing—Ms. Stern was raped and we are going to treat this case like a sex crime.'

12

Rape. That was the first time anyone had used that word, and it landed like a grenade in a foxhole. In an uncomfortable silence, everyone in the room looked at each other until Blade broke the spell.

'The fact is, someone had sex with that poor girl and it was without her consent. Where I'm from, that's called rape,' said Blade.

'Oh my God,' said Lourdes, making the sign of the cross.

'Dr. Crawford, you said earlier that by your calculations, Ms. Stern was probably attacked last year sometime between April and June, correct?'

'Correct.'

'We'll need a list of every man who's come in contact with the mother during that time frame,' said McQ. 'Every visitor, tradesman or employee. If there's a guy who waters your plants, I want a name. If there is a man who pulls weeds out in your parking lot, I want to know who he is. And, I want the names of every male patient.'

'But, all our male patients have traumatic brain injuries,' said Angela.

'I don't care,' said McQ. 'We're going to check everyone's DNA. No exceptions.'

'Won't that take weeks or months?' said Angela. 'We really need to get this wrapped up. I can't have this black cloud hanging over us for months and months while we wait for DNA results. The longer it takes, the more negative press we're going to get. There could be lawsuits.'

'It doesn't take months anymore, not even weeks,' said Blade.

'Technology is a beautiful thing,' said McQ. 'Some big city police operations have portable machines about the size of a large desktop printer that do certain DNA checks practically in real time. They can analyze the DNA in a swab and produce a profile on a DNA strand in less than two hours. Prosecutors have been using this kind of machine for about five years and the results are incredible and reliable. Rest assured, DNA—she don't lie.'

'In Atlanta, we could run someone's DNA while we were interrogating them and know if he or she was our perp before we finished the interview,' said Blade. 'Of course, those aren't connected to CODIS yet, the FBI database, but it will be eventually.'

'Do we have that capability here in Oceanside?' asked Angela.

'Not yet,' said McQ, 'but we can still get the results pretty quickly in most cases.'

Detective Blalock's phone buzzed. 'It's SVU,' she said, reading the text message, 'they want to know if we need a rape kit.'

'I think that ship has sailed. The attack was too long ago,' said McQ. 'Ms. Stern has been bathed and cleaned and delivered a baby. It's highly unlikely we'd recover anything. Would you agree, Dr. Crawford?'

'Yes. I'm afraid you're right.'

'I'll tell them,' said Blade, while texting her response. 'Dr. Crawford, we'll also need every male medical staff member's name including any doctors or nurses that work here from the hospital next door. Don't forget about the workers in food services, laundry, and housekeeping. No one is off limits.'

'I'll give you everything we have,' said Angela. 'It may take a little time but I'll put extra staff on it.'

'We've got time,' said Blade. 'Can we see Ms. Stern?'

A few minutes later, Jenny O'Hearn was summoned to escort the two detectives over to 3 West. When the group walked into Eliza's pale-yellow room, a dozen stuffed animals had been placed strategically around the space making it surprisingly cheery. In the hospital bed, twenty-one-year-old Eliza Stern lay silently with various tubes and electrodes attached to different parts of her body. An empty crib was positioned next to the bed.

'Look at that girl,' said McQ, walking over to Eliza's bed and looking down at her. 'She's not much younger than my own daughter. My kid just got engaged and has her whole life ahead of her. You got cheated, Eliza, didn't you?'

'She was only ten when the accident happened,' said Blade. 'Poor kid.'

'It's so sad,' said Jenny. 'She never got to live her life and now this happened.'

'What kind of an animal would do this?' said McQ, moving closer to Eliza and leaning over her. 'I'm making you a promise, Eliza. I'm going to find out who did this to you and put them away for good. You can count on that.'

'We both will,' said Blade, putting her hand on her partner's shoulder. She knew the older cop well. He was tough as nails on the outside but a total creampuff on the inside and he had a huge soft spot for young people and kids.

13

Later that day, Angela led Detectives McQuillan and Blalock to a plain vanilla medium-sized rectangular conference room. Inside there was a large table and eight chairs.

'This will be your space for as long as you need it for the investigation,' said Angela. 'There's also a smaller conference room across the hall that you can use as well. You can interview people here and you'll be able to lock up the rooms when you leave. That way you can store things safely.' She handed McQ and Blade a set of keys. Then she passed a copy of the spreadsheets Jenny had started to compile.

'We've narrowed down the list of visitors, vendors and others to 284 men that we know entered Oceanside Manor within the designated three-month period last year,' said Angela. 'This list includes staff, both medical and non-medical; delivery people, maintenance workers, clergy, visitors and relatives.'

'It's a start,' said McQ, coming to grips with the daunting task in front of him.

'Do you need us to include the names of our board members?' asked Angela.

'If they're male and over the age of ten, they go on the list,' said Blade, jumping in before her partner could answer.

'Ten?' gasped Angela. She closed her mouth and closed her eyes anticipating the fallout she would have to endure once that tidbit of news hit the board. She was about to leave the room when the detectives asked her to stay for a moment.

'We have a few other questions,' said McQ. 'We'd like to tap into your expertise.'

Angela nodded.

'You said you're an OB-GYN by training, correct?' asked Blade.

'I used to have an obstetrics practice. But, the hours got too demanding,' said Angela. 'Delivering babies is great when you're in your twenties and thirties, but as you get older, those hours get really tough. I couldn't handle the sleep deprivation. I thought moving into hospital administration would bring balance into my life. Look at me now.'

'We had a few questions about Eliza Stern, her pregnancy and the birth,' said Blade. 'How was it possible that Ms. Stern, on a feeding tube and presumably not eating the way a prospective mother should eat, could deliver a healthy baby?'

Angela took a few seconds before she answered the detective. 'Think of Eliza as kind of an incubator. A baby doesn't need much to grow. Calm and quiet and a steady flow of calories and liquids is all it takes. Eliza provided all that.'

'But, she was getting a minimum amount of nutrition and you said earlier that the baby looked cherubic,' said Blade.

'Sustaining a pregnancy doesn't take much if the womb is intact,' said Angela. 'There are women who deliver healthy babies in war zones. Starving refugees have healthy babies while in overcrowded camps. Eliza was fed regularly through a feeding tube and got sufficient calories, vitamins and nutrients that were enough to sustain a growing fetus. Patients who don't move, like

Eliza, have almost no caloric expenditure. Most of her food went to the baby.'

'Not a single person on staff noticed anything?' asked Blade. 'I know we discussed this earlier, but that's the piece that keeps rattling around in my head that doesn't compute.'

'I know to the lay person, it sounds inconceivable,' said Angela, 'but remember, no one was looking for or anticipating a pregnancy. That notion was so far out of the realm of possibilities that I guess it just didn't occur to anyone. Our staff sees Eliza several times a day. No one was looking for that.'

'But the woman was close to nine months pregnant,' said Blade, shaking her head in disbelief.

'Detective, our staff doesn't check for cataracts or tennis elbow either,' said Angela, getting annoyed. 'One of our patients may very well have cataracts and may be completely blind but it really doesn't matter when one is in a vegetative state so we don't check for it. A pregnancy fell into that same bucket.'

'I suppose that makes sense,' said Blade, clearly not convinced.

'She also carried extremely small. It can happen,' said Angela. 'I've had patients over the years who were in their seventh or eighth month and didn't know they were having a baby. They just thought they had gained a little weight.'

McQuillan had not said a word throughout the discussion. Normally, he would take the lead when he and Blade tag-teamed, but this was a subject where he felt out of his depth and he left it to his capable female partner.

'Let me ask you something else,' said Blade, scratching her head. 'How is it possible for a woman in a coma to vaginally deliver a baby? If her brain isn't working, how does that happen?'

'Detective, the human body is a miraculous instrument,' said Angela, getting excited. 'In a persistent vegetative state, like Eliza is in, your organs still work, and your fertility is functioning. While her brain is asleep, the rest of her body knows exactly what to do. That's why she's still breathing, circulating blood, excreting waste. Everything else is working. If a patient is unconscious and unable to push, delivery can be difficult. We would have to rely on medication to strengthen the contractions—oxytocin would be administered. That would bring on contractions strong enough to move the baby out through the birth canal. But, in this case, we didn't have to do that. Her body expelled the baby on its own.

'The nurses only realized what was happening after Eliza was well into her labor. She was already ten centimeters dilated when I got to her and we didn't know how long she had been at that stage. I got there just in time after they called me. The baby started crowning within minutes of my arrival in her room.'

'Good thing you were in the building,' said McQ.

'I'm glad I was,' said Angela.

It had barely been forty-eight hours since Eliza Stern had delivered her baby boy but to Angela it felt like years. Later that evening, on her way home that second surreal day, she stopped at a strip mall to pick up some food for dinner. It was late and she was tired when she stopped at the cash machine at a nearby Chase branch. When she checked her balance, their joint checking and savings account was down to one hundred and seventy-five dollars.

There should be at least three thousand dollars in this account. What happened to all of our money? The branch was closed so she called her husband but it went straight to voicemail. Wondering if their bank account had been compromised, she drove home as fast as she could, telling herself there was a logical explanation for the missing money. *David probably paid a bill that he forgot to tell me about.*

Out of habit, she grabbed the mail out of the mailbox hanging on the gray clapboard next to her front door as she entered her house. Her husband was waiting in the kitchen with cheese and crackers and an open bottle of red wine.

'I know you've been having a rough time at work so I cooked a nice dinner for you,' he said, smiling and reaching for her.

He always does this. It's like he has a sixth sense whenever the anvil is about to drop on his head.

'We won't have any hospital talk tonight,' said David, smiling. 'We'll just have a nice dinner and you can take your mind off everything.'

Angela glared at her husband. 'I stopped by the bank on my way home,' she said as David cut a piece of cheese and tried to give it to her.

'I don't want it,' she said, pushing his hand away. 'I went to get some cash. There's less than two hundred dollars left in our bank account. Where's all of our money?'

'Oh that, I'm just juggling around a few accounts to cover our bills, love. It should all gel out in a couple of days.'

'We can't keep doing this, David. Our credit rating is terrible. You've got to stop.'

'I promise, I'm getting us back on track,' he said, holding up a folder. 'I've got a system.'

Angela shook her head as she absentmindedly opened a few of the bills that were in her hand. 'How are we going to pay our bills this month? You want to tell me that? What did you do with the money?'

'Don't get yourself worked up about this, love, I'll take care of everything. I always do.'

Furious, she opened a statement from Florida Sun Pass. It showed the tolls for the past month. There were a half dozen trips to Hialeah, Hollywood and Coconut Creek. All locations that had casinos and dog tracks.

'I'm trying to keep a roof over our heads and you're screwing with me every step of the way,' Angela said, her voice getting louder. 'Just when I think we're starting to make headway, I go to the bank and our account is empty. Do I need to take your bank card away like a child?'

David hung his head and his eyes filled with tears.

'We can't keep going on like this, David,' said Angela. 'It's got to stop!'

'It's just that I get so frustrated when I can't write,' he said. 'Sometimes, I sit here and I feel like slamming my head into the wall. Going to the casinos or the tracks helps me take the edge off. I thought if I did this one race that I'd be able to make enough to pay back what I lost.' A single teardrop ran down his cheek into his salt and pepper beard. 'I got a tip. It was supposed to be a sure thing. I'm sorry, Angie. I'm so sorry.'

In almost every way, Angela Crawford was a force to be reckoned with, but her Achilles heel was her husband. Her soft spot for David ran long and deep and no matter how hard she tried, she couldn't stay mad at him. She still saw that handsome, dashing young author she had fallen in love with so many years before.

'It will be all right, babe, don't cry,' Angela said, putting her arms around her husband. 'We'll be okay. I get paid in two days.'

'I'm sorry, Angie. Forgive me?'

'Promise me, no more. I mean it.'

'I swear. Scout's honor.'

'You were never a Scout.'

14

On the third morning after the birth, Jenny O'Hearn and Lourdes Castro were summoned by the police to the temporary police conference rooms at Oceanside Manor. Blade took Lourdes into one room while McQ took Jenny into the other. Both nurses were asked if they had any idea what happened or saw anything unusual going on in the hospital prior to the birth of the baby. Neither had anything material to offer.

'Why did you call Dr. Crawford to assist you? Was there no other doctor available?' Blade asked Lourdes.

'That's a no-brainer. I knew Dr. Crawford was a trained OB-GYN and that she always worked late,' said Lourdes. 'She doesn't practice medicine anymore but when she did, she was really good, had a great reputation.'

'That's a lot of years of study to give it up. Why doesn't she do that anymore?'

'Delivering babies takes its toll,' said Lourdes. 'Who wouldn't get tired of getting up in the middle of the night, not getting enough sleep, and always being on call? She once told me the hours were affecting her health. I think she stopped practicing about twelve years ago and got her degree in hospital adminis-tration. I'll tell you one thing, she's a damn good administrator because she understands the needs of the patients *and* the medical staff.'

'A sign in the lobby says Oceanside Manor's chief adminis-trator is a Dr. Frank Farwell. Who is he?' asked Blade. 'And, where is he now?'

'Dr. Farwell went to Ecuador for about a year. Dr. Crawford is just the *acting* administrator while Dr. Farwell is on his sabbat-ical. He's supposed to be back in a few months,' said Lourdes.

In the other conference room, McQ was having a similar conversation with Jenny O'Hearn.

'Tell me how it all started,' said McQ.

'When Nurse Castro and I realized that Eliza was in labor, there wasn't time for anything. I'm not an obstetrical nurse but I know when a baby is about to be born. We both knew Dr. Craw-ford was probably in the building because she always works late so we called her and she came running within minutes.'

'Did the delivery go smoothly?'

'I haven't really been to any deliveries before,' said Jenny. 'I take care of people with brain injuries, but there didn't appear to be any complications. Dr. Crawford knew what she was doing.'

'As far as you could tell with your trained medical eye, the baby and mother were not in any distress?' asked McQ.

'I didn't say that,' said Jenny. 'Eliza was sort of twitching and she made some low moans. I remember asking Dr. Crawford if we should give her something for the pain but she didn't want to. She said she didn't know what she was dealing with and given all the other drugs Eliza was on, she didn't want to add anything. I think she was afraid it might hurt the baby. In retro-spect, I think that was the right call.'

≈

Back in the other room, Blade was nearly finished with Lourdes.

'Just a few more questions. Who else had access to Eliza Stern?' asked Blade.

'Not too many people work on our wing,' said Lourdes. 'The patients there don't require much nursing. Mainly checking delivery devices, making sure tubes aren't clogged, changing beds, that kind of thing.'

'In terms of staff, who's assigned to that floor?' asked Blade.

'There are eight rotating floor nurses on twelve-hour shifts and one head nurse during the week, that's me, and another one on the weekends. Ten nurses in total.'

'There's always at least one nurse on 3 West at all times, is that correct?'

The head nurse stared at the detective and pursed her lips.

'Yes. Unless…' said Lourdes.

Unless?'

'Unless a lot of people call in sick and we're short-handed. When that happens,' said Lourdes, 'I double or triple up my team so that I have one nurse covering two or three floors at a time.'

'How often does that occur?'

'Look, it's not supposed to happen, ever. You do what you gotta do,' said Lourdes. 'Sometimes I get one, two, three nurses all with the flu at the same time and somebody quits or has a death in the family and I have no coverage. What am I supposed to do? People get sick. People die. I have to make it work.'

'Dr. Crawford said her best guess as to when Eliza Stern conceived was most likely last year between April and June,' said Blade. 'During those months were there any times where you had people out sick and your nurses were covering more than one floor?'

'Probably,' said an exasperated Lourdes, throwing up her

hands. 'I'd have to check my old work schedules but people calling out sick happens every other week.'

'What about the aides? Are they always around?'

'During the day the aides are there, but at night it's only a night nurse.'

'Who might be on several different floors?' asked Blade.

'If they're covering for sick colleagues, yeah.'

'So, there could have been days where no one was within earshot of Eliza for hours?'

'I wouldn't put it that way,' said Lourdes.

In the other conference room, McQ continued to grill Jenny.

'If there are a lot of staff out sick, how long could 3 West go uncovered?' asked McQ.

'It's not exactly *uncovered*,' said Jenny defensively. 'It's only when we're short-staffed, which kind of happens a lot. But there's someone on a floor below or above. I've worked that shift plenty of times. I spend about half an hour on each floor before I go to the next. Nothing bad has ever happened.'

'On the overnight shift, do you go room to room?'

'No. I usually go to the central nurses' station on the floor where I can watch a monitor of patient vitals in every room. To be honest, it's pretty quiet at night. I usually watch Netflix,' said Jenny.

'If someone's covering three floors and they're up on 5 West. How long might it be before they're back on 3 West again?' McQ asked Jenny.

'It varies.'

'Give me a range.'

'I guess it could be as short as an hour and as long as three or four hours,' said Jenny.

'When people are out, there might be no personnel on 3 West for as long as four hours?' asked McQ.

'Yes, sometimes five,' said Jenny.

Blade had only a few more questions as McQ entered the interrogation room and took a seat.

'Nurse Castro,' said Blade, 'how many of your nurses and nurses' aides are men?'

'I knew that's what you were thinking and you're completely wrong,' said Lourdes. 'I know each one of them really well. Those guys have been with me for over five years. Neither of them would do something like that.'

'I'm going to need their names, please,' said Blade.

'They're both married. They've got kids. They didn't have anything to do with this,' replied Lourdes.

'Names, please.'

For Head Nurse Castro, this line of questioning didn't sit well. She loved every member of her team like they were her own family. She was the mother hen and they were her chicks. Both of the male nurses and their families celebrated Christmas with Lourdes' family and she was even a godmother to one of their kids. Giving up their names felt like she was giving up one of her own children.

'I realize this is uncomfortable for you,' said McQ gently. 'If they're the good guys you think they are, it will all be over quickly and we'll move on. You need to let us do our job.'

'Willie Maguire and Jorge Santiago,' she said, lowering her voice to a whisper.

Later that day, the detectives continued their investigation in their temporary conference rooms at Oceanside Manor. Two uniformed police officers were stationed out in the hallway outside the rooms prepping nervous people, answering questions and keeping general order.

'What's this all about? I don't know nothing about nothing,' said one tall, older man who worked in maintenance. 'I fix furnaces and broken chairs. That's it. I gotta get back to work.'

'Sir, the detectives are interviewing everyone who works at Oceanside Manor,' said the police officer. 'You've got nothing to worry about. Just routine questions. Your supervisors have been informed and know you are here.'

In order to keep a lid on what had happened and not raise suspicion or stoke rumors, the detectives elected to talk to everyone, not just the men. They also figured there might be a woman who witnessed something unusual.

A young policeman stepped out of the conference room and into the hall. 'Reginald Smith?' he called out to the crowd.

An aide, a young black man wearing blue scrubs raised his hand and was directed to the larger conference room. When he entered, McQ and Blade exchanged a look. Reginald Smith wasn't their guy. The father of Eliza's baby was definitely white. Still, they asked the aide a few questions, made him sign a statement and sent him on his way.

15

Tommy Devlin wasn't the fastest rising star on *The Oceanside Bulletin* editorial staff, but he was the most tenacious. Once he bit, he sunk his teeth in so deep, you needed a surgeon to get him off you. It took him a while to warm up to a story but when he did, if he thought it would put him in the limelight, he was all in. Tommy Devlin had one overarching goal in life—he wanted to be famous. If you stood between him and the story that could get him there, he'd steamroll over you without thinking twice. When he smelled a juicy headline, he was a heat seeking-missile—single-focused and intrepid.

Single, thirty-six and handsome in a calculated, smarmy sort of way, Tommy had been pounding the pavement for the *Bulletin* for nearly seven years. When he joined the editorial team, he considered them a third-rate news organization. He planned to use his position at the *Bulletin* to springboard himself into a bigger playing field. He wanted to write for a newspaper like the *New York Times* or a national magazine like *Forbes*. He thought himself good-looking enough for prime time and his ultimate goal—a regular spot on cable news and maybe even his own show one day on CNN. Unfortunately for Tommy, he had a knack for rubbing people up the wrong way and opportunities that presented themselves usually soured after he pissed somebody off. The fact that he wasn't able to leapfrog out of the *Bulletin* like he had planned became a source of great frustration for him. He believed he was destined for and deserved to be in the big leagues.

This particular day, he was at his desk eating a ham and Swiss cheese sandwich with extra mayo, washing it down with a can of Red Bull when the call came into the overcrowded, dingy news bullpen. Tommy answered the call with a mouth full of food. It was some guy who worked in food service at Oceanside Manor, the extended-care facility next to the hospital. The guy was calling in a tip. At first, Tommy thought the man sounded like a moron and he tried to get him off the phone so he could finish his sandwich.

'I'm telling you, man, there's been some strange things going on here this week,' said the food services guy. 'People are whispering all kinds of crazy stuff and there are cops all over the place. They're interviewing like every person who works here. Even the guys who mow the lawns.'

'Do you know why?' asked Tommy Devlin, mildly interested as he reluctantly put his sandwich down to grab a pen.

'I don't know,' said the man. 'What's in it for me?'

'My eternal gratitude,' said Devlin. 'We don't pay for tips. If that's what you're looking for, you came to the wrong place. Call the *Enquirer*.'

'I was just asking. No harm in that. I mean, what if you did pay for tips and I left money on the table. Then, I'd be a big loser.'

'Yeah, you'd be a loser. But we don't. If you want to talk to me because you want to do the right thing, I'm here. If not, I'd like to finish my lunch,' said Tommy about to hang up.

There was a long pause as the would-be tipster considered his options.

'Okay, I'll tell you what I know,' said the man on the phone. 'It's something to do with a baby.'

'What do you mean "something to do with a baby?"' asked Devlin. 'Isn't that a place full of old people?'

'There's a lot of old people in here but there's some younger ones, too,' said the man on the phone. 'Oceanside Manor is for people who are, you know, brain-dead, nothing going on upstairs, vegetables. All I know is that I heard people saying something about a baby and pretty soon all these cops showed up. We don't have no babies here. Something strange is going on.'

Tommy smelled something. When he finished the sketchy call with the tipster he walked directly over to his editor's desk.

'I just got a line that something weird is going on over at that extended-care facility next to the hospital. You know the place, Oceanside Manor.'

'I know it. What do you mean by weird?' asked his editor, looking up from an article he was reading.

'That's all I've got so far,' said Devlin. 'My source said there were a bunch of cops over there and they're interviewing all the employees, even freelancers. The guy said there's a baby involved.'

'Isn't that place a nursing home? Why would there be a baby there? You think it's something?'

'Could be. I don't think it's nothing.'

'Grab one of the photographers and go see what you can find out. Bring back something for tomorrow's paper.'

Tommy Devlin tapped one of the photographers on the shoulder and the two headed across town. When they drove through the front entrance of Oceanside Manor, several police cars were outside. Parking in front of the old brick building that at one time had been the hospital, before the new one had been built next door in 1998, they got out and walked towards the front doors. A uniformed police officer stood in the center of the lobby. Tommy recognized him. Oceanside wasn't that big a town and Tommy had been working the crime beat for a long time. He knew all the local cops and they knew him and most of them had his number. It was common knowledge that Tommy would sell his own grandmother if it would give him a leg up and a front-page story. The police were always guarded about what they said to him.

'Hey, Officer Manzer,' said Tommy, smiling as he stuck out his hand. The officer reluctantly shook it and cautiously smiled back.

'Doesn't take long for bad news to travel, I see,' said the policeman. 'What brings you down here, Devlin?'

'Got a tip. What's going on down here? Awful lot of cops around the place.'

'Routine stuff.'

'Routine? Three squad cars in the parking lot?' said Tommy. 'You've got cops standing guard in the lobby. Doesn't seem *routine* to me. I doubt you're here to collect unpaid parking tickets.'

'I'm not at liberty to discuss anything at this time.'

'Then it *is* something?' said Tommy, his head cocked to one side. 'From what I heard, you're interviewing a boatload of people. Someone told me the police were meeting with every person on the staff. That right?'

'I can't confirm or deny anything. Orders. Sorry,' said the officer, looking away, wishing Tommy would disappear.

'I heard this has something to do with a baby. They got a baby in this place? I thought Oceanside Manor was for old people. Isn't this a nursing home?'

'I have no comment on anything, Devlin,' said Officer

Manzer, getting testy. 'You're going to have to leave the building, now.'

'Relax, I'm going. I'll just nose around outside a little. That's okay, isn't it? It's a free country, right?'

Devlin and his photographer walked out through the automatic sliding glass doors into the parking lot. The photographer turned around and took a photo of the red brick building while Devlin waited for new people to walk in or out. A few minutes later the electronic doors of Oceanside Manor opened again and two young women in lab coats emerged, headed towards the parking lot. The reporter spotted them and followed.

'Excuse me, ladies?'

The two women spun around.

'I'm Tommy Devlin with *The Oceanside Bulletin*,' he said, smiling and handing them each a business card. 'You work here at Oceanside Manor?'

They both nodded.

'Cool. What's going on? Why are the police here?'

The two women looked at each other quizzically.

'We don't know,' said the shorter one. 'We got an email saying the cops needed to interview everyone who works here. They didn't tell us why.'

'Did they interview you yet?' asked Devlin.

'Yeah,' said the short woman. 'They just asked me some basic stuff, you know, like what my schedule was and had I seen anything unusual around the building.'

'Did you?'

'No.'

'How about you?' said Devlin to the taller woman.

'Same thing,' said the taller one. 'I didn't see nothing.'

'You know anything about a baby?'

The two women looked at each other for a moment as if they were trying to communicate telepathically.

'Well...I heard somebody say something about a baby,' said the taller one. 'And, they've cordoned off 3 West. No one except the people who work on that floor or the cops are allowed up there.'

'Is that pretty unusual?' asked the reporter, getting more interested.

'Extremely unusual.'

'I heard someone found a dead baby,' the shorter girl blurted out.

'That's what I heard, too,' said the taller one, her eyes growing wide. 'I heard somebody found a dead baby's skeleton buried inside of a wall.'

Tommy Devlin's mouth dropped open while he wrote as fast as his pen would move.

16

Eliza Stern's court-appointed attorney, Elliot Meyers, waited in an interrogation room at the Oceanside Police headquarters for a meeting with Blade and McQ. Short, bald and pudgy, Elliot was co-operative, but guarded.

'Thanks for coming in, Mr. Meyers,' said McQ. 'We figured it was better for you to come here rather than fight with the circus over at Oceanside Manor. Yesterday, there were already a few reporters poking around and we're trying to keep a lid on this for as long as possible to keep the chaos to a minimum.'

'I appreciate your discretion, detective,' said Meyers. 'This is all a terrible business. That poor girl. Are you any closer to knowing what happened? It's an outrage, is what it is.'

'We're working on it,' said McQ. 'There are hundreds of people to be interviewed. We've just scratched the surface. It may take a few weeks before we get to everyone.'

'Naturally, my concern is for my client, Ms. Stern. I spoke with a Dr. Horowitz, the attending physician,' said the attorney. 'According to him, healthwise, Eliza is fine. What remains to be decided is, what happens to her baby.'

'I believe child services was called,' said McQ. 'For the time being, given that the child was slightly premature, they're keeping him with his mother so they can monitor him and make sure there are no complications.'

'My client has no other close family members,' said Meyers. 'Only one or two distant relatives who didn't know Eliza before the accident and they've taken no interest in her since. Right after the crash, they crawled out of the woodwork. Once they learned there was no money in it for them, they disappeared. I can assure you, they will not want the baby. I suspect the child is headed into foster care.'

Blade shot her partner a look.

'Mr. Meyers, can you tell us what exactly your role is and what you do for Eliza Stern now?' said Blade.

'I was appointed by the courts after the family's car accident when it was determined that Eliza would not be coming out of her comatose state,' said Meyers. 'There was a settlement from their insurance company which provides enough money to maintain her in Oceanside Manor for as long as she lives.'

'If she dies, who gets the money?' asked Blade.

'No one,' said the lawyer. 'It's open-ended. As long as she stays alive, they keep paying. If she dies, their obligation is complete.'

'What about if she has heirs, like a child,' asked Blade.

'There was no provision made for that as it wasn't something anyone...anticipated,' said Meyers.

'It would be in the insurance company's best financial interest if Ms. Stern expired, correct,' asked Blade.

'That's true. If my client died, the insurance company would be off the hook,' said Elliot Meyers. 'Are you suggesting that somehow there was a conspiracy on the part of the insurance company to impregnate my client with the hopes that she'd die?'

'We're not suggesting anything,' said McQ. 'We just want to

understand all the players and who might benefit from the situation.'

'Mr. Meyers, according to the hospital records,' said Blade, sifting through some papers, 'you come here fairly regularly. Why do you come to Oceanside Manor?'

'To see my client, of course.'

'But your client's in a coma,' said McQ. 'Couldn't be a very productive visit.'

'Look, detectives, my office is right here in town and once every quarter, I stop in and talk to her, as her attorney,' said Meyers. 'I have a soft spot for her. She was a kid when she was brought in here. We have a nice little chat. I tell her what's going on in the news, how I'm taking care of her bills and how things are going in the world. Been doing it for over ten years.'

'Once a quarter you spend alone time here with your client?' asked McQ.

When he heard McQ's comment, Elliot Meyers furrowed his brow and looked at each of the detectives. 'Wait a minute. You're barking up the wrong tree,' said Meyers, his palms in the air.

'Do you hear any barking, Detective Blalock?' said McQ to his partner.

'I don't hear a thing,' she said, laying on her thickest southern drawl. 'When mah partnuh barks up a tree, he howls. He ain't howling right now. You'd know it if he was.'

'If you're trying to insinuate that I had anything to do with Eliza Stern's pregnancy, you're out of your mind. Take it any further and you'll have a lawsuit to contend with.'

'Now don't get your tail all in a bunch, Mr. Meyers,' said Blade slowly and cheerfully. 'We're just having a friendly, neighborly conversation.'

'Are we through here?'

'One more question,' said McQ. 'You've been handling Ms. Stern's affairs for ten years and visit her four times a year. That would mean you've had about forty *meetings* with her. Is that correct?'

'I guess so. Are we finished now?'

'There's a part B to my question,' said McQ. 'During your visits with Eliza, were you always alone?'

'Yes.'

'One of the floor nurses said,' McQ continued, while reading from a piece of paper in his hand, 'that you'd tell them you were going to confer with your client and you were not to be disturbed. The nurse said you always closed the door to the room. Now, why would you close the door, Mr. Meyers?'

17

After Elliot Meyers left the police station in a huff, threatening multiple forms of legal retribution, McQ and Blade headed back to Oceanside Manor for an afternoon of interviews. With so many people to interrogate, the chief of police decided that they would conduct most of the interviews over at the long-term facility.

Blade pulled their Toyota Camry out of the police station parking lot and pointed the nose of the car west towards Oceanside Manor.

'How about making a little detour on our way across town,' said McQ, pointing to his watch. 'We've got a few minutes.'

Blade glanced sideways at her partner. 'What heart healthy establishment do you want to go to today?' she said with a mix of amusement and disapproval.

'I've been thinking Chick-fil-A might brighten our day.'

'Does your cardiologist think so, too?'

McQ squirmed. Sometimes being with his partner was like being with a wife.

'I'll stop today because we're under the gun, and we're not going to have time for a lunch break,' said Blade, lecturing. 'But going forward, we agreed you get only one fast food stop per week. You hear me? I promised Marie I wouldn't let you eat all that crap.'

'Yeah, I got it,' said McQ with a sad but resigned expression on his face as they pulled up to the drive-through lane.

'Welcome to Chick-fil-A,' said the talking sign. 'What can I get for you?'

'Let me have a spicy deluxe sandwich with pepper jack cheese, no lettuce,' said McQ.

'God forbid you ate some greens,' said Blade under her breath.

'What are you talking about. It comes with a pickle.'

Blade rolled her eyes.

'I'll also take an order of waffle fries.'

'Anything to drink,' said the sign.

Blade squinted at her partner.

'A *diet* lemonade,' said McQ.

The car lurched forward in the drive-through line.

'You think because you ordered a diet lemonade it counteracts all the junk you eat?' said Blade, shaking her head. 'You and Marie come over for dinner tomorrow night. You know what a great cook Eve is, she'll make you a healthy vegan meal. I promise, you'll love it.'

McQ finished the last bits of his sandwich as they pulled into the Oceanside Manor parking lot. Four squad cars were parked outside the front entrance. Several reporters and a news van pulled into a spot as the detectives walked across the blacktop to the front door of the facility.

Within a minute they were surrounded by eager media folks. Some were from the local paper and a couple were from the cable news channels. Standing at the center of the pack was Tommy Devlin.

'Look who's already here,' said McQ.

'It's your good friend, Mr. Devlin,' said Blade with a laugh. 'That boy can smell a dead possum on the road before the crows get wind of it.'

'No kidding,' said McQ. 'He's a mercenary.'

The two detectives walked through the crowd deflecting questions from the reporters and entered the building. They waved to the officer standing in the lobby and went up a flight of stairs to the staging area where all employee interviews were being conducted. Opening the heavy metal door from the stairwell, the detectives looked down the hall. Dozens of people were seated in chairs along the walls. Some reading, some talking—most were screwing around on their phones. A uniformed female officer was at the other end of the hall doing preliminary interviews.

'Looks like you have things under control,' said McQ to the younger officer. 'How many people have you logged in so far?'

'We've only gotten general info from the staff that was on duty this week. Maybe fifty people in total, twenty-two of those are men,' said the officer. 'Figured we'd start there. I've color coded them into four batches, A–D. Some because of ethnicity or lack of physical ability are on the D list, meaning *highly unlikely*.'

'The hospital admin, Dr. Crawford, has her staff pulling together lists of visitors, freelancers, and outside vendors,' said McQ. 'They'll pass those names off to us as they compile them. Should have some of it by end of day today.'

McQ picked up a stack of folders with individual names on each one. He separated out the ones color coded with red and handed one to Blade.

'Is there an Emanuel Silva here?' Blade said loudly so everyone in the long hallway could hear.

A man's hand shot up.

'Come with me,' said Blade, waving her hand.

Silva followed the detectives into the conference room. In his thirties, he was wearing baggy jeans, a utility belt with tools hanging from it and had a beeper on the breast pocket of his shirt. His eyes darted around the room when they closed the door. He was shaking slightly and sweat stains were visible under both of his arms.

'Have a seat, Mr. Silva,' said McQ. 'Can I call you Emanuel?'

'Call me Manny. That's what everyone calls me,' said the man.

'So, Manny, tell me what you do here.'

'I'm the on-staff handyman. I do everything from changing lightbulbs to fixing TV's to unstopping toilets,' said the young man.

'You spend any time over on 3 West?' asked McQ.

'No more than anywhere else in the building. Lightbulbs go out pretty much all over the hospital. This is an old building. Something's always breaking.'

'You ever go into Eliza Stern's room?'

'I've been in every room in this place,' said Manny. 'I don't know who that person is. I don't pay attention to the names of people. I just fix what's broken.'

'According to the notes in this file, one of the nurses said she remembered seeing you up in room 312, Eliza Stern's room. She said it was about ten months ago and she asked you what you were doing in there. Do you recall that, Manny?'

A row of sweat formed on the man's upper lip.

'Manny, I hope you don't mind me saying this but you seem a little nervous. Are you nervous?' asked McQ. 'We're just having a friendly chat. Is there something you want to tell us? Something you want to get off your chest?'

The young man looked at each of the detectives, visibly anxious.

'I don't know anything,' said Manny, looking down at his

feet. 'Sometimes, I eat my lunch in the rooms with some of the patients and just talk to them. I tell them my problems and my secrets because I know they won't tell anyone. I find it relaxing.'

'Now, what kind of secrets might you be keeping, Manny?' asked Blade.

The agitated young man looked like he was about to explode.

'Look, I don't want no trouble. I do my job. I got a wife and a two-year-old daughter to take care of.'

'We don't want any trouble either but it feels like you're hiding something from us,' said McQ. The two detectives stopped talking and waited. After almost a minute of silence, Manny cracked.

'Okay, okay. Three years ago, I overstayed my visa. I was supposed to go back to Brazil but I didn't. I do a good job here. I've got a family. I don't want any trouble with immigration.'

McQ let out the breath he had been holding and looked at his partner with a tinge of disappointment.

'Manny, we have no interest or inclination to contact immigration,' said Blade. 'We've got a crime to solve and that's all we care about. Do we understand each other?'

The young man nodded and from then on was more forthcoming. After another fifteen minutes of questions, Manny Silva was dismissed.

Blade picked up another red dotted folder and went out into the hallway.

'Jason Branko.'

A man with light brown hair in his thirties, sitting at the far end of the hall stood up, grabbed a backpack on the floor next to his chair and followed Blade into the conference room.

'Mr. Branko, may I call you Jason?' said McQ.

'Yeah, sure.'

'Jason, tell me what you do here.'

'I work in food service. I help prepare the food and then I also deliver meals to the patients.'

'Right. There's something that's confusing me a little,' said McQ. 'According to the notes in your file, several people said that you were seen coming from 3 West with your food tray trolley.'

'Yeah, so?'

'I think what he's getting at, Mr. Branko, is that all the patients in 3 West are incapacitated,' said Blade. 'None of them are conscious. They wouldn't get food trays, would they? They have feeding tubes, do they not?'

'I guess so. I don't know if they have feeding tubes or not,' said Branko. 'I just deliver food where I'm told.'

'What's confusing me is why you would be anywhere near 3 West?'

Until that moment, Jason Branko had been non-committal and aloof. Once the detectives pointed out that no meals would have been delivered to that floor, he knew the jig was up and came clean.

'I'm not supposed to do it but...there's a few girls who work as aides on that wing that I kind of like. I bring 'em free lunch when I'm working. I grease their wheels a bit. Cheaper than taking them out for dinner, you know what I mean? It's like I'm treating them to a meal but the hospital is paying for it. They order whatever they want, I deliver it and later on they're very grateful to me.'

'I've always said nothing turns a girl on more than Jell-O and little cups of orange juice,' said Blade to her partner.

After several more minutes with Branko, McQ let him go.

'Quite the Romeo,' said McQ to his partner once they were alone. The rest of the afternoon produced more of the same. After they interviewed every single man waiting in the hallway, they were no closer to a conclusion than before they started.

18

In the three days since she had delivered Eliza Stern's baby, Angela's life had been turned upside down. The board was breathing down her neck. The entire staff of Oceanside Manor was in different stages of interrogation by the police. Through it all, Angela was still trying to run the place while taking care of her patients. While balancing all the internal chaos, she was also trying to keep the press at bay for as long as possible. Once they got their claws into this story, she knew they would be relentless. Despite her best efforts, inquiring phone calls from the newspapers and TV stations had increased exponentially each day.

'What's going on down there?' barked board president, Bob Beckmann, over the phone on that third day. 'My office just got a call from the *Miami Herald.*'

'I don't know how much longer we can keep the press out of it,' Angela replied. 'They smell something rotten and they're not letting go—like sharks circling around chum. At best, I think we've got until tomorrow. Stuff is already leaking out.'

'What are the police doing?' said Beckmann.

'They have a lot of people to interview.'

'Why is it taking them so goddam long?' demanded Beck-mann. 'I'm thinking the press release should go out tomorrow.'

A few minutes later, Angela's call with the board president ended the way it always did—him yelling, complaining and issuing an edict of some kind before he hung up on her. This call was no different. Angela looked out the window and realized it was already dark outside. With no more energy left, she packed her bag to go home. Before she left the building, she went up to 3 West to check on Eliza and the baby. As she had mandated, a registered nurse was on duty in Eliza's room and was holding the baby and singing to him when Angela walked in.

'Dr. Crawford,' said the nurse, surprised and a little embarrassed that Angela had caught her singing. 'I-I didn't know you were still here. I'm on the night shift.'

'And, quite the singer, I see,' Angela said, smiling.

The night nurse blushed red and giggled. 'My kids always loved it when I'd sing to them. I figured since this little guy doesn't have a mom who can sing, I would,' said the night nurse.

Angela looked at the infant cradled in the woman's arms.

'Can I hold him for a minute?' Angela asked, smiling for the first time all day.

'Of course, Dr. Crawford.'

The nurse stood up with the baby in her arms so Angela could take a seat in the rocking chair that had been installed in the room the day before. The nurse carefully handed over the baby.

'He's a cutie,' said the night nurse, stepping back to give her boss some space.

'He sure is,' said Angela, not taking her eyes off the little boy. 'He's truly a miracle.'

'Dr. Crawford, are you going to be here for a while?' asked

the night nurse. 'I was wondering, would it be okay if I left you for a few minutes to use the ladies' room?'

'Of course, take as much time as you need. I'm not in any rush.'

The nurse trotted off as Angela rocked the child in her arms.

'Are they taking good care of you here, my little man?' asked Angela softly, using a baby voice. Slowly, she touched the baby's nose and examined each of his tiny pink fingers and his even tinier fingernails. 'You're really perfect, aren't you? And, you're such a good baby, too. All the nurses say you hardly ever cry and that you're a good eater.'

She continued to rock in the chair and began to sing to the baby. 'Twinkle, twinkle, little star, how I wonder where you are. Up above the sky so high, like a diamond in the sky...'

Angela looked up and saw the night nurse standing in the doorway smiling at her.

'You look like you know your way around babies,' said the nurse. 'Do you have kids?'

Angela smiled ruefully. 'We wanted them but I couldn't so instead I went for the big career. But I love kids, especially babies.'

'From the way you look right now, I'll bet you would have been a great mother,' said the nurse. Catching herself, she added, '...if you had been a mother. I mean...being a mother isn't the only path...I mean...'

'It's okay,' said Angela, her eyes never leaving the baby. 'I know what you meant.'

She continued to rock the baby for a while longer and then glanced at her watch. She had been there for almost forty minutes and it was nearly nine. 'I guess it's time I went home. I'll be back here in ten hours, anyway.' She gave the baby a kiss on his forehead and handed the little boy to the nurse.

When she walked into her house that night, her husband

was in the kitchen waiting for her. He had saved a dinner plate wrapped in foil and had it waiting on the counter for her as he often did. When she saw the dish, she realized how hungry she was. David didn't do much to help pay the bills, but at least he knew his way around the kitchen, and she was grateful one of them knew how to cook. *He may not contribute much to our finances*, she told herself, *but at least there is always something good to eat when I get home from work.* She took whatever solace she could in that.

19

DAY 4

When Blade and McQ arrived at the hospital that morning, a new stack of names and folders were waiting for them. The chief of police had added an overnight team to the investigation because of the time sensitivity of the case. The night crew had vetted and sorted through a ton of information. Now, it was up to Detectives McQuillan and Blalock to weed through what had been compiled the night before. They had the first batch of names that included non-employees—outside contractors, visitors, clergy and others.

That morning, the detectives interviewed eleven men from a variety of companies—grounds maintenance, fire alarm, hospital supply and an office cleaning crew. Not a single one of them set off McQ's inner bullshit meter which he considered infallible.

'You think any of the guys we interviewed today are good for it?' said a disappointed McQ to his partner.

'Nope. It was pretty clear none of them had any idea why they were here. Who's next on deck?' said Blade, looking through another folder.

'A priest, a rabbi and minister walk into a critical care facility...'

'The hospital chaplain?' said Blade, doing a fist pump.

'Bingo. Should be interesting. I don't know if you've heard,' said McQ, 'but the clergy hasn't got a very good reputation when it comes to this kind of thing.'

'You don't say?' said Blade with a grin.

Five minutes later, Father Harold Heathwood sat across the table from the detectives.

'Father, you also work out of St. Mary's Church up north of Palm Beach, right?' asked McQ.

'That's right, detective. I minister at a number of hospitals and senior facilities. Oceanside Manor is just one of many.'

'Not to be indelicate father, but what kind of *ministering* do you do with unconscious people?' asked McQ.

'Even if they're sleeping, they're still God's children,' said the priest. 'I talk to them. I give them hope.'

'You know you give them hope because...?' said Blade with one raised eyebrow.

'I believe I do. It's about having faith, detective.'

'I believe that I'm going to win the lottery when I'm buying my ticket,' said Blade. 'I have complete faith in that as I hand over my five dollars, but that doesn't make it so.'

'Eliza Stern was born and raised a Catholic. I try to give whatever comfort I can to that poor young woman,' said the priest.

'How exactly do you comfort her?' asked Blade.

'I pray with her. I hold her hand and read from the bible. I tell her that God is watching over her and loves her and that one day she'll be rejoined with her family in heaven.'

'Do you ever touch her in any way other than holding her hand, father?' asked McQ.

'Of course not, detective. I understand why you have to ask

but I assure you, nothing inappropriate ever happened. I am after all, a priest.'

'That's why I'm asking,' said McQ with a bit of rancor. 'I went all through the Catholic school system which makes me a bit of an expert.'

After a few more questions and answers, the detectives released Father Heathwood.

'What's your bullshit meter telling you now?' asked Blade.

'He's not our guy,' said McQ. 'He's a pompous creep but my ears didn't itch and you know my ears always itch when I'm getting close to something. Who's up at bat next?'

'Peter Parris, he's the brother of Martin Parris, another patient on 3 West. Martin is in the room right next to Eliza,' said Blade, flipping through the file. 'According to the visitor logs, Peter Parris visited his brother frequently, almost every week and he spends long hours reading to him. From a logistics perspective, he could have easily slipped out of his brother's room and into Eliza's without anyone noticing.'

'Don't keep me in suspense. Let's bring him in,' said McQ as his stomach grumbled. 'Before you do, you got anything to eat in your pack?'

'An apple.'

McQ made a sour face as Blade went to get Peter Parris.

Three minutes later, the two detectives were staring across the table at a tall, very thin young man with reddish blond hair.

'What's going on,' asked Peter. 'There's all sorts of crazy rumors going around.'

'What have you heard?' asked McQ.

'Someone said a body was missing from the hospital morgue next door,' said Peter. 'But if that's what it is, why would you want to talk to me? I've never been over there. I just come here to Oceanside Manor to visit my brother, Marty.'

'I understand you come here quite often,' said McQ, looking him dead in the eye.

'Every week.'

'That's a real commitment,' said McQ, tilting his head to one side.

'Marty isn't just my brother, he's my identical twin.'

'Now there's a coincidence,' said McQ. 'Your twin brother is in a coma and right next door to him is a woman in a coma who was also an identical twin. What are the odds of that?'

'Slim to none, I'd guess,' said Peter. 'I had heard that Eliza was an identical twin, too. One of the nurses told me about her. I felt sorry for her.'

'Why is that?' asked Blade.

'I visit my brother every week. I read to him and tell him stories about what's going on in our family. But she has no one. Nobody visits her or spends time with her. Sometimes, I'd go into her room and talk to her, just to let her know that someone cared. That I cared.'

'How often did you visit with Eliza and how long would you stay?' asked Blade, suddenly more interested.

'It varied. Sometimes, I'd stop in to see her for a few minutes. Other times, when I didn't have to be anywhere else, I'd stay with her for half an hour and just talk. Sometimes I'd hold her hand. I think she knew I was there. It must be awful with no one to love you.'

'Did you ever lay down on the bed with Ms. Stern?' asked Blade. 'You know, maybe just to hold her and let her know you were there for her?'

Peter's eyes widened and he looked genuinely surprised. 'Did something happen to her? Do I need a lawyer?'

'That's up to you, Mr. Parris,' said McQ. 'Eliza is fine. You're not being charged with anything. We're just asking some general questions.'

'I would never hurt Eliza. In a weird way, I always felt very connected to her because of my brother. I thought maybe they communicated with each other in that cosmic coma realm that they're both inhabiting. You think that's possible?'

'Yeah, sure,' said McQ, giving his partner the eye.

20

After McQ and Blade finished with Peter Parris and several other relatives of patients, they waited for Steve Horowitz, the attending physician, to arrive from the hospital next door.

'Is this going to take long?' said Dr. Horowitz, walking in twenty minutes late, eyes on his phone. 'I've got a lot of patients to see today and I'm supposed to leave for a medical conference in New Orleans tonight.'

'Doctor, I'm going to ask you to please put your phone away while we conduct this interview,' said McQ. 'We need your full attention.'

'I can multitask,' protested the doctor clutching his phone. 'You have to be able to do that when you practice medicine.'

'Bless your heart. Can you operate on two people at the same time, too?' said Blade, wearing her big South Carolina smile. 'Still, despite your extraordinary brain capacity, we need you to put your phone away while we ask you some questions.'

Horowitz made an irritated face as he put his phone into his breast pocket. 'I'm keeping it on vibrate,' he announced, 'in case anyone needs me.'

'That's fine,' said McQ with a weary look. He was tired. Since this case started, he and his partner had worked eighteen-hour days. 'Dr. Horowitz, you want to tell me what your role is here at Oceanside Manor and if and when you ever treated Eliza Stern?'

'I'm on staff next door at Oceanside Medical. I divide my time between the emergency room there and supervise the care of some patients here at the Oceanside Manor annex. I mainly work with those who have *recently* been admitted,' said Horowitz. 'After they've been here a while, the nurses have the routine down and the patients don't need that much intervention or input from a physician.'

'Can you give me an overview of the patient population you treat here at Oceanside Manor?' asked McQ.

'Almost all the people who are residents here have traumatic brain injuries,' said Dr. Horowitz. 'Some from accidents—car crashes, drowning, electrocution. There are those who had strokes or internal issues that caused a brain hemorrhage. And, there are even one or two who landed here because of a drug overdose that led to a catastrophic incident. Most of the patients who end up here, have no chance of any meaningful recovery due to the severity and permanence of their injuries. This place is kind of the last stop on the train, if you know what I mean.'

'I see,' said McQ, taking notes. 'Did you supervise the care of Eliza Stern?'

'She's been one of my patients.'

'How often did you see her?'

'About once a week, I do rounds and check charts,' said Horowitz. 'Detective, what you don't understand is that the condition of these patients rarely changes. The facility's job is to make sure their feeding tubes and catheters were working and that the patients are clean and as comfortable as possible and that's kind of about it.'

'When you did your rounds, did you do them alone?' asked Blade.

'Sometimes. It depended on the day,' said Horowitz. 'Look, this place is a business, like all medicine is today. They keep staff levels low in order to make a profit. Most of the time, I checked on patients by myself. Rarely was there a nurse with me.'

'What about when you checked on Eliza Stern?' said McQ.

'She's on 3 West. That wing has the most severely compromised patients, you can hear a pin drop over there. Jenny O'Hearn and Lourdes Castro are the nurses who work on that floor. They're both diligent and competent. Sometimes, when I checked on Eliza, Nurse O'Hearn accompanied me.'

'But you just said that the staff was so lean, you were usually alone,' said Blade, leaning forward. 'Now you're saying that Nurse O'Hearn was with you when you examined Eliza?'

'I know where you're going with this,' said Horowitz. 'Obviously, we all know that some guy raped Eliza Stern and you're trying to find out who that is. Read my lips, it wasn't me and I was never alone with Eliza.'

'And, why is that?' asked McQ.

Horowitz appeared uncomfortable and looked around at every corner of the room. McQ glanced over at Blade.

'Dr. Horowitz?' said McQ. 'Is there something you want to tell us?'

Horowitz took a deep breath and let it out. His initial look of irritation was replaced with one of resignation. 'I was never alone with Eliza Stern because...I was having an affair with Jenny O'Hearn and she was always with me,' said Horowitz. 'The patients on 3 West are so compromised that we used to meet in some of their rooms and...well...you know.'

'No doctor, I don't know,' said Blade. 'Illuminate me.'

Horowitz grimaced and waited a beat. 'We'd have sex, detective. Jenny and I would go into Eliza's room every few days and share a moment. Satisfied?'

'Why always Eliza's room?' asked McQ.

'A few reasons,' said the doctor. 'The patients on that floor require little maintenance so rarely would any other staff be around. Also, Eliza had no relatives or friends. There was virtually no chance of being surprised by a visitor or well-wisher. And, her room was at the end of the hall near the staircase so we could easily get in and out.'

'Let me get this straight,' said Blade, unable to control her eyebrows from arching. 'You'd have sex with Nurse O'Hearn, check your patient and move on to another patient?'

'Pretty much.'

'When was the last time you had a romantic encounter in Eliza's room?' asked McQ.

'It's been at least six months,' said Horowitz. 'Jenny and I ended it a while ago.'

'Oh yeah,' said McQ. 'Now, why is that?'

'She met someone else and said she didn't see our relationship going anywhere.'

'I wonder why,' said a deadpan McQ.

'She was hung up on the fact that I'm married,' said Horowitz.

'Some women are so petty,' said Blade, shaking her head.

Horowitz's confused expression told them he wasn't sure if the detective was mocking him or agreeing with him.

'She started seeing this other guy and told me it was over between us.'

'How did you feel about her ending it?' asked McQ.

'I was cool with it being over,' said Horowitz. 'Jenny is hot but there are plenty of nurses who go for doctors, married or not. I didn't need all the headaches. Besides, there were some rumors that Jenny used to have a drug problem. As a physician, I can't afford any whisper of drugs connected to my reputation.'

'Of course not,' said Blade supportively. 'That's entirely

understandable. Sex with a nurse on the floor of your comatose patient's room is fine but drugs...well that's a bridge too far.'

Horowitz looked at Detective Blalock unsure of the true intention of her comments.

After the physician answered a few more questions, he left and the detectives did a post-mortem of their meeting.

'That guy is a piece of work but I'm on the fence about him,' said Blade.

'He might have been getting it on with the nurse but that doesn't preclude him from also having some extra-curricular time with Eliza Stern. Horowitz clearly likes to play the field.'

'He had the access,' said Blade, 'and his moral compass is definitely askew.'

21

Tommy Devlin had stood out in front of Oceanside Manor waiting for his big scoop for so long, he was afraid he would get picked up for loitering. Getting a statement from anyone who went in or out of the facility had resulted in very little usable material. Nobody was talking and the ones who were, didn't know anything. His editor at the *Bulletin* was breathing down his neck, demanding to know when Devlin was going to deliver his big story. Short answer, he wasn't. He had nothing.

Only the day before, a couple of girls had given him a tip about a baby's skeleton being recovered from inside of a wall in the hospital. His eyes nearly bugged out of his head when he heard it as he envisioned the shocking headline with his name attached to it. A story like that would bring a huge circulation bump to the paper and put him on the front page for weeks, maybe even months. After a little checking, it turned out the baby in the wall story was completely bogus, another fake rumor, one of many that had been circulating. Apparently, the girl who shared that tidbit heard one thing and thought she heard something else, repeated it, and the next thing you knew, they had all concocted one giant, horrific but entirely untrue story.

When Devlin first took her statement, he was pumped—it was juicy. But as he continued to press the women on the facts, something didn't add up. He'd been a reporter long enough to know when a line didn't feel right. Thankfully, he didn't embarrass himself by taking it to his editor without verification.

Three days of a huge police presence at Oceanside Manor and Devlin was still without his big story. Still, he knew something was there. His byline from the day before reported there was 'something going on at Oceanside Manor' but didn't reveal any facts. The hospital and police continued to keep a tight lid on whatever it was. The information blackout only increased Devlin's desire to get his story. The lack of transparency on the part of the police tripped his insatiable curiosity gene into high gear. His editor wanted the juice and Devlin would be damned if he didn't deliver it with extra pulp.

He called the facility administrator, Angela Crawford, and got lucky when she answered her own phone. When Devlin identified himself as a reporter from the *Bulletin*, she mumbled something about being in a meeting and hung up. He was used to that. More people hung up on him than a robocall. He had to make at least twenty calls to get one person who'd agree to spill the beans. It went with the territory and he was cool with it— most of the time.

It was about 2:30 in the afternoon when the same two girls who had told him about the baby in the wall, walked out of the front entrance of Oceanside Manor and waved at him as they strolled towards the parking lot.

'Hey, girls,' shouted Devlin, running after them. 'Got a minute?'

'We're not supposed to talk to anyone,' said the tall girl,

turning away. 'Our supervisor told us not to engage with reporters under any circumstances.'

'Hey,' said Devlin, turning on what little charm he had, 'who said anything about engagement? I'm not asking you two to get married. I'm just wondering what's going on inside this place. Why so many cops?'

'We still don't know,' whispered the short girl. 'Nobody tells us anything.'

'I tried to corroborate that baby inside the wall story you told me; didn't check out,' said Devlin, shaking his head.

'I told you not to say that,' said the short girl, letting out an exasperated breath as she shot her taller friend a look. 'She always let's her imagination run away with her. I'm constantly reining her in.'

'I thought it was true,' said the tall girl. 'Somebody told me that. How should I know?'

'You think everything is true,' said the short one. 'You think all the women on *The Bachelor* really like the guy. Give me a break. It's totally fake.'

'It is not. They do like him,' protested her friend. 'You're so cynical.'

'Ladies. Ladies. Let's get back to the topic at hand. Why is the place crawling with cops? There's been a police presence here for three full days. Why here? Something must have happened.'

The short girl looked over at the red brick building and moved closer to Devlin as if she was going to impart the world's greatest secret. 'I don't know if this is why the police are here, but I heard that it has something to do with one of the nurses— Jenny O'Hearn,' said the short girl in a loud whisper.

'Jenny O'Hearn?' Devlin repeated as he wrote the name down.

'She's a floor nurse on 3 West,' said the short girl.

'She thinks she's all that,' said the taller girl. 'Kind of stuck up, I'd say.'

'Did something happen to her? Why would the cops be here about her?' Devlin asked.

'I don't know,' said the short girl. 'But what I do know is that Jenny O'Hearn had an affair with one of the doctors on staff, Dr. Steve Horowitz. Horowitz's wife, by the way, is currently expecting twins.' The short woman nodded her head for emphasis.

'Interesting,' said Devlin, 'but I don't think an extra-marital affair would warrant a full police investigation. A divorce lawyer, maybe, but the cops, not so much.'

'That's all I know,' said the short girl as she and her friend walked away. 'And don't quote me, I detest gossip,' she said, calling over her shoulder.

'Me too,' Devlin called out as the women got into their car.

As far as he was concerned, he had nothing to quote, but still, he didn't completely discount what he had learned. After years walking the crime beat, he knew that every piece of information added up to the sum of the whole—you can't discount anything. He leaned up against a tree to get out of the sun and made a mental list of what he knew so far.

Half of the Oceanside Police Department is camped out at an extended-care facility housing mainly brain-dead people. The cops aren't talking and they're interviewing a lot of people. The baby skeleton story was a bust—unreliable sources. The head of the hospital hung up on me and no information is being released. A nurse, who works on the third floor of the facility is allegedly doing the nasty dance with a Dr. Horowitz, whose clueless wife is just about to deliver twins. Ha! When Mrs. Horowitz finds out about the nurse, they're going to need a cop. Note to self—find out if Mrs. Horowitz is really in the dark? My gut tells me this is something...something big.

22

Walking back from the ladies' room, Angela stopped at a hall window and looked out, almost in a trance. She watched several more news trucks pull into the hospital parking lot and unload equipment as dozens of reporters and cameramen scurried about setting things up. Food trucks, having identified a new market of hungry customers, had also joined the melee. Angela shook her head as a hand gently tapped her shoulder.

'Dr. Crawford,' said her assistant, Vera. 'You have a three o'clock conference call with Bob Beckmann.'

Startled, Angela looked down at her watch. It was 2:59. She sighed, thanked her assistant for reminding her and marched towards her office. As soon as she closed her door, her phone rang. She looked at the ID and made a sour face, it was Beckmann.

'Good afternoon, Bob.'

'What's going on?'

Adrenaline pumped as she ran her fingers through her hair. Beckmann always rattled her, making her anxious and animated. 'We're moving as fast as we can,' said Angela. 'My staff is weeding through names, dates, job orders, deliveries, time sheets. It's a lot. We're not automated like they are next door at Oceanside Medical. Remember, you and the board didn't approve the budget for that last year. We have to do everything by hand.'

'Are you complaining?'

'I'm just telling you the reality,' Angela snipped.

'You know what the reality is?' said Beckmann, his voice starting to amplify. 'You've got a freak show going on over there, Angela. Women in comas having babies, sickos running around loose, and reporters camping in our parking lot. I drove by earlier today and there was a taco truck doing brisk business in front of Oceanside Manor. We can't have that.'

Angela took a deep breath before she responded. 'We're doing the best we can.'

'Which isn't good enough and means you're nowhere.'

'The police have been interrogating people for fifteen hours a day,' said Angela. 'I don't know how much longer we can keep this story under wraps. Bits and pieces have already leaked. Reporters and news crews are all around the building asking questions. The truth is going to come out.'

'We can't let that happen,' said Beckmann. 'Call the PR firm. Tell them I said to "push the button" tomorrow midday. They've been sitting on the release we crafted with the lawyers just waiting for my signal. Tell them it's time to roll it out, we need to get ahead of this story. Before it breaks, you need to inform the staff. Meet with your people first thing in the morning.'

23

Sitting on the worn oatmeal-colored sofa in the familiar waiting room that evening, the sound of world music coming from hidden speakers was barely audible. It was set just loud enough to block out any noise coming from behind the closed office door. An essential oil machine pumped a light scent of patchouli into the air. For probably the fiftieth time, Angela examined the oversized adventure photographs that lined the walls. She had been seeing Virginia for years and had grown fond of the therapist's no-nonsense approach and her adventurous spirit. Blown-up photos of diving, mountain climbing, kayaking and white-water rafting had been taken by the therapist on her many global excursions. Angela didn't have Virginia's keen sense of adventure, but she deeply admired people who did. More single-goal oriented, Angela focused her energy on her husband and medicine and that was enough for her. Besides, these days, they had no money for extravagant vacations. David had seen to that.

The door to Virginia's office opened slowly and a teenage boy of about seventeen shuffled out looking like a deer in headlights. For a split second, the kid reminded Angela of her brother, Michael. The kid looked right past her at his mother who was signaling from out in the hallway through the glass door and the boy left. A moment later, Virginia stepped out of her office and waved to Angela.

'Give me a minute,' she said as she hurriedly walked by. 'I've got to wee or I'm going to burst.'

Angela turned her attention back to the soothing pictures. Virginia had taken a great photo of tropical fish on one of her diving trips to the Caribbean. *How wonderful and quiet it must be deep down in the water. No phones ringing. No one asking questions. No board of directors—only quiet.* Lost in her thoughts, she was startled when Virginia burst back into the waiting room with her customary smile.

'Angela, you're up,' said Virginia, walking back into her office with Angela following obediently behind.

'How are you?' said Virginia as they both sat. Virginia looked directly into Angela's eyes.

'I've been better.'

'I've heard there's quite a scuttlebutt brewing over at Ocean-side Manor.'

'It's an awful mess. One of our non-responsive patients went into labor four days ago.'

'How far along in her pregnancy was she when she was admitted?' asked Virginia.

'You don't understand, this particular patient has been with us and in a coma for twelve years.'

'Holy shit,' said Virginia, her eyes opening wide. The second after her words left her mouth, she caught herself. 'Sorry, that wasn't very professional of me at all. You caught me by surprise. What I meant to say was, "Oh my, how did that happen?"'

'We don't know yet,' said Angela, shaking her head. 'There's a massive investigation going on right now. I haven't had a minute to breathe. It's a miracle I was able to make our session today. I've been working twenty-hour days this week. I'm exhausted but I really needed to see you.'

'I can imagine,' said Virginia. 'Sounds like you have your hands full. What do you want to talk about today? Work or home?'

Angela paused for a moment. 'I think a little of both,' she replied.

'Let's start with what's going on with your job and after we can talk about David,' said Virginia.

Angela brought her therapist up to speed on the many challenges she was facing at the hospital with managing the staff, the board, the patients and the police. Virginia gave Angela gentle suggestions for coping with her new set of challenges.

'How about trying it this way,' said the therapist, leaning forward. 'Rather than looking at it as one giant insurmountable problem—and don't get me wrong, it is most definitely a biggie —try breaking everything into small pieces and manage each one individually. You'll find it more expedient and easier to accomplish small goals.'

Angela nodded dutifully.

'Now, what's going on with your husband?' the therapist asked.

'Nothing, that's the whole problem.'

'Can you give me a little more?'

'He's the same only it's getting worse. It feels like it's been going on for so long,' said Angela. 'I go to work and he doesn't do anything all day. He hasn't written a word in years except for an occasional corporate freelance project and even those have dried up because he doesn't meet deadlines. He's been gambling and losing money at the casinos after he's promised me he'd stop. He might as well flush our money down the toilet or set it on fire. Some months, I can barely pay our bills and I'm a freaking doctor.'

'Do you still love him?'

'I'm still in love with Professor David Crawford, the man I met in college. David the novelist, the jokester, the confident guy who was going to take on the world and win a Nobel Prize for literature. Every girl I went to college with had a crush on him and he chose me. But the man I have now is so different from the one I married.'

'You think the old David is still in there?'

'I thought if I gave him enough support, everything would eventually come together and he'd be able to start writing again. His writing was how he defined himself. Without that identity, he's blowing aimlessly in the wind.'

Virginia nodded in support. 'Perhaps he peaked too soon having a best-selling novel in his early twenties. Sometimes, success too early and too fast overwhelms people and sends them down the wrong path. It's hard to top a meteoric juggernaut that one achieved at twenty-four.'

'That's what I think, too,' said Angela. 'When his second book tanked, people in the publishing industry stopped calling and he lost his mojo. Add to that, all the years of stress, with us trying to have a baby. My husband really wanted to be a dad. I think he's still really sad that he's not. Being a father would have given him the purpose that he seems to be missing.'

'We've talked about this before. You still won't consider adoption?'

Angela looked at her therapist with resolve and shook her head. 'You know why I don't want to. My brother and I were adopted and it was hell for my parents after my brother started to lose it. When you adopt you don't know what kind of gene pool you're fishing in. I won't put myself through that.'

24

DAY 5

As Beckmann had ordered, the next morning Angela called an all-hands meeting of Oceanside Manor staff and carefully explained the particulars of the miraculous birth and the baby that now resided on 3 West. She answered dozens of questions and tried to rally her troops and put their concerns to rest. Getting teary as she spoke, she committed herself and the hospital to rooting out the problem and putting new procedures in place to make sure nothing like this would ever happen again.

'There is no place for something like this in our facility,' said Angela. 'Families entrust the care and well-being of their loved ones to us and we cannot fall short. Right now, we need to make things right so our families regain the confidence in Oceanside Manor that they once had. We'll all be under a lot of scrutiny and stress for the next few weeks. I'd like to ask each of you to co-operate fully with the police and provide them with whatever they need so we can put this awful situation behind us. We will get to the bottom of this, I promise you.'

'What do we tell the families of the other patients?' asked a nurse. 'There are going to be a lot of questions.'

'That's being handled,' said Angela calmly. 'The hospital attorneys and I have been reaching out to the families privately by phone. A letter is being sent out from the board to each family by email as we speak. Please refer all questions from patient families or their attorneys to me.'

Working with their PR agency, the following press release was sent out over the wires.

For Immediate Release.

Contact: Dr. Angela Crawford, MD, Acting Administrator, Oceanside Manor

Email: aacrawford@oceansidemanor.org

OCEANSIDE MEDICAL CENTER/ OCEANSIDE MANOR

POLICE INVESTIGATION UPDATE

Oceanside Manor, affiliated with Oceanside Medical Center, has been in business for close to 25 years, and has an unblemished reputation for providing high-quality care for our patients. Our patients' health and safety are always our first priority. We are proud of our long history in caring for the intellectually and developmentally disabled.

Recently, we became aware of an incident regarding the health and safety of one of our residents. We have taken steps to review our systems, protocols and staff to make sure that all of our patients are getting the safest and best possible care. We strive for excellence in patient care and offer our profound apologies to all of our families, our clients/patients/residents, to the community and our agency partners.

As soon as we were made aware of the problem, we gave our full cooperation to the Oceanside Police Department and will continue to work with investigators in every way possible.

We have increased security measures to ensure the safety of

all our patients and are in the process of reviewing and improving what is already an in-depth vetting process for caregivers at Oceanside Medical Center and Oceanside Manor. Mistreatment or assault of a patient in our care will not be tolerated. Every patient is entitled to and deserves a safe environment.

A copy of the Oceanside Manor press release was forwarded from the newspaper's editor to Tommy Devlin. The reporter had ignored his beeping phone because he was in the middle of schmoozing one of the young female police officers he had cornered outside the police headquarters building.

'What's going on over at Oceanside Manor,' said Devlin. 'My gut is screaming right now.'

The officer remained silent and simply stared back at the persistent reporter.

'C'mon, Janice. How long have we known each other?' said Devlin, laying it on thick.

'About a month,' said the policewoman, looking around for another cop to rescue her.

'Exactly. We're practically family,' he replied with a grin.

The female police officer smirked. Everyone in the Oceanside PD knew Devlin. He was relentless, and sometimes abrasive but he made up for it by being occasionally entertaining. It was common knowledge there was nothing he wouldn't say if he thought it would get him the story.

'I'm not at liberty to talk about it,' said the cop. 'You're going to have to wait like everyone else.'

'C'mon, Janice, help out a fellow Irishman,' he said.

'I'm Italian.'

'Irish, Italian, same thing. My people came here because of a potato famine and yours because of a pasta famine,' he said with a hopeful grin as he reached for the vibrating phone in his pocket. Looking at the screen, he quickly scanned the press release from Oceanside Manor that had just been sent to him.

'Holy shit,' said Devlin as he read. 'What the hell does this mean? Assault of a patient? Isn't everyone at Oceanside Manor totally out of it?' The reporter looked up at the officer's face and tried to read it.

'Don't look at me,' she said, backing away, her hands in the air. 'If you want information, talk to the chief. I'll have my head handed to me if I open my mouth.'

'They put out a press release, it's all public now. So, you can tell me.'

'Nice try, Devlin. You're an investigative reporter. Go investigate,' said the police officer as she turned and walked back into the station.

Devlin ran across the street, jumped into his car and raced back to the Oceanside Manor building as fast as possible. This was going to be big.

25

After a long afternoon hanging around the hospital parking lot, Tommy was only able to gather crumbs of benign information that the hospital administration and the police would divulge. Somehow, he pieced together a story for the morning edition of the paper.

WOMAN IN 12 YEAR COMA HAS BABY
By Thomas Devlin, Jr.

After an unprecedented breach of security, police investigators have begun to gather DNA from all male parties who worked for or visited the Oceanside Medical/Oceanside Manor extended-care facility, where a twenty-one-year-old woman who has been in a vegetative state for almost twelve years, gave birth to a healthy baby boy last week.

A spokesperson from the Oceanside Police said Wednesday that the woman and child, who was delivered on January 13, remain in the hospital and both are in good condition and that 'the sexual assault investigation will likely take some time.'

'This is not a simple process,' said Mayor Tim Davidson.

'This crime happened over an extended time period and there are a large number of individuals that need to be vetted. The police department has had to cast a very wide net.'

The police would not comment further on whether anyone had been asked for DNA samples.

The woman in question, has been a patient at Oceanside Manor since 2005, according to court records. It has been reported that she entered the facility after a catastrophic car accident on the Florida Turnpike outside of Orlando that killed both of her parents and her twin sister. The accident left the mother of the baby in a permanent vegetative state. The woman has no other relatives.

Board President of Oceanside Manor, Robert Beckmann, would not take phone calls but directed people to a hospital spokesperson, Acting Facility Administrator, Angela Crawford, for further information.

'Oceanside Manor will do everything in our power to help uncover the full accounting of this horrifying situation. This has devastated everyone involved, from the victim to our own hospital staff,' said Angela Crawford, MD. 'I want to assure our families and the public, we will get to the bottom of this situation.'

When Tommy Devlin's story went out onto the wires, it was picked up by every national and international news organization within an hour. Cable shows grabbed it and for the first time in months, the relentless bi-partisan political in-fighting that had become a staple of the evening news was pushed to the back burner. Eliza and her baby were front page in every national newspaper. She was the lead story on the radio, TV, and internet. The birth was the topic of conversation in company lunchrooms, on social media and at cocktail parties. Tommy Devlin himself was even interviewed by national news shows as the 'local reporter on the ground in Oceanside.' There was talk of Devlin appearing on CNN. In a nutshell—the story went viral in a nuclear way. Eliza Stern and her baby were in the dead center of a conversation happening around the world and everyone asked the same question in different languages—what kind of person would do something like that?

Devlin didn't really care one way or the other who or why someone would have sex with an unconscious woman. It was irrelevant to him. What mattered was that he was now at the center of the news universe. People around the world wanted to know his opinion about what had happened and he planned to milk the story for all it was worth. From his vantage point, Eliza Stern and her baby had become his golden goose. He laughed when he thought of the irony of it all. Some guy got his rocks off with a comatose woman and Devlin might very well end up on CNN. His whole life was about to change and he figured he had Eliza Stern and a yet unknown pervert, to thank for all of it. *The world works in mysterious ways*, he chuckled to himself as he returned a call from Reuters.

26

A few days into the investigation, McQuillan and Blalock had come to a mutual conclusion on how to proceed. It became apparent that the only way they were going to find the person who raped Eliza Stern was to get a DNA sample from every male who had set foot in Oceanside Manor over a three-month period the year before. It was probably a wider range than necessary but if there was the slightest possibility that the conception calculations were off, they expanded the time, just to be on the safe side.

'Even so,' said Blade, 'some nut job could have gotten in through an improper channel and there may be no record of him at all. Seems to me, if I was going to do something like this, I'd want to remain invisible so there would be no record of my presence.'

'It's possible our perp snuck in undetected,' said McQ, 'but right now we've got a partial working-list of seventy-three males who we know for sure were in the building during that period of time. There are still more names to vet but let's swab the ones we've got and see what crawls out. If we're lucky, one of them is the baby daddy and we can stop looking for that needle in a haystack.'

'Legally, they don't have to give us their DNA,' said Blade.

'I know that, and you know that, but I'm hoping most of them don't know that.'

'If I were the baby daddy, I wouldn't give my DNA up. But, I guess for the guys who are employed here,' said Blade, 'it would look really bad if they didn't. If they're innocent, they should naturally want to do the swab and clear themselves.'

'From your mouth to God's ears,' said McQ with a knowing smile.

Later that day, an Oceanside police team was assembled to methodically take all samples from those willing to give it. A line of men in all shapes and sizes formed in the hallway by the conference rooms being used by the police. The line was so long it twisted around the corner.

One by one, each man stepped into a small private room, the door was closed and cells were gently scraped from inside their cheek, collected, bagged and labeled. It took a few hours but the officers worked efficiently and without much conversation in order to get a job of this magnitude completed and samples off to the Palm Beach County police lab.

Until the investigation was over, no one other than hospital staff and immediate family members of patients were allowed into the facility for any reason. All deliveries and 'other business,' would be conducted and logged in the lobby. While things were surprisingly orderly inside the Oceanside Manor building, outside it was pure pandemonium. It had only been a few hours since Tommy Devlin's story broke. His front-page article was the catalyst triggering the global media world's descent on the normally sleepy Oceanside. Reporters and news crews ten deep camped out on all the main streets in town. Local residents were annoyed their town had become overcrowded, while the restaurants, bars and delis were delighted. For some entrepreneurs, this 'immaculate conception' at Oceanside Manor was great for business.

News of the baby had spread like wildfire within the walls of Oceanside Manor and throughout their sister hospital, Oceanside Medical. Nurses and doctors from all departments stopped by the room to see the tiny baby the world was so curious about. As Angela had mandated, the child received 24/7 care and was rarely put down, falling asleep in the arms of one nurse or another. The hospital staff had decorated the room. Many brought in baby things they had at home and created a mini-nursery in Eliza's room. Colorful animal decals were placed on the wall next to the baby's bassinet and a musical mobile hung over the crib. Stuffed animals of every shape and size lined the walls of the room and soft twinkling music played in the background. A rocker and a changing table had been moved into the room and fully stocked with diapers and lotions. The staff even fought over who got to hold or feed the newborn on any given hour. Outside the hospital, a steady stream of flowers and baby toys piled up near the front entrance from well-wishers and lookey-loos. Oceanside Manor had become a media and tourist mecca and the tiny baby boy was the star attraction.

Even Angela, despite all the stress, found herself over on 3 West taking her turn at feeding the infant, who the hospital staff had already nicknamed, Eli, after the baby's mother. While the country and the world's fascination with the scandal grew, Eliza Stern lay nearby, motionless, as strangers fed her son.

When Angela took her turn to hold and feed the baby she looked carefully at his tiny head. It had only been six days since the little boy was born but he already looked so different from that first day. When he first came out, he had just a little fuzz on his head but already more was coming in. She smiled at him.

Look how nice and chubby you are now. Your face has changed. You are a beautiful boy.

She gazed down at the infant in her arms and wondered what it would be like to have a child in her own home. She had thought those maternal feelings had vanished after all the years she and David had tried to have a child. Now, holding him and contemplating all she had been through, feelings stirred inside of her.

That evening when Angela left the building to go home, she had to fight her way through throngs of reporters and cameras all clamoring to get a statement or picture from her. The hospital board and the company attorneys had been very specific about interactions with the press. There were not to be any, until there was some closure on what had happened.

'You understand me, Angela?' Bob Beckmann had said at an emergency offsite meeting of the board that she had been summoned to. 'Say nothing to anyone. When you come in or out of the building, look straight ahead and walk. Don't stop. Don't smile. You're a horse with blinders on. Clear?'

'Clear.'

'It hasn't even been twenty-four hours since this thing broke in the press and they're covering it in New Zealand. Can you believe that? My wife's sister is on vacation there and she saw it on the news. New Zealand. Who even knows where that country is anyway?'

'I believe New Zealand is southeast of Australia, Bob,' volunteered another board member.

'I don't give a shit if it's northwest of the north pole,' shouted Beckmann. 'Bottom line, it's on the other side of the world and Oceanside Manor is on the front pages of their newspapers. Everyone needs to keep their head down until we figure this out. If there's nothing else, and I hope to God there isn't, let's adjourn.'

'There is one more thing,' Angela began, bracing for his reaction while at the same time, looking forward to it. 'I hate to be indelicate, but I'm afraid the police have asked that all of you provide your DNA samples to them.'

'What the hell are you talking about?' demanded Beckmann.

'According to our records, the board had one of your quarterly meetings with Frank Farwell in the building just before Dr. Farwell left for Ecuador,' said Angela. 'The date of that meeting fell within the time period that's being investigated.'

'Why didn't anyone tell me about this?' said Beckmann.

'I'm telling you, now,' said Angela. 'The police want your sample.'

'This is outrageous. You think that one of *us* attacked a woman in a coma?' said Beckmann. 'Whenever we had our meetings at Oceanside Manor, we all came and left together and went to lunch—together. There would have been no time for any one of us to wander off.'

'Don't shoot the messenger,' said Angela, turning her palms up, secretly pleased the police request for DNA had irritated Beckmann so much. 'They're taking samples from every male who was in the building during those twelve weeks. You're a male and you were in the building. It's not my call, it's a request from the police. We can't expect all of our employees to do this if our administrators and board won't.'

Beckmann grumbled as he and the other board members made some calls and arranged for their samples to be taken somewhere other than at Oceanside Manor. That kind of publicity, they didn't want or need.

27

Inside and outside the hospital everyone was losing their minds except for Jenny O'Hearn. She remained calm and focused as she poured over documents in a small records room on the third floor of the facility. Due to privacy laws, the hospital would release only material absolutely essential to the investigation. It was Jenny's task to keep those protocols in mind while she compiled the list and ruled out those who didn't fit the profile. She looked down at the column of names. *One of these men is the father of Eliza's baby. One of them is a rapist.*

The small file room she was using had at one time been a staff break room before the hospital commandeered it for storage. Angela had turned the space over to Jenny while the project was ongoing, and the rest of the staff was told it was 'off limits' to all other personnel. It was now filled with boxes containing operational documentation; schedules, supply orders, patient dietary requirements, and so on. She pulled out a long cardboard box sitting on a metal shelf along the walls and dragged it with a thud onto the metal table in the middle of the room. The table was a remnant from the days when staff used to eat their lunch in there. She opened the box. It was filled with employee schedules from the previous year and she separated the men from the women. Spotting another carton of files on a higher shelf, she climbed up on a chair and pulled it down. It contained one of the things she needed, visitor and vendor logs. She began to sort through those.

Sadly, she noted as she read the visitor logs, most of the patients at Oceanside Manor didn't get many visitors. During the ninety-day period that she was focused on, there were only forty-four different visitors and only eleven who went to 3 West. She also noted that Eliza Stern had only one visitor during that time period, her attorney, Elliot Meyers. According to the records, Meyers spent over an hour with Eliza—alone.

For the entire day, Jenny combed through box after box of documents. She wrote a note to herself. 'Check the mail delivery guy. He comes every day but doesn't always sign in on the log books because the front desk knows him and waves him in.'

Absorbed in countless files, she was startled when her phone rang. It was her boyfriend, Danny. Seeing his number pop up on her screen made her smile. After all the missteps she had with men in the past, Danny was possibly the real deal. They had only been going together for a few months but he was always so good to her, she had already decided he might be 'the one.'

'Jenny, whatcha doing?' he said, chuckling. Danny was always laughing. That was one of the reasons she liked him so much. He could always make her smile.

'I'm up to my eyeballs in files. Literally.'

'Still?'

'You have no idea. There are thousands of data points to be matched. I'm doing it all by hand. This is the kind of thing that would normally be done by a computer. My eyes aren't even focusing anymore.'

'Poor baby. I'll have dinner ready for you when you get here.'

'Have I told you today that I love you?'

'No.'

'Well, I do.'

28

Late that afternoon, McQ and Blade's car pulled into the Oceanside Manor parking lot for a five o'clock meeting with Angela and board president, Beckmann. The hospital was ready to pass on the names they had compiled and now the police would start banging on some doors.

Blade put the car in park and looked at her watch. It was four forty, still twenty minutes until their meeting.

'You ready to go in?' she asked her partner.

McQ looked over at her and picked up his half-finished cup of almost cold coffee out of the cup-holder and took a final gulp.

'We got a minute. If we get there early, they're only going to make us wait in the lobby. Let me finish my donut,' he said as he unwrapped a half-eaten gooey chocolate mess covered with sprinkles.

'Does Marie know you're still eating those?'

'Hey, this past weekend she decided *we* were going gluten free,' said McQ. 'I didn't have any gluten for three whole days.'

'And, how did you feel?'

'I felt like crap,' said McQ. 'I really think my body *needs* gluten.'

Blade gave her partner a withering look.

'No, seriously. I could barely hold my head up. When Marie took a shower I ducked out and got myself a bagel,' he replied as he stuffed the remainder of the donut into his mouth. 'I almost forgot to tell you. Got a call on the prints they took from Stern's room. There were over thirty different sets. They were able to match all of them to staff except for one.'

'Our perp?'

'Could be,' said McQ, 'but something tells me it's not going to be that easy and we've still got to identify who those prints belong to.'

'Any new theories you want to share?' said Blade.

'Logistically,' said McQ as he swallowed, 'it's most likely someone on staff because they would have frequent and easy access. A visitor or an outside employee would have to be really stealthy and know exactly when and where they could commit the act without getting caught. That seems too convoluted to pull off for an outsider. My money is on an inside job.'

'But it *could* have been someone from outside,' said Blade. 'That's still a possibility.'

'That's what makes this whole investigation so unwieldy.'

'Here's a creepy thought,' said Blade. 'How do we know the perpetrator only did this the one time? Maybe he had sex with Eliza numerous times, but this was the only time she got pregnant.'

'What if whoever did this tried it with other brain trauma patients besides Eliza,' said McQ. 'Dr. Crawford said she was going to have all the female patients on 3 West checked for pregnancy and signs of any physical or sexual disturbance.'

'Can you imagine if there are more?'

Minutes later, the two detectives waited in Angela's office while she went down to the lobby to get Beckmann. Behind the administrator's desk, McQ noticed a picture of Angela and, he presumed, her husband, all dressed up at some black-tie event. Out of professional habit, and because he couldn't help himself, the detective studied all of Angela's photos until she entered the room followed by the perpetually scowling board president. Beckmann walked past the detectives and sat in Angela's chair at her desk, forcing Angela to sit on a nearby window ledge.

'Take my chair,' said McQ, getting up.

'I'm fine here,' said Angela.

While the seat jockeying was going on, Jenny O'Hearn knocked on the office door holding an armful of manila folders.

'Come in, Jenny. We're about to start,' said Angela, waving the young nurse into the room. 'Grab a chair from out front.'

'I've got it,' said McQ, who stepped out of the office and returned with a chair and placed it next to Angela.

'Detectives,' said Beckmann, 'it's been almost a week since this terrible business started. I trust you're close to making an arrest.'

'Mr. Beckmann, there are a lot of moving pieces in this case,' said McQ. 'We've been waiting all week for the data and logs from your people so we can run down leads. With all the health privacy laws, our hands have been partially tied. I think we're going to get everything we need today from Ms. O'Hearn.'

Jenny smiled and nodded eagerly.

'You mean to say you haven't been doing anything except waiting for us to provide you with information,' asked an incredulous Beckmann. 'You're the cops, not us.'

'Mr. Beckmann,' said Blade, jumping in and laying on her southern drawl. 'We've had the entire Oceanside Police Department standing on their heads trying to get to the bottom of this unfortunate situation. As my partner already said, because of United States health privacy regulations, we've had to move very slowly and carefully. Now, I'm assuming Ms. O'Hearn here will be able to provide us with all relevant employee work schedules, patient-visitor log files and other assorted vendor lists in order for us to do a thorough and precise investigation.'

Beckmann glared at Blade but uncharacteristically, said nothing. Angela laughed to herself. *Nicely done, Detective Blalock. I need to take a page from you on managing that pompous ass.*

'Jenny, why don't you show us what you've got,' said Angela. 'She has fairly high confidence that she's got a substantial and accurate list for you.'

Everyone's eyes turned to the young blond nurse.

'I could have missed something and I'm going to spend the next few days digging a little more but I think, detectives, what I'm about to give you is pretty solid,' she said as she dropped some thick files on the desk near McQ and Blade.

'How many people did you uncover?' asked McQ.

'A lot: 274,' said Jenny with an air of confidence.

Blade whistled. 'That's a lot of people.'

'Too big a challenge for a small-town police department, detective?' said Beckmann. 'Maybe we should call the FBI, bring in the big guns.'

McQ and Blade exchanged a look. 'Mr. Beckmann, I think Detective Blalock's reaction to the big number had more to do with her surprise at the largesse of *your* security breach,' said McQ with authority, 'not that our police department can't handle it.'

'Let's get the show on the road,' said Beckmann. 'Every minute this case goes unresolved the reputation of the hospital goes further into the gutter. Already, some of our biggest financial donors have started to walk away. That can't happen. Do I make myself clear?'

'Crystal,' said McQ, his steely eyes looking right through the board president causing Beckmann to squirm. *Exactly what I thought, he's a big pussy. I bet his wife has to cut up his meat for him before he eats it.*

29

While his wife's world at the hospital spun out of control, David's routine remained painfully the same as it was the day, week, month and even year before. He cleaned up the breakfast dishes, read the news on his phone and sat down at his computer to work on his manuscript, the same as he did every morning. Each day, for five years, he'd type a few words or sentences into his computer, read them over and usually erase them. He'd do a few more sentences, delete some of them and keep one. After several hours of writing he'd discover he'd only accumulated one or two paragraphs and when he reread it, he'd decide it was crap and delete the entire page. That was pretty much how every morning went.

David's mind drifted back to the early days of his career. It was easier reminiscing about his past Camelot than confronting his current dismal professional reality. Everything had happened so goddamned soon for him—faster than anyone expected, and maybe that was at the root of the problem.

College had been a magical time. He was handsome, charming and smart and without much effort, good grades and friends came easily. Interested in writing, at the end of his junior year, David showed some of his short stories to his favorite English professor, Dr. Anastos, head of the English department.

'I like this one, David,' said Dr. Anastos, holding up a short story called, *The Savior Falls*. 'It's got grit and asks some provocative questions. I want you to submit it to that writing competition I told you about.'

'They must get thousands of entries,' said David.

'Listen to me,' said Dr. Anastos. 'You've got real talent. I don't think I've ever said that to any of my students.'

When David left his professor, he was walking on air and the next day he mailed in his entry. Months later, quite unexpectedly, he got a letter.

Dear Mr. Crawford,

The National Literary Guild is delighted to inform you that you have been selected to receive this year's first prize in the short story category.

He ran across campus to the English department to find Dr. Anastos. The older professor was sitting at his desk grading papers when a breathless David flung himself into the teacher's doorway.

David waved the envelope as he tried to catch his breath. 'The short story contest, I won first prize!'

Dr. Anastos's face broke into a huge smile. 'First prize! If I remember correctly, part of the prize is you'll get a literary agent, too. You're on your way.'

In early spring the following year, a week after his story was published, David got a call from Corbin Rotero, a seasoned New York literary agent. He had read David's winning story and wanted to work with him.

'Have you given any consideration to writing a full-length novel?' asked Corbin.

'All the time,' said David. 'I've got a million ideas.'

After graduation, he began working on a novel that would eventually be called, *Where the Falcons Go*.

For the next two years, David worked diligently on his manuscript sending bits and pieces to Corbin as he finished them. Right before his twenty-fourth birthday, David finished his manuscript, sent it off to his agent and held his breath. For two weeks, he waited by the phone until finally he got the call.

'It's brilliant,' said Corbin, 'one of the finest pieces of fiction I've read in a long time. You've blown me away and that doesn't happen very often. I'll bet I can even get a bidding war going from the top five publishers.' Within two months, Corbin scored with several major publishing houses bidding for David's book and a six-figure deal was signed.

When *Where the Falcons Go* came out eighteen months later, it was a hit. Magazines called him the next F. Scott Fitzgerald and his book was translated into seven foreign languages.

After a year of interviews, awards and basking in literary glory, David began working on his second novel but something was wrong. Where words had at one time sprung from his fingers, now it was like they were lodged in his knuckles. It would take him weeks to write one chapter. Eighteen excruciating months later, he delivered his new manuscript to his agent.

'I liked your other one better, but we'll sell this one on your name alone,' said Corbin. 'A publisher will take it and consumers will buy it because of your first book.'

Early reviews were scathing and in no time at all, David's second novel was on the sale table in book stores.

Fortunately, while he was writing his second novel, David had gotten his masters' degree in journalism and had started teaching at his alma mater. The New York literary community may have had David Crawford in the rear-view mirror, but he was still a big deal on the college campus and enjoyed a kind of elite status there.

Over the next seven years, David wrote another novel but no one wanted to publish it.

It was around that time that he met a young pre-med student, Angela Asmodeo, who was taking one of his English classes. He thought she was beautiful the minute he laid eyes on her.

That was so many years ago. On this morning, David went through his daily fruitless literary gymnastics and eventually got up from his desk in frustration. Washing his hands in the bathroom, he looked at the familiar face in the mirror. *When did your hair get so white?* His hair, mustache and beard were prematurely white, but the skin on his face was taut and his eyes were still twinkly blue and bright. He stared at his reflection and was overcome by a feeling of self-loathing.

'You think you can write?' he said out loud to his image in the mirror. 'You don't have talent. You're a fraud. You thought you were such a big deal when you published that first book. You were so full of yourself and now you can't string two words together.'

Feeling the walls closing in on him, he had to get out of the house. He splashed water on his face, grabbed his car keys and headed out the front door. Before long he found himself on I 95 driving south towards Davie, Florida. He knew exactly where he was going, where he always went when he felt like he couldn't breathe or live up to his own expectations. When he was in the middle of a game at the Hard Rock Casino, he wasn't a 'has-been' writer anymore, he was the master of his universe with Lady Luck sitting on the arm of his chair. Sometimes, when she was smiling down on him, he won big. At that moment, he felt lucky. Truth be told, that's how he felt every time he drove down to the casino. On some level, he knew he was no better than the guys who buy the lottery tickets with all the money from their social security checks when they should be paying their rent or making a car payment. He knew this but he couldn't help himself. He truly believed each time he went to the casino, that was the day he was going to beat the house. But it never, ever was.

While he parked his car in the casino lot, he envisioned winning the big jackpot. He could see himself scooping up mounds of chips and cashing them in for tens of thousands of dollars. Then, he'd buy his wife something special, a gold bracelet or maybe diamond earrings—big fat ones. Angela deserved it, he thought, putting up with him all these years. She had thought she had married a future Pulitzer Prize winner. Now, all he wrote were the occasional corporate training manual and he didn't get too many of those anymore. He turned off his car and inhaled. Today was going to be different. He could feel it. Today would make up for all the years he had disappointed her.

The sliding front doors of the casino magically parted as David approached the entrance. A gladiator entering the Colosseum, he was alive again. At the casino, he wasn't mocked by the vengeful words on the page. Here, he was a player and the possibilities were endless. The mere thought of winning made him high. Feeling his mojo return is what always brought him back to the roulette wheel or blackjack table. Setting foot inside the building, he heard the bells of the slot machines ring. Blood coursed through his veins and his endorphins began to flow. Sure, he'd been on a losing streak, but a long downward period only made his inevitable win that much sweeter. Enveloped in the fantasy of conquering the table, he was sure this was the day he had been waiting for.

As he walked through the different rooms of the casino, the catcalls of the players, the music of the slots and even the stale smell of the room activated the dopamine in his brain. He was flying—nothing would stop him from his destiny today. He started to walk towards the blackjack tables when an arm grabbed him from behind.

'What are you doing here, Mr. Crawford?'

David spun around. It was Vinny, the six-foot-four security guard who worked at the hotel. If Vinny hadn't worked for the hotel, he might have been a professional wrestler.

'I'm here to try my luck like every other person in this place,' said David innocently. 'Only difference between me and the rest of these jokers is, today, I'm going to win.'

'Sure, it is, Mr. Crawford. But you're not supposed to be in here.'

'I don't know what you're talking about?'

'C'mon, we had this talk the last time you were here. You took a casino loan and you ain't been paying it back in a timely manner. Boss said you can't play here until you're all paid up.'

'I think there's some misunderstanding, Vinny.'

'No misunderstanding. The boss was very clear. I need you to turn around now and head out that door,' Vinny said as he gripped David's upper arm and led him towards the exit.

Once they were outside Vinny let go and David dramatically rubbed his shoulder as if he had been injured during their walk.

'It's nothing personal, Mr. Crawford. You're a nice guy. Business is business and you owe the casino money. It's that simple. Pay off your bill and you'll be welcome here again.'

David stood up as straight as he could in order to maintain whatever dignity he thought he had left. 'Thanks so much, Vincent. Good advice. I'll be sure to get a check out to the casino in the morning. See you in a few days.'

'Sure, Mr. Crawford. See you, but only after the check has cleared, okay?'

30

That evening, back in the supply room, Jenny dug through more boxes filled with disorganized documents. It was a tedious job but she had enjoyed being in the inner circle at the hospital—sitting in with the board president and all the higher-ups, everyone wanting to know her opinion. It felt good.

'You've surprised me in a good way, Jenny,' Angela had said when they had a moment alone earlier that day. 'I knew you were a diligent nurse but your work on this very difficult project has been stellar.'

'Thank you, Dr. Crawford, I've tried really hard,' Jenny had replied with a big grateful smile.

'Keep it up,' said Angela as she paused a moment. 'Something is puzzling me. This has nothing to do with anything you're working on, but I noticed in your personnel file, you took time off for about three months a couple of years ago. Mind if I ask what you did?'

Jenny took a deep breath and her eyes narrowed. 'Dr. Farwell didn't tell you?' asked Jenny.

'Tell me what?'

Jenny looked down at the floor.

'What is it?' asked Angela, now intensely curious.

'It's all over now, and there's no reason for concern, but for a time I had a little bit of a substance abuse problem,' said Jenny, red-faced. 'Mainly sleeping pills like Ambien and a bad choice on my part to try something at a club one night. It got the better of me and affected my work. I talked to Dr. Farwell and the hospital put me in rehab for three months.'

Angela's face showed genuine surprise. *Jenny doesn't seem like the type. She comes off as so wholesome. I guess everyone has their secrets.*

'And everything's fine now?' asked Angela, tilting her head.

'Yes, all good.'

'Wonderful,' said Angela. 'Anyway, you're doing a terrific job.'

Later, Jenny had called Danny and told him all about Dr. Crawford's compliments and he, always supportive, had been so proud of her.

'I told you that you could do it,' her boyfriend had said. 'All your insecurities were for nothing. The work you did will give the cops the leads they need to break this case wide open. When they catch this guy, they'll have you to thank for it.'

Jenny reminisced for another minute about the wonderful man now in her life and was filled with gratitude. Her previous boyfriend, Brian, had been the polar opposite. She had been with Brian for five years. They used to smoke weed and get high together and when they weren't high, he was just plain mean. One day, she realized that the only time he was nice was when he was flying. That chapter of her life was thankfully over now that Brian was out of the picture.

She pulled out another heavy box from the shelf and dragged it over to the table and found more 3 West floor work orders, patient information and directives; dietary requirements, medicine changes, along with daily protocols for patients. She hadn't seen any of this stuff before.

The interior of this box and a few others like them, were in no order—paper just dumped in willy-nilly. Patient records had been mixed in with other patient records and there was no rhyme or reason whatsoever. It was like someone took a pitch-fork and just heaved documents into boxes. *Clearly this hospital needs a better record-keeping system.*

By nearly midnight, after five hours of digging, she came across one of Eliza Stern's daily medical schedules mixed in with the rest.

That's strange. Why would that order be in here? The document was dated from May of the previous year during the window when Eliza Stern had become pregnant. Jenny examined the paper and wrinkled her forehead. *This makes no sense.* She folded the document in half, put it inside a manila folder and tucked it into her bag to look at more carefully later on.

31

That same night when Angela was standing in their kitchen as David cooked, she told him about everything that had unraveled since that morning when the press broke the story.

'The floodgates of hell opened today and all the demons flew out shooting poison darts in every direction,' said Angela. 'I needed a security escort to go in and out of the building. The word "chaos" doesn't do justice to what was happening. People shoved cameras in my face and shouted horrible things. There was even press there from China. Can you believe that? China! At one point, the police had to intervene because the reporters and photographers surrounded me.'

'Do you want me to take you to work in the morning and pick you up at night? I could park by that back entrance and you could go in by the rear door. The reporters won't be camped back there.'

Angela smiled appreciatively at her husband. The gallant man she married had been her knight in shining armor, but she rarely saw that version anymore. *If only he would finish writing his damn book, maybe he'd find himself and we could be normal again. I want the man he was when we fell in love—confident and strong. He needs a purpose and I may have found one.*

'Let me see how it goes tomorrow. If it's not any better, I'll take you up on your offer,' said Angela. 'I'm hoping it will die down as time passes, but you never know. Some stories stay alive for a long time and take on a life of their own.'

'From a writer's perspective, I think the reason the press and everyone else is so infatuated with this story is because it's such a hideously disgusting tale that generates all sorts of awful visuals. That's why it's piqued everyone's interest.'

'That's probably it,' said Angela. 'I'd like to talk to you about something else.'

'Shoot.'

'You know how I was the one who delivered Eliza Stern's baby.'

David nodded.

'The last six days have been crazy but the staff has really come together and rallied,' said Angela. 'I'm so proud of them. They've turned Eliza's room into a sort of nursery and people have volunteered to hold, feed and change the baby. He gets more attention than a prince.'

'That's a good thing, right?'

'It's a very good thing. We've kept the baby with Eliza to keep an eye on him and to provide him with skin on skin contact with the mother. We've even had him breastfeed with her. We're not sure how premature he was, but our guess is about three to four weeks.' Angela paused and let out a breath as she got to the real point of her speech. 'I had a visit this afternoon from a Ms. Jablonski,' said Angela. 'She's the intake case worker with the Palm Beach County Child and Family Services unit assigned to this case.'

'Okay?'

'I didn't think they'd move so swiftly given the kind of care we're providing to the baby,' said Angela. 'She came to Ocean-side Manor today to check on him and to let me know that it would only be a matter of days before they took him. It's criminal for that sweet little boy to start his life in foster care, don't you think?'

'There's no family member who could take him?' asked David.

'Eliza's entire family was killed in a car accident and as far as we know, there were no other close relatives. In all these years, she's never had a family member or a friend, come to visit. If there is a relative, they're distant or want nothing to do with her.'

'That's so sad,' said David, shaking his head. 'I've heard awful stories about children in the foster system. Sure, there are some good foster families but there are some very bad ones too. Some people do it just for the money.'

'He's such a beautiful baby. You should see him. Big chubby cheeks and he makes the cutest faces. I've spent some time taking care of him myself.'

'Really?'

'I don't know why but I feel a connection to him. Maybe because it happened in my hospital or because I delivered him or both. He has no one in the world to look out for him. He's all alone.'

They sat in silence for about thirty seconds when finally, David spoke. 'I've got a thought. Hear me out, Angela,' he said. 'We've always wanted a baby. Why couldn't we foster him?'

'I don't know,' said Angela, turning away and looking out the window. 'That's a huge commitment and you know how I feel about adoptions.'

'You never wanted to adopt because you said you'd never know what kind of a gene pool you'd be getting. Right?'

'Exactly.'

'But in this case, we do know the mother,' said David. 'We know she's not crazy or a drug addict.'

'But the baby's father is a rapist,' Angela said, turning back to her husband. 'You want a child whose birth father assaulted a woman in a coma? What if the father's predilection is passed on to the son.'

'You're borrowing trouble,' said David. 'It's a proven fact it's not only nature that forms people. Nurture has just as much to do with the outcome as genes. Maybe more. We can do this, Angie. We could give that little boy a home.'

David stared at his wife. For years he had tried to get her to agree to an adoption once they knew they would never be able to have children of their own. She had always been emphatically opposed to it, wouldn't even discuss it, but this time, he sensed a crack in her armor.

'I suppose, we could foster him for a while and see how it goes. We wouldn't have to commit to anything permanent,' said Angela, tapping her nails on the kitchen counter.

'Exactly.'

'The baby *is* special. Everyone says so. He's completely healthy,' said Angela in measured tones as if she were trying to convince herself. 'I guess when you think about it, he actually had the safest and most perfect womb to grow in.'

'We're in agreement?' asked David, smiling.

'If we don't take him,' said Angela, 'he's going to be thrown into the foster system. I can't stand the thought of that little boy being shuffled from one disinterested or possibly abusive home to another. We'd have to talk to our lawyer about this and I'd have to let the board know our intentions.'

'Of course,' said David, getting excited.

'We'd need to ask a few logistical legal questions because the baby already has a mother and we'd have to know what that means in terms of a future adoption.'

'You would consider adoption?'

'I didn't say that,' said Angela, 'but I would consider temporary fostering and we'll see how it goes. That's all I can commit to right now.'

'I can live with that.'

'Since the baby's mother is under Oceanside Manor's care, if I say for medical reasons we need to keep him longer, it could buy us the time we need. Then we can do whatever paperwork is necessary to be approved as a foster family by child services.'

'Are you *really* sure about this?' asked David.

'Yes, but you have to be sure, too. A lot of the childcare is going to fall on you since I'm at work Monday through Friday. Are you certain you're okay with that?'

David started to laugh and shake his head in disbelief coupled with joy. 'Absolutely. One thousand percent sure.'

'In that case, tomorrow morning, I'm going to go see Sharon Anderson,' said Angela. 'You remember, she was often my obstetrical nurse when I first opened my practice.'

'I do remember her,' said David. 'Nice woman.'

'Sharon now works for the Palm Beach Social Services department. I did her a few favors over the years and she owes me. If anyone can help us pull this off, she can. I'll bet she can move us to the front of the foster line.' Angela looked at her husband. 'Are we seriously going to do this?'

'I'm all in,' said David, smiling. 'I can't believe I'm going to be a father at the age of fifty-three. It's a good thing I've got long living in my family tree.'

'We're just fostering,' Angela reminded her husband. 'Adoption is a long way off.'

'I know,' said David, grinning from ear to ear. 'Am I not allowed to be happy?'

Angela crossed the room and threw her arms around her husband and kissed him.

'We're going to do this,' said Angela, gazing into her husband's blue eyes. 'You know something, I always thought you'd be the best dad that ever lived.'

'I'd like the chance to prove you right,' said David as they hugged each other again.

32

Before she went to work in the morning, Angela made a detour to the office of Social Services of Palm Beach County to pay a surprise visit on her old colleague, Sharon Anderson. Fifteen years before, when Sharon was a nurse, she had worked alongside Angela in the delivery room and assisted on many births. When Sharon turned forty, she shifted gears, went back to school and got her masters and after that her PhD in social work. The two women had always had a good professional relationship and Angela had been one of Sharon's references for graduate school. When Sharon applied for her current job within the state division of social services, Angela wrote a beautiful testimonial letter for her that helped the nurse land the position. Now, Angela was going to ask her to return the favor. If anyone could help, Sharon could.

When Angela popped her head into Sharon's beige government-issued cubicle, the social worker was both surprised and delighted. After they exchanged a hug and a few family inquiries, Angela got to the point of her visit.

'I need your help,' Angela said in a loud whisper.

'Does it have anything to do with all that business I've been hearing about on the news?' said Sharon. 'What a tragedy.'

'It's been a nightmare and it is related,' said Angela, choosing her words carefully. 'Not to the police investigation but it *is* connected.'

'If I can help you, you know I will.'

'As I'm sure you heard,' said Angela, tapping her nails lightly on Sharon's desk, 'one of our patients delivered a baby last week. A boy. Right now, he's being looked after round the clock by a team of nurses and doctors. He's getting the absolute best care. But soon he'll be moved into the foster system.'

'If there are no family members willing to take him, that is what will happen,' said Sharon. 'That's how it works.'

'There is no family that we know of. Everyone at the hospital has become so attached to him. He's really darling. I've given this a lot of thought and my husband David is on board. Sharon, we want to foster the baby and then if all goes well, adopt him.'

Sharon's jaw dropped. She hadn't seen that coming at all. During the years she had worked with Angela, she had always admired the physician's medical skills and bedside manner. But Angela never struck her as particularly maternal. She thought Angela's career had always come first, although she vaguely remembered hearing a rumor that the Crawfords had gone through infertility treatment. She wondered if Angela had been all business only because she couldn't have a baby.

'I didn't think you wanted children.'

'For years, I didn't. My career and my husband were always enough for me. When I was about thirty-three and my biological clock started ticking, I changed my mind.'

'I had no idea,' said Sharon.

'David always wanted kids so we started trying and eventually found out we couldn't,' said Angela solemnly. 'We even tried *in vitro* but that didn't work either.'

'It must have been difficult for you.'

'I thought I had moved on and accepted that children weren't on the cards,' said Angela. 'This miracle of a little boy appeared out of nowhere, and somehow I know I'm supposed to be his mother.'

'There's a lot of things that would have to happen before you could adopt.'

'As soon as the baby's strong enough,' said Angela, getting more animated and smiling, 'instead of putting the baby in foster care, David and I could foster him in my home and take care of him there. Who would be better than us? I'm a doctor. I can take care of his every need and my husband works from home. David would be the primary caregiver.'

'This is all highly irregular,' Sharon said.

'That's an understatement. Wouldn't it be better for the baby to be in a home where he's loved, versus in some institutional setting or with a family who's doing it for the money?'

'Of course it would. I'm sure you'd be a terrific mother,' said the social services director. 'I can't promise you completely smooth sailing on this, but I can pull a few strings to make you the provisional caregiver.'

'That would be amazing,' said Angela, smiling.

'For the time being, you'd simply be classified as a foster family,' said Sharon. 'There will be reams of documents to fill out in order for you to be eligible to foster a baby. I can fast-track your application to allow the baby to be in your care while his case is moving through the system. From what you've told me, the good news is, you don't have to worry about someone coming forward and exercising their parental rights. That's what adopting parents worry about the most. After a certain period of time, you can then apply for the legal adoption.'

'How long does that take?'

'It can take years,' said Sharon. 'But the courts would most likely grant the adoption in your favor if the child has been thriving while in your care.'

'What do I need to sign?' said Angela.

33

Jenny hoped she would finish her research project by the end of the week and get back to what she loved, nursing. As each new name surfaced, she would systematically pass it on to the police. At one point, Jenny got excited because she thought she had figured out who did it. According to the work schedules, there was one male nurse who was on duty at all the right times and dates. She really thought he was the one and was about to call the detectives but stopped when she came across another box of payroll stubs that painted a different picture. Turned out, the male nurse she suspected to be the rapist, had been on the schedule but had a death in the family that month and other nurses took over his shifts. He wasn't even on the property for four weeks.

When her stomach started to growl, Jenny checked the time. It was half past two and she hadn't had any lunch. Not wanting to stop because she thought she was close to something, she looked around the room for something to eat. Nurses and aides often used this room for private phone calls on break or lunch or even a quick nap when needed. She hoped someone had left a package of something edible behind. She opened up all the cabinets and drawers and let out a little cry of joy when she found a sleeve of saltines.

After consuming six or seven crackers her mouth was dry. She took a big swig from her water bottle and it went down the wrong way which made her cough. Getting up to clear her throat, she paced around the room until the coughing subsided. Out of the corner of her eye she noticed a tall, slim beige file cabinet tucked behind a larger one. She didn't even know that cabinet was there until that moment. Curious, she opened a drawer and looked through the names in the files. One name looked familiar.

'Kramer, Paul.' She took the file out and opened it.

Paul Kramer? I know him. I took care of him once when I filled in for one of the nurses on 4 East. He's the guy who almost drowned but never regained consciousness. Why are there patient files mixed in with the operations files? These should be in the records department, not in here. Jeez! Oceanside Manor has some serious record-keeping issues.

Jenny sifted through the cabinet until she glanced down at her watch. She had just wasted thirty minutes on something not germane to her task. She shut the drawer and went back to examining the work schedules and visitor logs. She was already in the Ks and certain she'd complete the Ls today, as she had promised Angela. Still hungry, she got up to get a few more crackers and the beige filing cabinet caught her eye again.

I wonder if Eliza Stern has files in there, too?

She opened the second drawer of the beige cabinet and ran her fingers through the Ss. Three quarters of the way back, she found 'Stern, Eliza.' She lifted the brown folder out of the drawer and sat down at the table. Slowly, she went through each page of Eliza's file. It covered the last two years. She carefully read all the notes written in Eliza's charts. Month after month, no changes. With dozens of papers in the file, in no particular order, Jenny flipped each one over finding nothing out of the ordinary. More than halfway through, she admonished herself for having just wasted nearly half an hour messing with Eliza's medication files. She was supposed to be going through staff and personnel files and she kept getting sidetracked.

This has nothing to do with my assignment. If I keep going off task I won't finish on time. Dr. Crawford is counting on me.

About to close the folder and get back to work, she turned over one last document. It was a routine weekly medication chart from a week in June of the previous year.

She looked over the medication directives. Everything looked totally normal, appropriate for a patient in Eliza's condition, except for one thing. Last June, according to this piece of paper, Eliza had received a new prescription of vitamins and supplements.

Who would have ordered that and why? None of the other patients get that nutrient mixture.

She looked on the form for a nurse's signature signing off on the new protocols but there was nothing more than a squiggly line that she couldn't make out.

That's so weird. Why would someone give Eliza that? It makes no sense.

Jenny googled the common supplements and vitamins prescribed on Eliza's chart to see if they had other uses—they didn't. According to Google, there was only one reason someone would take them.

34

The overcrowded bullpen in the police department was buzzing with activity. While she studied her computer screen, impatiently clicking on various links that lead to dead ends, Blade shook her head, rubbed her eyes and groaned.

'Stop moaning, Anita,' her partner said without looking up from his computer. 'You sound like a wounded animal.'

Blade made a face and turned back to her screen. After a few minutes she pushed her chair quietly back, turned and stared at McQ's back.

'I know you're looking at me, Anita.'

'How did you know? Sometimes you freak me out. You're like a witch.'

McQ turned and faced his partner as he clasped his hands behind his head and smiled. Blade was fiercely chewing the inside of her lip. He knew his partner's moves as well as he knew his girlfriend Marie's. When Blade was hiding something, she picked at her nails and looked at her feet. When she was frustrated, she chewed on the inside of her right cheek and when she had no patience for bullshit, she sweet-talked the bullshitter like a southern belle just before she went for their jugular.

'What's eating you?' asked McQ with a paternal smile.

'Eleven men have refused to give their DNA,' said Blade. 'That's a lot of people to not be able to rule out. We've got to get them to give a sample or we'll never close this case.'

'Let's wait and see what comes back from the lab from all the samples we did get,' said McQ. 'You never know, we may already have our daddy.'

'If you were the father, would you have given your DNA?' asked Blade.

'Not a chance,' said McQ. 'But our perp could be a Simple Simon who just likes incapacitated women but has no understanding of how DNA works. That's what I'm banking on. Who are the holdouts?'

Blade turned back to her computer and pulled up a list.

'Looks like all staff members have been swabbed,' she said.

'They didn't have much of a choice,' said McQ. 'Crawford told the entire staff that if they didn't submit, they would be dismissed and she meant it. Who else is left?'

'Looks like seven outside maintenance and temporary staff —two plumbers, an air-conditioning guy, two temps who worked in food service when some of the regulars were out with the flu, and a guy who waters the plants.'

'That's seven. You said there were eleven. Who are the other four?'

'Patient relatives,' said Blade. 'Kevin and Tim Mulcahy, sons of a coma patient on the second floor and Raymond Barbero, the father of a patient on 3 East. But Barbero is nearly eighty.'

'I know a couple of eighty-year-olds who are major womanizers. If he is mobile, we can't rule him out because he's eighty, not in the age of Viagra. If he can get up, he can get it up.'

Blade let out an exasperated sigh. 'Last but not least, Peter Parris, the twin brother of Martin Parris, who is also a permanent resident on 3 West. If you remember, when we interviewed him, we both thought he was a legit possibility. He would have had easy access from his brother's room next door.'

'I'll take the plumbers, the air-con and plant guys. You do the food service temps and let's see if we can get some of them to have a change of heart.'

'What about the patient relatives?'

'I'll take the Mulcahy brothers and old man Barbero,' said McQ. 'You can have Parris.'

Later that day, while McQ and Blade worked the phones trying to sweet-talk eleven men out of their DNA, the lab reports they had been waiting for arrived. The two boxes were dropped on the detective's desks making simultaneous thuds as they landed.

Both detectives in the middle of a DNA phone pitch looked up when they heard the noise. Realizing what had just arrived on their desks, McQ signaled to his partner with a circular hand gesture to wrap it up. Minutes later, both detectives dug into the lab results. Within a short amount of time the results were clear. After testing over two hundred DNA samples, the lab had determined there was not a single match. Not even close.

'Damn,' said Blade as she read the last page summary for the third time.

'You didn't think the perp was going to be in the first two hundred, did you?' said McQ. 'It's never that easy.'

'I hoped.'

'Hope for the best and prepare for the worst. There's still eleven more people to vet. It ain't over yet. How did you make out with Peter Parris?' asked McQ.

'Doesn't want to give his DNA,' said Blade. 'He said he doesn't even use Facebook, values his privacy. He's not going to play nice with us.'

'We'll circle back on him later. In the meantime, both plumbers reluctantly agreed and so did the Mulcahy brothers,' said McQ. 'They'll meet us over at Oceanside Manor to do their swab later this afternoon.'

'How did you get them all to say yes?'

'I told them they had to.'

'But they *don't* have to,' said Blade, sitting up straight and looking directly at her partner.

'I know that and you know that, but they don't know that,' said McQ.

'What happens when they find out?'

'Then it will be too late.'

35

Nearing the end of their shift, Blade pulled their unmarked car up in front of Oceanside Manor. She noticed the news van and reporter count had grown even larger than from the previous day.

'Would you look at that,' she said to her partner. 'Those reporters are multiplying like rabbits.'

'This thing is mushrooming. It's become an international story,' said McQ, popping an antacid tablet in his mouth as they got out of the car. 'I got a cousin in the army stationed in Stuttgart, Germany. He called me last night to tell me Oceanside and the baby story was all over the German news.'

As the two cops crossed the parking lot, several reporters with cameramen in tow, including Tommy Devlin, ran towards them.

'Detective McQuillan,' said Devlin, pushing his way to the front of the pack. 'Do you know who the father of Eliza Stern's baby is? If you don't know, when will you know? When are the police going to make a statement? Where's the baby right now?'

Stone-faced, McQ and Blade moved silently through the crowd of relentless newsmen and women and into the building. The Mulcahy brothers, and the two plumbers were waiting in the lobby and were directed into a private room for the official swab. When that was completed, the detectives went to check on Eliza Stern. Climbing the steps to 3 West, they found the new mother where she always was, in her bed, forever silent.

'If she only knew all the chaos that's going on,' said Blade. 'Hundreds of people are trying to unravel what happened to you, Eliza. If only you could tell us.'

'She'll never get to hold her son,' said McQ, shaking his head.

After they left Eliza's room, the detectives walked down to the administration floor. They had a few new questions for Angela. It was after five and the doctor's assistant had already left for the day, leaving the path to her office wide open.

'Wasn't expecting you, detectives,' said Angela, looking up and seeing the two police officers in her doorway. 'Any news?'

'We were in the building and had a couple of questions for you,' said Blade. 'Got a minute?'

Angela took off her reading glasses and smiled ruefully.

'Not really,' said Angela with a sigh. 'What can I help you with?'

McQ shared the topline DNA results with the administrator.

'That's disappointing,' said Angela. 'I thought for sure we'd get closure from the DNA. Now what?'

'We've still got about a dozen more people to check out, we're not close to being done on that angle,' said McQ.

'I asked Jenny to triple check the data she's been working with,' said Angela. 'Though unlikely, it's possible she may still turn up something or someone new.'

McQ nodded. 'Is there any way we may have overlooked someone? Could a person have used another way into the building that we might have missed? Is there an outside vendor that might have been overlooked or a temporary worker that was accidently omitted?'

'We've checked all the names six ways from Sunday,' said Angela. 'We gave you the names of some people that fell outside of the time frame for conception, just in case we were slightly wrong on the dates. We even put the pizza delivery guy on the list and we're positive he never went past the front desk.'

Blade looked over Angela's head and noticed for the first time that the medical degrees on the wall were not hers but for a Francis Farwell.

'Dr. Crawford,' said Blade. 'Francis Farwell, he's the Oceanside Manor administrator who's on sabbatical in Ecuador, right?'

'Yes. Frank is my boss. I'm filling in for him while he's gone,' said Angela. 'Clearly, that was the worst decision of my life.'

'Exactly when did Dr. Farwell leave for Ecuador?' asked Blade, leaning forward.

Angela flipped through the pages of her desk calendar.

'Here it is. Frank's last day on the job was May 30th. I think he left for Ecuador on June 1st or 2nd,' said Angela.

'Then technically, Dr. Farwell could have been here when Eliza Stern was attacked,' said McQ.

'That's exactly what I said to him after he told me this was my mess to clean up and not his,' said Angela, scrunching up her face.

'Is there a picture of Dr. Farwell around here?' asked Blade, looking around the room.

'When I moved in, that loquacious windbag had multiple pictures of himself on all four walls of this office,' said Angela, getting up and walking over to a large wooden credenza. 'His degrees on the wall were one thing, but I wasn't planning to look at Frank's fat bloated face every day for more than a year.' She reached into the drawer and lifted out a stack of framed pictures and handed them to the detectives. The photos showed a rotund middle-aged man with thinning red hair. McQ felt his ears get hot and itchy and he locked eyes with his partner.

'Your ears are bright pink,' said Blade.

'We're going to need a sample of Dr. Farwell's DNA,' said McQ.

36

The day after discovering the notes about the new vitamins and supplements given to Eliza Stern, Jenny went to Eliza's room to look around—for what, she didn't know. When she entered, she saw that the baby's crib was empty.

He's probably down the hall at the nurses' station. They don't put that kid down for a minute. He's going to get spoiled with so much attention.

Each day, Eliza's room morphed further into baby land. The walls were now covered in moons, stars and rainbows. A baby lamp had been added and a giant black and white panda sat on the floor next to the crib. With each nursing shift, additional baby items were left by well-meaning staff. Lourdes Castro finally put a stop to it because there was simply no room to move.

Methodically, Jenny searched Eliza's room, opening every drawer and closet, looking for some kind of amorphous clue. After searching for fifteen minutes, she was chilly and buttoned her sweater and thought to check Eliza's temperature. She placed the back of her hand on the immobile woman's forehead. Eliza's skin was cool to the touch and Jenny looked around for something to cover her patient. Opening the closet, she saw a pink blanket way up on the top shelf. She pushed a chair over, climbed up and reached for the blanket. After she pulled it from the high shelf, she spotted a small medicine bottle wedged way in the back in a gap between the shelf and the rear of the closet wall. Reaching in, she pulled out an unopened bottle of liquid medication. The label was clear and she knew what the drug was.

Why the hell would this be in here? Can it be used for something else?

She pulled out her phone and searched on the uses for the drug in the bottle and could find only one reason to have it.

That's the second time this week I found something that wouldn't be used for this patient population.

She put the bottle of liquid into her pocket and looked around to see if there was anything else she had missed. She searched every inch of Eliza's room a second time but found nothing more.

I've got to talk to Dr. Crawford tomorrow. None of this makes any sense.

37

When Jenny got to her apartment that night it was late, but her boyfriend, Danny, was waiting outside for her with a pizza, diet coke, a box of glazed donuts and a kiss.

'I am so glad to see you,' said a smiling Jenny, returning the kiss. 'Another long and crazy day.'

'I'm told pizza can fix anything,' he said, waving the box as the two walked into her apartment and turned on the lights.

Flipping on the television to watch the news, they ate without much conversation.

'This is unusual,' said Danny, his mouth full of pizza.

'What?'

'You're not talking. That almost never happens.'

'I'm tired. Long and weird day.'

Jenny took another bite of her slice and drifted off in thought.

'Supposed to get a lot of rain this weekend,' said Danny, trying to make conversation. 'I was thinking that maybe we could go...'

'I think the man who impregnated Eliza Stern didn't mean for it to happen. He just wanted to get his rocks off and go on his way. But what if, later on, he realized she was pregnant and it would lead back to him?'

'I was wondering how long it would take you to get on to this topic. Why don't we talk about something else for a change?' said Danny.

'It must mean he works at the hospital or at least he's there all the time. What if it's a nurse, an aide or even a doctor? What if it's someone I know?'

'If it was a nurse or a doctor, of course you'd know them,' said Danny.

'Today, I was poking around in Eliza Stern's room.'

'Why are you doing that? That's what the cops are there for.'

'Stay with me for a second,' said Jenny. 'So, I'm in her room. Just looking around to see if there was anything that was missed.'

'You think you're better at this than the police?'

'I'm a medical professional and they're not,' said Jenny. 'There are things I would notice that the lay person wouldn't, not even a cop. While I was in Eliza's room, I noticed she was cold, so I climbed up on a stool to get a pink blanket from the top of her closet. Something glimmered and I found this.' Jenny held out a small medicine bottle in her hand for Danny to see. 'You know what this is?'

'I don't but I know you're going to tell me.'

'It's Pitocin,' said Jenny matter-of-factly.

She moved closer to her boyfriend and continued talking. 'Pitocin can be used for a number of things but one of the main things is to induce labor,' she said. 'What if the person who had sex with Eliza Stern realized she was pregnant. Then, what if he tried to induce an abortion to get rid of the baby so it couldn't be traced back to him.'

'You'd have to be a medical person to know how to do that,'

said Danny, a look of disgust on his face. 'I certainly wouldn't know how to pull that off.'

'What if it was Dr. Horowitz?' said Jenny, her eyes bugging out. 'He's always hitting on all the nurses and aides. He even flirts with the college volunteers. He'd know how to administer and use Pitocin. That makes total sense and it would explain everything. I'm sure the last thing Steve Horowitz expected was Eliza getting pregnant.'

'You're jumping to conclusions without much information. Besides the baby wasn't aborted,' said Danny. 'The baby is alive.'

'Maybe whoever got Eliza pregnant was going to use the Pitocin but chickened out,' said Jenny, on a roll. 'Or maybe they got fired or got a new job and figured they were in the clear, long gone by the time the baby came around.'

'Didn't you tell me that you and Horowitz once had a thing?'

'It was nothing,' said Jenny coldly. 'Horowitz has a thing with every woman on staff under forty.'

'Did you tell the police about the Pitocin?'

'Not yet, I discovered it right before I left work,' said Jenny. 'I'll tell Dr. Crawford in the morning. I kind of feel sorry for her — she's got a lot on her plate right now.'

'If you're right about this, it could be huge,' said Danny.

'Maybe it wasn't Horowitz, but I'll bet money it's someone on the medical staff at Oceanside Manor or Oceanside Medical. I know the cops were looking at maintenance people and gardeners, but in order to use Pitocin and induce an abortion without killing the patient, you'd have to really know what you were doing. There would be a lot of blood.'

38

When McQ and Blade arrived at work in the morning, there was already an urgent message from Angela Crawford saying she needed to see them immediately and asked if they could all meet in her office at 9:15. After checking in with the chief, the two detectives drove across town to Oceanside Manor.

At ten after nine, Vera sat them in Angela's office and the two detectives waited patiently for the administrator to arrive.

'Looks like her highness had more important things to do today,' said Blade, looking at her watch. 'It's 9:41. She did say to be here at 9:15, right?'

'Calm down, Anita,' said McQ. 'The lady is clearly frazzled. On top of everything else, she has this whole facility to run. She's under a lot of pressure.'

'Look at you, Mr. Magnanimous,' said Blade, laying on the drawl. 'Since when did you become so patient and less parsimonious with your valuable time?'

'Magnanimous. Parsimonious. A few new scrabble words, perhaps?' said McQ with a grin. 'Has Eve been making you practice with your vocabulary flash cards again?'

Blade stuck her tongue out at her partner. A moment later, there was a commotion outside the office, it was Angela barking orders at staff. 'Schedule a call tomorrow afternoon with Bob Beckmann, any time after two. Cancel my lunch today and reschedule it for next week. Hold all my calls until the detectives leave.'

A moment later, Angela burst into her office carrying several tote bags filled with files. 'Detectives, I'm sorry for being so late. The Stern situation has completely dominated my life this past week. Things have been unfortunately falling through the cracks.'

'You called us Dr. Crawford, so we're here,' said McQ.

'Any developments on the case since we last talked?' said Angela.

'Nothing significant since yesterday. We're still interviewing people,' said Blade.

'You said there was something important you wanted to talk about,' said McQ.

Angela reached into her bag and pulled out a small clear bottle, the kind used for drawing medicine with a syringe, and placed it on her desk.

The two detectives stared at the bottle and looked at each other and shrugged.

'Do you know what this is?' asked Angela.

McQ leaned over and picked up the small bottle and his ears started to itch, but he uncharacteristically ignored the feeling.

'The label says "Pitocin,"' said McQ. 'I don't know what that is.'

'Jenny, the nurse who is doing all the research for us, found it yesterday in Eliza Stern's room. It was stuck in the back of a closet shelf. She gave it to me early this morning.'

'What is Pitocin used for?' asked Blade.

'It's most often used to start labor but it can also be used to induce an abortion,' said Angela. 'Jenny thinks that the man who raped Eliza might have been trying to get *rid of the evidence* linking him to the baby. That's her theory, and I think she could be right.'

'Let me get this straight,' said Blade. 'Y'all think the perp had his way with Eliza, later he realized she was pregnant, and tried to get rid of the baby by inducing an abortion?'

'That's the working theory,' said Angela. 'It makes sense, don't you think?'

'It would mean whoever did it wasn't an occasional or one-time visitor,' said McQ.

'That's correct, detective,' said Angela. 'If Jenny's right, whoever did this had regular access and had been around for a while and knew they'd be able to get back in and administer the Pitocin.'

'I suppose it's possible,' said McQ, scratching his head. 'Could the Pitocin have been in Eliza's room for some completely benign random reason?'

'In a regular hospital maybe, but not here in Oceanside Manor,' said Angela, shaking her head. 'All of our patients are significantly disabled. No one is having babies here. Pitocin is only used in reproductive medicine.'

'What about visiting medical students or interns?' asked Blade. 'Couldn't one of them have had it in their pockets and dropped it? Maybe one of the aides or cleaning people just picked it up and stuck it in the place Jenny found it.'

'After what we've all been through this past week,' said Angela, 'anything is possible.'

McQ took the vial of Pitocin and bagged it. 'Maybe we can still get a print off of it,' he said.

'Don't forget, we still need Frank Farwell's DNA,' said Blade. 'If he's a match, it blows a hole in your hypothesis. If he was in

South America when Eliza gave birth, he couldn't have administered the drug.'

'That's true,' said Angela, making a face. 'I video chatted with him to get some advice right after I delivered the baby. He was definitely in Ecuador. I had the pleasure of watching him wolf down some disgusting street sandwich covered in red sauce, most of which ended up on his face.'

'There's clearly no love lost between you and Farwell,' said Blade. 'Were you able to reach him yesterday to inform him we want his DNA sample?'

Angela nodded. 'It wasn't pretty. He went ballistic when I told him what you wanted.' She smiled. 'That was the only happy moment of my day yesterday. Frank calmed down after I told him all the hospital board members were asked as well. He only agreed to co-operate because he had no choice, not because it was the right thing to do.'

When they got back to the police station, McQ reached out to the FBI to arrange for someone at the U.S. Consulate in Guayaquil, Ecuador to meet up with Frank Farwell the following week and get his sample and have it shipped back to the United States.

39

Jenny had met briefly with Angela at 7:45 that morning and had given her boss the small vial of Pitocin she had found in Eliza Stern's closet. She didn't mention the vitamin and nutrient order changes on Eliza's charts. She wanted to do a little more digging before she presented her findings. By 8:45, Jenny was back at work in the little supply room. She took out the old paper change order for Eliza Stern's vitamins and nutrients and spent the next hour poring over papers in the remaining bins and cabinets. Finding nothing further about Eliza's medication change, she decided it was time to call Angela and let her know what she had found. She wasn't sure if it was anything, but she thought it might be something.

The phone on Angela's desk rang just as three corporate attorneys had arrived to walk her through the legal ramifications of the Eliza Stern situation. She signaled for them to come into her office while she picked up the ringing phone. Her assistant, Vera, had an emergency root canal that morning, and Angela was on her own.

'Angela Crawford,' she barked into the phone while motioning for the three lawyers to sit down.

'Dr. Crawford, it's Jenny.'

'I'm about to start a meeting in my office,' said Angela quietly. 'Can I call you back later?'

'It's just that I found something kind of odd. Can you come down to 3 West, I need to show you something,' said Jenny. 'I'm in the little supply room, you know the one, right next to the stairwell. I found this document because I got hungry yesterday and started looking for something to eat and—'

'I've got people sitting in my office,' said Angela brusquely, rolling her eyes for the attorneys' benefit.

'There was a weird change in Eliza Stern's protocols. Somebody added a bunch of things to her meds last spring,' said Jenny. 'I need to show you.'

Angela smiled at the three hospital lawyers in dark suits sitting in front of her.

'Jenny, can you sit tight?' she said half-whispering. 'I should be free in about two hours. As soon as my meeting here finishes. I'll come down to see you.'

'Okay.'

'I'll try to wrap things up here as quickly as I can,' said Angela. 'And thanks for being so thorough. I didn't mean to sound abrupt before. I appreciate everything you've been doing. Do me a favor, don't say anything to anyone until you show me what you have, okay? We don't need any more rumors circulating until we know exactly what we're dealing with.'

'I won't say a word.'

With two hours to kill before her meeting with Angela, Jenny looked around for more schedule changes. The more she thought about it, the more peculiar it seemed.

It makes no sense, unless...

40

Cracking open the stairwell door, the intruder took one last look up and down the halls to make sure no one was around. Whipping out a syringe, the needle was stuck into a bottle containing clear liquid and drawn into the syringe's vial. When it was completely full, and the air was squeezed out with a squirt, the cap was replaced. The injection device was placed in a side pocket. A bottle of ether and a terry cloth rag were in the other side pocket along with a small but heavy bronze statue, just in case the ether didn't do the trick. The intruder left the stairwell and quickly walked across the hall to the door of the small supply room.

With her back to the door, Jenny O'Hearn was deeply engrossed in thought while trying to absorb all the new information she had discovered. Perhaps that's why she didn't hear the soft swoosh of the hospital door to the supply room open or the silent footsteps of the intruder creeping up behind her. She only realized someone else was in the room when the gloved hand covered her mouth and she smelled something noxiously sweet.

The smell was followed by the sensation of falling. She grabbed for the hand that covered her mouth as her legs buckled from underneath and everything went dark.

41

Angela's meeting with the lawyers ended sooner than anticipated. She had wrapped the meeting up early because she had other fires to put out and suggested they reconvene the next day. Minutes after the lawyers departed, she answered a call from Bob Beckmann. She looked at her watch while Beckmann droned on about how a hospital *should* be run. She yessed him to death to shorten the pointless conversation so she could get down to the supply room and see what Jenny wanted to show her. It had already been more than two hours since the young nurse had called her.

'I understand, Bob,' said Angela, trying to get off the phone. 'I can assure you we're doing everything possible. I've met with the lawyers and with the PR group and I've got everything under control. Everyone on staff has made themselves completely available to the police. I'm confident we'll soon figure out who did this and why.'

'I already know why. You've got a pervert running around over there.'

'I've got a 12:30 budget meeting that's just about to start,' Angela said, lying to get off the call. A moment later Beckmann mercifully hung up on her as he always did and Angela went to find Jenny. She walked down the halls from the east wing over to the west, passing several nursing stations.

'Good afternoon, Dr. Crawford,' could be heard every few yards. 'Good afternoon,' Angela replied. She took the elevator up to the third floor. When she got to the nurses' station on 3 West, Lourdes Castro was on duty. Angela inquired about a few different patients and got a status update on one patient who had been in a fair amount of distress the night before.

'Mr. Wong is okay today,' said Lourdes. 'Last night something was off, but he seems fine now.'

'How's our baby?' said Angela.

'He's wonderful,' said Lourdes, her face breaking into a smile. 'There's a pediatrician from the hospital checking him out right now in Eliza's room. At least Eliza's baby is thriving.'

'I'll stop by and see him and Eliza after I meet with Jenny,' said Angela. 'Can you show me where the small supply room is that Jenny is working in? She wanted to show me something.'

'I'll take you there,' said Lourdes.

Angela followed the older nurse down the hall. They turned left at the intersection, passed an exit sign and the stairwell and were soon standing in front of another door.

'This is it,' said Lourdes as she pushed the door open. 'Jenny, Dr. Crawford is here to...oh my God, Jenny!'

Jenny O'Hearn's lifeless body lay on its side on the cold white terrazzo floor. Angela ran over and grabbed her wrist to check for a pulse.

'There's no pulse,' she screamed to Lourdes.

Angela checked again. Nothing. When she rolled Jenny over, she saw a hypodermic needle and a tourniquet on Jenny's upper arm.

'Lourdes, get help! Call a code blue and have the emergency room get me a dose of Narcan. STAT!'

'Oh my God, Jenny,' wailed Lourdes. 'This can't be happening. Not to Jenny.'

'Now, nurse, now!' screamed Angela.

Lourdes ran down the hall shouting orders at various aides while Angela started CPR and tried to get Jenny's heart going. Twenty seconds later Lourdes returned.

'They're coming,' she shouted, out of breath. 'The EMS crew should be here in less than a minute.'

Angela continued to administer CPR but without the Narcan, she knew it was probably pointless.

'Oh my God, that poor, sweet girl,' said the older nurse, looking down at Jenny's pale, limp body. 'Is she breathing?'

'No,' said Angela between breaths.

'Oh my God,' cried Lourdes again, tears running down her cheeks.

'Nurse, I'm trying to save her life,' said Angela, still pumping Jenny's chest. 'Either help me or get out.'

Thirty seconds later, an EMS team rushed into the room followed by Dr. Horowitz. Soon the EMS guys moved into position.

'How long has she been this way,' asked one of the EMS technicians while the other took over the CPR.

'I found this,' said a panting Angela, holding up a vial of Dilaudid and the tourniquet. The technician looked at it and nodded. 'Overdose,' he said to his partner as he pulled out a shot of Narcan and plunged it into the muscle of Jenny's upper thigh. Everyone waited as the EMS guys continued CPR and assisted with the breathing. After three minutes, the Narcan elicited no reaction from the young nurse.

'She's not responding,' said the EMS tech.

'Give her another dose,' demanded Angela. 'Sometimes patients respond to a second dose, isn't that right?'

Dr. Horowitz pulled out a second Narcan syringe and this

time plunged into the muscle on Jenny's upper arm while the techs continued CPR. Two more minutes passed and finally Jenny took a breath.

'We've got a pulse,' shouted the EMS technician with a smile on his face.

'Thank God,' said Lourdes, wringing her hands.

The technicians busied themselves with additional testing and prepared Jenny to be moved.

'Do you know how long she's been like this?' asked the EMS tech.

'I spoke with her two hours ago,' said Angela. 'This must have happened sometime since then. Did anyone see her in the halls in the last hour or two?'

Lourdes started to cry. 'I can't believe it. This isn't right. Jenny didn't use drugs. I would know if she did. We were very close. She's like a daughter to me.'

Angela shook her head and sighed.

'Thank God you two got here when you did,' said Steve Horowitz. 'Another five minutes and I don't think we would have saved her.'

The EMS team loaded Jenny onto a gurney and prepared to move her out of the room over into the ER next door.

'Is she going to be all right?' asked Lourdes. 'She looks so pale.'

'She wasn't breathing for a long time,' said the technician. 'We won't know for a while. What we do know is that she's alive right now.'

They pushed Jenny's body out the door and raced down the hall with Dr. Horowitz right behind them.

'This doesn't make any sense,' said a crying Lourdes, leaning against a wall to steady herself. 'I'm telling you, Jenny didn't use drugs.'

Angela closed the door and turned to the weeping nurse.

'This goes no further because I'm breaking confidentiality rules, but about Jenny and drugs, that's not true. Jenny was treated for substance abuse a number of years ago.'

Lourdes' mouth dropped open.

'It was brief, the hospital dealt with it and Jenny bounced back. We all moved on. As far as anyone knew there were no other incidents. I guess when you've been an addict it's always lurking underneath.'

'But not Jenny…' Lourdes started again, tears spilling down her cheeks.

'I can't talk about this right now. I've got to call her family,' said Angela, grimacing. 'I suppose I need to call the police, too,' she said with a sigh as she opened the door and ran to catch up with the gurney.

42

The EMS squad raced into the ER with a clatter and moved the wheeled stretcher into a berth. Within seconds, many hands attached tubes and monitors onto Jenny O'Hearn's small, still body. An oxygen mask was placed over her face as the soft blip of the heart monitor pulsed in the background.

Dr. Horowitz came in right after the EMS team and stared down at the young nurse. It was hard to believe that the lifeless body of the girl in front of him was the vibrant, saucy girl that he had spent good times with in empty hospital rooms and closets. At that moment, he knew he probably shouldn't have tainted her and felt a pang of guilt.

All the young nurses looked up to the doctors and it was so easy to pick them off. Jenny was so eager to please that he barely had to wink at her before he had her in his arms behind some old filing cabinets in the back of an empty storage room. His wife was pregnant with twins, and she had made it clear that she was always hot and uncomfortable and didn't want him to touch her. What was he supposed to do for the entire nine months? He told himself his affairs with Jenny and the other nurses and aides were really just to help his wife out, so he didn't have to bother her with his physical needs. Still, he actually liked Jenny.

'How is she?' said an anxious Steve Horowitz to the attending ER doctor.

'Hard to say until we run some tests,' said the ER doctor. 'We know she injected Dilaudid but we don't know how much or how long she was lying there unconscious. The EMS team said they gave her two shots of Narcan. That's not good. She was really gone.'

'I'm going to stay here with her for a while,' said Horowitz. 'I just don't get it. She wasn't currently using drugs, I would have noticed. I know what that looks like and Jenny's eyes were always clear.'

'I've been working in the ER here in Oceanside for ten years,' said the ER doc as he walked to the doorway. 'There's a big drug problem down here in South Florida and a lot of opportunity to get drugs in this town if you want them. I'm sorry to say, I see this all too often.'

'I had heard she had dabbled with drugs a few years ago,' said Horowitz. 'But I saw no signs of it now.'

'Some people hide it really well,' said the doctor about to walk out of the room, 'especially a nurse, they'd know how to get it and how to hide it.'

Steve Horowitz sat by Jenny's bedside for twenty minutes remembering how their long flirtation went on for weeks until it came to a head.

'But you're married, Dr. Horowitz,' Jenny had said, pulling away from him after he cornered her in a vacant hallway.

'That doesn't change the fact that I still find you extremely attractive,' he had said. 'I'm married, not blind.'

Jenny laughed and walked away as she wheeled a food cart down the hall to a patient's room. Later that same day, he walked into a break room and found she was the only other person in there.

'You got a new haircut since this morning,' he said.

'Did it on my lunch break.'

'I like it. It looks good.'

'Thanks,' she said, smiling as she looked into his eyes.

'It's sexy. Very French.'

Jenny giggled. 'Merci.'

He remembered that moment well. The air felt so thick he could almost cut it with a knife. He felt his heartbeat quicken and his palms grow moist. She continued to stare up at him with her big aqua-blue eyes flecked with yellow and blinked several times making her appear even more innocent and vulnerable. When she licked her lips, he reached over and gently grabbed her upper arm and pulled her towards him.

'You're so beautiful,' he whispered while she looked up and parted her lips. He wasn't sure if that was a signal for him to kiss her but decided it was. He leaned over and took her mouth into his. After several seconds passed, Jenny pushed him back and straightened her hair and shirt.

'We can't do this,' she said, shaking her head as she walked out of the room leaving him alone and wanting more. After that, Steve Horowitz couldn't get Jenny O'Hearn out of his head and spent the next two weeks in hot pursuit until she, overwhelmed and flattered by the physician's persistence, succumbed. For both of them, it had been worth the wait. After that, at least for a time, they couldn't keep their hands off each other.

For the next few months the two of them would steal away into a supply room, a walk-in closet, an empty car—wherever they could grab a few seconds alone. Jenny was charming, sweet and childlike, which turned Horowitz on. In his arms she felt tiny, like a little doll, as opposed to his fat wife who looked and felt like a baby elephant with two kids growing in her swollen belly.

For Jenny, Dr. Horowitz was the ultimate trophy—a doctor. He was on the top of the totem pole. Every nurse wanted to snag a doctor, preferably a single one who they could marry. Despite the fact that Steven Horowitz had a wife already and would soon have two children, there was something about him that Jenny couldn't resist. Maybe it was his MD or maybe it was just that he was so insistent she was the most intelligent, beautiful and sexy creature he'd ever known. His adoration was intoxicating. For a while, Jenny was all in with her secret married doctor boyfriend and he was of a similar mind—at least until his twins were born. Horowitz had promised himself that once the babies arrived, he'd stop all his nonsense and reacquaint himself with his fat and often demanding wife.

Then, everything came crashing down. The last time they had been together, Jenny had asked him about their future.

'What's going to happen to us now?'

'I told you, I just need a little more time,' said Steve, getting prickly. 'My wife needs a lot of support at the moment. You've got to give me a little breathing room.'

'You said you and your wife barely spoke to each other, and if she hadn't gotten pregnant you were going to divorce her. You swore to me the only reason you were staying with her was because she was a high-risk pregnancy,' said Jenny.

'Can we talk about this another time?' said Steve, looking around worriedly as other hospital staff passed by within earshot. 'Wait until after the babies are born. I promise then we can make our plans.'

'Despite what everyone around here says about you, and they say a lot,' said Jenny, 'I believed you. Be straight with me, if we're not going to be a couple, I think we should end this before it goes any further.'

Horowitz remembered how he had enjoyed every minute he had spent with the young nurse, every stolen kiss, each transgression. It had been exciting, fun, silly, sexy and secret.

Now, he was looking down on this same woman, attached to so many tubes, electrodes and machines and no one knew if she was going to live or die. There was a knock behind him and he turned his head. Lourdes was standing in the doorway.

'Anything change?' she asked.

'No, she's not regained consciousness,' said Steve.

'What did the doctor say?' asked Lourdes.

'He didn't know anything. It's a waiting game. It's possible she'll die or she won't ever wake up.'

Lourdes walked over to Jenny's bed and took her hand in hers and rubbed it.

'C'mon, Jenny, you're a strong girl. You can do this,' she whispered. 'We need you to come back to work.'

'I don't understand any of this,' said Steve. 'Did you know anything about Jenny using drugs recently?'

Lourdes moved closer to Steve and spoke very softly so no one else would hear.

'I never saw that sweet girl be anything but cold sober,' said Lourdes, inching closer to Horowitz and positioning her mouth a few inches from his ear and whispering. 'Dr. Crawford told me that Jenny had a history of drug use and the hospital had even sent her to rehab several years ago. Must have been before we started working together.'

'I had heard something once a long time ago,' said Horowitz, beginning to squirm, 'but I never saw any evidence of it.'

'No one did,' Lourdes replied, tearing up again as she looked down at her young friend.

43

Jenny's overdose had taken McQ and Blade by surprise. As the two detectives walked briskly towards Oceanside Manor's front entrance, in his peripheral vision, McQ saw Tommy Devlin and his cameraman interrogating a man wearing scrubs.

'Would you look at that, Anita,' whispered McQ to his partner and tilting his head in Devlin's direction. 'Freakin' Devlin already smelled this one. How did he do that? We got the call about the nurse's overdose ten minutes ago and Devlin beat us down here. The guy is practically psychic. It's downright creepy.'

'Maybe he was already here,' said Blade. 'From what I can tell lately, this parking lot is where Devlin reports for work every morning. I suspect he also has a lot of *friends* around town who tip him off when something happens. He's been relentless and riding this story for everything it's worth. I heard he wants to be on TV permanently.'

From the other side of the parking lot, as if Devlin had a sixth sense they were talking about him, he ditched the guy in scrubs and made a beeline over to them.

'Detectives, ya got a minute?' asked Devlin with a smarmy smile.

McQ gave Blade a weary look and turned to face the reporter. 'Actually, we don't,' said McQ as he and Blade continued into the building.

'Not a problem,' shouted Devlin as the two cops walked past him. 'I'll be waiting here when you come out.'

'I'm sure you will,' McQ said over his shoulder.

When they approached reception, they were told to go next door to the ER at Oceanside Medical. As they turned to leave, Angela Crawford came walking directly towards them, passing through small groups of hospital personnel all talking in hushed tones.

'I was the one who found her,' Angela said, tears in her eyes. 'She called me a few hours before saying she'd uncovered something peculiar regarding Eliza Stern. I was in the middle of a meeting with the hospital's lawyers so I told her I'd come to see her in a couple of hours. When I arrived at the room with Nurse Castro, Jenny was on the floor with a syringe of Dilaudid in her arm.'

'Was she breathing?' asked Blade.

'No. I checked for a pulse and couldn't find one,' said Angela, visibly shaken. 'I screamed for help and told them to call the emergency team from the hospital next door right away while I started CPR. A few minutes later, Dr. Horowitz relieved me and administered a shot of naloxone, you'd know it as Narcan, an opioid antagonist used for the reversal of an overdose.'

'We're unfortunately all too familiar with Narcan. Did Ms. O'Hearn respond right away?' asked McQ.

'No,' said Angela. 'Dr. Horowitz had to administer a second dose. At first there was no response but finally she coughed and took a breath.'

'Being a nurse in a hospital, would she have had access to these kinds of drugs here?' asked McQ.

'In a normal hospital she would have some access although controlled substances are highly monitored. We're not a traditional hospital, we're a resident care facility,' said Angela. 'We don't have a lot of those types of medications here, but there's probably a small amount of Dilaudid available. It's an opioid used for pain. To answer your question, it *is* possible she got it here, somewhere.'

'And could she have gotten access to it over at the hospital, too?' asked McQ.

'It wouldn't be easy. Those kinds of drugs are all locked up, but I guess it's possible,' said Angela.

'Were you aware of Ms. O'Hearn ever using drugs before?' Blade asked.

'There are hospital privacy laws. I'm not sure I'm at liberty to discuss personal medical records.'

'Dr. Crawford, we need to know how this happened,' said Blade.

Angela let out a sigh. 'I wasn't in this administrative role at the time, but according to the employee files, my predecessor, Dr. Farwell, put Jenny into a drug rehab program several years ago. He might be able to give you more information on that.'

McQ and Blade each made some notes and continued their line of questioning.

'Dr. Crawford, you said that Jenny had called you because she had found some important information,' said McQ. 'Do you know what it was?'

'Not really,' said Angela. 'I was in a meeting with our lawyers. It was something about medication that she said she had to show me. That's why I was going to see her.'

'Here's what puzzles me,' said Blade. 'She knew her boss was coming to talk to her and she had something important to tell you. Why would she have chosen that moment to take such a powerful drug knowing you were on your way?'

'Those are both questions I keep asking myself,' said Angela, shaking her head and getting teary. 'She wouldn't tell me on the phone exactly what she'd found. She said I had to see it. Jenny taking the drugs when she knew I was coming to meet with her struck me as odd, even reckless. If I had known her drug problem had resurfaced, I could have done something to help her. I just didn't know.'

'Drugs are unpredictable,' said McQ to Blade. 'How many overdose calls do we get every week? Too many. I'm sure none of those people thought they would end their party night in a hospital and those are the lucky ones.'

'Let's hope Ms. O'Hearn survives,' said Blade.

44

'I want you to know, detectives, that my daughter wasn't using drugs,' said Jenny's father before anyone spoke in the hospital waiting room. He, like her boyfriend Danny and her mother, was exhausted and looked pale. 'Something about this whole thing is all wrong.'

'I'm very sorry for what happened to your daughter,' said McQ. 'By all accounts, Jenny was well liked, highly regarded by her peers and...'

'I'm telling you, Jenny wasn't using drugs,' interrupted Danny. 'She was a vegan. She was totally into unprocessed food, yoga and meditation. She didn't even drink much.'

McQ felt his ears warm up and start to itch—his internal alert system was starting to ring. 'According to hospital files,' said McQ, 'Jenny *had* a drug problem several years ago. The hospital even put her in a rehab program.'

'Detective, I'll admit my daughter did occasionally use light drugs recreationally when she was in high school and college and while she was seeing that loser, Brian Finn,' said Jenny's father. 'She mainly smoked pot and drank too much. A few years back, after she started working at Oceanside Manor, she went out to a club with some friends. One of them gave her some-thing, a pill. It was stupid and she should have said no, but she took it. The reason the hospital put her into rehab was because the morning after she took the pill the drugs hadn't worn off completely and Jenny was supposed to be at work at 7am. Still feeling the effects of the drug, she went to work anyway because she feared she might get fired if she called in sick. Apparently, she had been warned about taking sick days already. It was a terrible idea for her to show up at the hospital in that condition. From what I understood at the time, she was so out of it that day at work that the only way she was able to keep her job was to agree to go into a drug rehab program. So, she did. But really, Jenny did not have a persistent drug problem. In fact, she never touched anything after that night.'

'Did your daughter have any enemies?' asked McQ.

'She didn't get along with her ex,' Danny said.

'Oh yeah, who's that?' asked McQ, poised to write down a name.

'Brian Finn, a real asshole,' said Danny as if he tasted some-thing terrible in his mouth.

'How do you know that?' asked Blade.

'Once, Jenny and I ran into him in the lobby of a movie theater,' said Danny. 'He asked me what it felt like to be the "transitional boyfriend." You know, like she was only dating me to get over him. Like I said—a real asshole.'

'When did Brian and Jenny break up?' asked Blade.

'About six months ago, shortly before I started going out with her,' said Danny. 'She told me Brian blamed me for their break-up. She said she had tried to end it with him long before I came along but he wouldn't accept it. I think she dated other guys towards the tail end of her relationship with him but I never asked. When we met, that was it for both of us. I really love her.'

'Do you know if Brian ever went to the hospital to see Jenny or picked her up from work?' asked McQ.

'I didn't know her when she was seeing him,' said Danny. 'Wait a minute, Jenny told me that last year when she got a promotion, the staff on her floor threw a little party in her honor. They gave her a teddy bear dressed in a nurses' uniform. She still keeps it on the dresser next to her bed. I think she told me her ex-boyfriend came to that party.'

When the detectives went back over to Oceanside Manor they were swarmed by several dozen reporters and their associated camera crews. The news crews kept coming. The Eliza Stern case and the subsequent overdose of Jenny O'Hearn had driven the reporters into a conspiracy frenzy. McQ and Blade deflected questions while trying to get from their car into the building. Once safely inside, Blade let out a deep breath.

'One of those reporters was from Peru. Peru!' said Blade in astonishment. 'Can you believe that?'

'This story has taken on a life of its own,' said McQ. 'You think Jenny O'Hearn's overdose is connected to Eliza Stern? It seems like too much of a coincidence.'

'I wouldn't rule it out,' said Blade. 'On this case, anything is possible.'

45

When the baby was two weeks old, a staff pediatrician at the hospital examined him and gave the little boy a clean bill of health. With the blessing of child services, Angela and David became temporary foster parents and the baby would be going home with them.

Since the Crawfords had made the decision to take in the baby, the atmosphere around their house had gotten decidedly cheerier. Angela hummed and David whistled as they readied their extra bedroom and turned it into a nursery. The walls were already painted a light blue so all they had to do was move some of the furniture out and install a crib, a changing table, a couple of baby paintings, some curtains, a mobile with tiny red and blue elephants and a small army of stuffed animals. Supplies of diapers, blankets and baby clothes were purchased. They were ready.

The morning the Crawfords were to bring the baby home, Angela grabbed the infant car seat she had waiting in her office and took it up to 3 West to collect him. The nurses and aides had tears in their eyes. They had all enjoyed having the baby on the floor and would miss him. Still, they were all relieved that he was going into a home and not into the cold, callous foster system where so many children slipped through the cracks. Over the past two weeks, the staff had observed Angela on her many frequent visits to see the baby and had all agreed, she would make an excellent mother.

David pulled their blue Mazda sedan around to the rear parking lot of Oceanside Manor and got out while he waited for his wife and new baby to appear. Filled with joyful anticipation while also being a little terrified, he contemplated what he had committed to. It was scary becoming a father for the first time in his fifties—but it was good scary.

Moments later, Angela emerged from the back door and David rushed over to help his wife. Together, they loaded the seat containing the infant into the car, clipped it in with the seat belt and took their new foster son home. David drove very carefully and slowly with his precious cargo on board, much more slowly than usual.

'David,' said Angela, 'you're going twenty miles an hour and the speed limit is forty. At this rate, we're never going to get home.'

'I don't want anything to happen to this little guy,' said David, looking at the baby in his rear-view mirror.

'The line of cars behind you is going to start honking any minute.'

'Let 'em,' said David, smiling.

When they arrived at their house, he parked carefully on their gravel driveway and ran to unlock the front door. When the door was open, he went back to help Angela bring the baby into his new home. Once inside, Angela placed the sleeping child, still in his car seat, down on their kitchen table.

'David, can you feel it?'

'Feel what?'

'The air in here. It's different. There's an electricity flowing all around us. We're a family. At last, we're a real live family. We have to savor this moment. This is our family's very first day. It will never happen again.'

David smiled, put his arms around his wife and gave her a long hug. It was the most peace and unabashed joy he had felt in a long, long time.

'It's a new beginning for us. I feel like I'm going to be able to write again,' said David. 'I think this is what was missing.'

'We need to pick a name for him,' said Angela softly, looking over at her new son. 'Everyone around Oceanside Manor has been calling him Eli, after Eliza. We should pick a name for our son.'

'I've been thinking about that,' said David. 'I think Eli is a great name and honors Eliza, the woman who gave us this amazing gift. Let's keep the name Eli.'

Angela looked at the sleeping baby for a minute and smiled. 'I agree. Eli Crawford it will be.'

'Sounds like the name of a famous writer,' said David, grinning.

'His father is a famous author, you know,' said Angela as she kissed her husband. They spent the rest of the night looking at their new baby and feeling like the luckiest two people on the face of the earth.

46

That first weekend, Angela had spent two whole days with Eli. While she would have preferred to take more time off to spend extra hours with him, given what was still going on at Oceanside Manor, time off was not possible. This first Monday morning, she thought about how lucky David was to be home with their son while she went reluctantly back to work.

When she walked into the kitchen that morning to grab a coffee and a piece of toast, David was already sitting at the table giving Eli a bottle. The gentle loving image of her husband with the baby nearly took her breath away.

It's all been worth it. This baby is going to make us right again.

'You look like you were born to be a father,' said Angela with a wink.

David looked up and smiled back at his wife. 'I can't believe how much I love this little guy after only three days. It's an incredible feeling. Already, I can't remember what it was like before we had him.'

'It's a whole new chapter for us,' said Angela, drinking in the image of her husband and new baby. 'Are you sure you're going to be all right by yourself today?'

'He's just a tiny baby. He'll sleep most of the time. All I have to do is feed him and change him. Piece of cake.'

'Okay, but tiny babies can make a lot of noise and need a lot of attention,' said Angela as she leaned over and kissed her husband on the cheek. She touched the baby's forehead and looked into the infant's eyes. 'His eyes are still blue. You think they'll stay that way?'

'Blue or brown. I don't care.'

'I'll try to be home by 6:30. I'll pick up dinner on my way. Call me if you run into any trouble. Wish me luck, I'm off to the snake pit.'

'Hey, Angie, I was thinking, I might even take a crack again at my writing today, when Eli is sleeping, of course. I got a new story idea last night.'

Angela smiled and gave her husband a thumbs up as she walked out the front door. *When all this crazy stuff at the hospital goes away, my life is going to be perfect.*

Consumed with new baby thoughts during her entire fifteen-minute drive to work, Angela was brought back to harsh reality when she saw the Oceanside Manor entrance sign and the parking lot already filled to capacity with news vans. Hordes of photographers with cameras gathered under the palm trees and across the blacktop making it difficult to navigate to her spot.

She turned off the engine, took a deep breath, grabbed her brown leather tote bag loaded with files and headed into the building. She had a lot going on today, most of it to do with Eliza Stern. Beyond Eliza, Angela still had a facility to run, and for the last two weeks almost everything else had been put on hold. Today, she had committed to complete the annual budgets and take care of a few other critical contracts that had been laid fallow since the day Eliza gave birth.

When she got to her office, Vera dropped a mini hand

grenade on to her schedule. Detectives McQuillan and Blalock had called, they were on their way over. Angela groaned, rolled her eyes and went into her office. Her master plan for getting back to hospital business had just been hijacked. Fifteen minutes later, McQ and Blade were shown into Angela's office.

'Dr. Crawford,' said McQ. 'We've gotten the DNA results back from over 200 people. Most were conclusive, but some we've had to send back for a retest. Every single person was interviewed, which was no easy feat given our time restraints. The governor of Florida, and the mayor and chief of police all want this thing put to bed ASAP.'

'No arguments from me. I couldn't agree more,' said Angela. 'We can't live with this chaos much longer. Not good for the staff and not good for our patients. And don't get me started on the outside vendors. We can't get anyone to make deliveries here anymore. They're all afraid someone's going to ask them for their DNA. I've had to send aides out to pick up supplies. Then there is that awful tragedy with Jenny.'

'I'm not going to sugarcoat this,' said McQ. 'We've eliminated a lot of people as the father of Ms. Stern's baby but we're no closer to identifying who it is. We only know who it isn't. After reviewing documents, security tapes and statements from employees, vendors and relatives, there are only a handful of possible suspects left.'

'Who?' said Angela.

'We can't reveal that at this time,' said Blade, 'but we could use your help on something else. One of your hospital employees did not submit to a DNA test.'

'What? I told everyone, nurses and aides included, that it was mandatory.'

'It wasn't a nurse or an aide,' said Blade.

'Who was it?'

'Dr. Steve Horowitz,' said McQ.

'You're kidding me,' said Angela, picking up her phone.

Ten minutes later, Steve Horowitz was shown into Angela's office. It was evident to McQ from the guilty look on the doctor's face that he had surmised why he had been called in.

'Before you say anything, I have my reasons,' said Horowitz.

'Can't wait to hear them,' said Angela, lips pursed.

Horowitz looked over at the two detectives, sweat beading on his upper lip.

'Well?' said Angela.

'It's personal.'

'In case you haven't noticed,' said Angela, 'we've been the headline on CNN for the past two weeks.'

Horowitz remained silent.

'Will you answer me?' said Angela.

Horowitz took a deep breath. 'I won't get into what it is but suffice it to say, there is a genetic mutation that has run its course through several generations of my family,' said Horowitz. 'I don't know if I have it but given all the issues in this country with health insurance, I don't want my genetic data out there or I might not be able to get health insurance. And my children might not be able to get insured either.'

'No one is going to see it besides the police,' said McQ. 'We're not a genetics company.'

'What planet do you live on?' said an incredulous Horowitz. 'Everyone is buying and selling personal data. If you don't think that someday your genetics will be used against you, guess again.'

'I'm afraid I'll have to insist,' said Angela.

'You can ask to have your DNA removed from our databases once you're cleared,' volunteered Blade. After a more pointed discussion and some thinly veiled threats from Angela, Horowitz dug his heels in and flat out refused to co-operate.

'This isn't helping your case, Steve,' said Angela. 'How do

you think it looks if you don't give the police your DNA after everyone else did?'

'Then everyone else is stupid and doesn't know their rights,' said Horowitz. 'I know my rights and I don't have to do it. Isn't that correct, detectives?'

'You're correct. You're totally within your rights, doctor,' said Blade. 'But it looks *really* bad.'

47

On David's first day alone with the baby, Eli had done little more than eat, burp and sleep. In the morning, David readied the formula, put a load of baby clothes in the washer and straightened up Eli's room until he was satisfied that everything was in its proper place. Eli's diaper had been changed twice and now the infant was sleeping quietly in the downstairs bassinet. David found himself staring at the tiny person in his charge, aware that he felt happier than he had in years. His whole body tingled with a sense of anticipation, similar to the way he felt when he was a grad student and had his whole life and career ahead of him.

With all the house chores completed by eleven, David sat down at his desk and opened his laptop. Before Eli, the mere act of sitting at the desk was only a reminder of his inability to write anything meaningful. Today, he felt different, a million ideas and thoughts coursed through his brain as if five novels were trying to push their way out all at once. He turned on his computer and opened a blank Word document, something he had done a thousand times with little result. He waited for the inspiration to hit him. Within seconds his fingers were gliding over the keyboard and paragraphs appeared on the screen. After an hour, he had written nearly ten pages, something he hadn't been able to accomplish in years. He sighed with relief.

Baby, I'm back.

48

Back at Oceanside PD headquarters, the Eliza Stern police investigative team had been assembled. McQ and Blade stood in the front of the room by a whiteboard, reviewing all of the information collected thus far.

'Where are we on the lab samples?' McQ asked one of the uniformed officers.

'We've ruled out more than 250 possible suspects and still have several more samples at different stages,' said the young officer. 'We're still waiting on the specimen kit from that doctor in Ecuador, Farwell. We've been told that the U.S. consulate in Guayaquil took the sample and it's being shipped as we speak.'

'And how many other samples are still outstanding?' asked McQ.

'If we include Farwell, that leaves four men whose DNA we have not been able to acquire and process. There's also Raymond Barbero, the father of an Oceanside Manor patient. He won't give it up, but he's pretty old,' said the officer. 'There's Peter Parris, the brother of the patient who's in the room next to Eliza Stern. He won't budge. There's also another man named

Peluso who refused to give a sample. He replenishes vending machines and coffee stations around the facility.'

'All four men couldn't be guilty,' said McQ. 'My hunch is that the three not guilty parties may have committed other crimes and don't want to incriminate themselves by putting their DNA into the legal system.'

'Let's look at this logically,' said Blade. 'Barbero is in his eighties and uses a cane. He's not nimble. He's not jumping up on hospital beds for sex. Have you seen him walk? He's very unstable. Just blow on him and he'll fall over.'

'I agree,' said McQ. 'Let's tentatively rule Barbero out for now. That leaves Farwell, Parris and the vending machine guy, Peluso.'

'I checked out Peluso. Looks like he's a family man, has a bunch of kids. Because of his job, he uses a lot of supplies,' said one of the younger female officers. 'With all that stuff, it would have been hard for him to disappear on Eliza's floor. They don't have any vending machines on that wing. The nurses would have noticed if Peluso was hanging around with all of his equipment. None of them remember seeing him.'

'Makes sense,' said McQ. 'Let's back burner Peluso, too. That leaves us with the mysterious Dr. Frank Farwell, who none of us have met. Farwell's been out of the country for many months but from a timing perspective, he could be our perp. Remote, but possible.'

'Then there's that oddball Peter Parris,' said Blade, writing his name on the whiteboard. 'Parris said he thought about match-making his brother and Eliza because they were both in comas.' Snickering erupted from the officers and spread across the room. 'Okay, quiet down people. We're still waiting for Farwell's DNA to get here from South America,' Blade continued as she wrote Farwell's name on the board. 'If we wind up ruling him out, the smart money is on Parris. And don't forget, we still haven't cleared the data-averse lothario, Dr. Horowitz.'

'Agreed. Let's move on. What do we know about Brian Finn?' asked McQ.

'As a reminder everyone, that's Jenny O'Hearn's ex-boyfriend,' said Blade. 'According to her current boyfriend, Finn is a bad dude. Did we confirm whether Finn was ever in the hospital during our three-month window?'

'Not yet,' said McQ. 'It's probably time to pay Mr. Finn a visit.' Minutes later the meeting was adjourned, each officer with their own set of tasks to accomplish.

Since they had found Jenny unconscious in the supply room over a week ago, she remained non-responsive and the doctors declined to make any predictions. She still had some brain activity but it was not at the levels the neurologists had hoped for. The big question everyone had was, if Jenny did wake up, would she still function the way she had before? The general consensus was that Jenny O'Hearn's prognosis was not particularly good.

Two hours later, McQ and Blade walked into J & M's Electronics store in Boynton Beach and asked the manager if they could speak to one of his employees, Brian Finn. At first Finn was belligerent, but after a little relentless badgering from the detectives, he opened up about his relationship with Jenny. He was clearly bitter and said he hadn't seen his ex-girlfriend since she dumped him.

'Yeah?' said McQ, looking in his little notebook for effect. 'According to our investigation, you ran into Jenny and her boyfriend, Danny Laffan, at the Cinemark movie theater.'

'Look, Jenny and I went out for a few years and I found out

she was cheating on me with all these different guys,' said Finn. 'I even heard, after the fact, that she was doing it with one of the doctors at the hospital while she was seeing me. Then she dumped me for that loser, Laffan.'

'You still sound angry,' said Blade.

'How would you feel? I'm the one who usually does the dumping, not the other way around. Besides that was ancient history, I'm totally over her,' said Finn. 'Now I'm seeing this other girl from Fort Lauderdale who's way hotter than Jenny.'

'You know Jenny's unconscious in the ICU right now?' said McQ.

'I heard,' said Finn, not very interested. 'Tough break. Maybe if she had stayed with me, this wouldn't have happened.'

After leaving the petulant Brian Finn, Blade and McQ drove back to the police station. 'So, sweet little Jenny O'Hearn ran around with a lot of men and had a drug history,' said Blade. 'Didn't seem like the type. Then, she finally dumped Finn for Danny Laffan, which I totally get because Finn is such a tool. But she also had an affair with Dr. Horowitz.'

'That's a lot of socializing given that she worked all day and went to school at night to get her masters,' said McQ. 'The more I think about Jenny and the overdose, the less it makes sense to me. It doesn't fit her profile. She was too driven.'

'You know how we women are, we're big old multitaskers. Women get things done,' said Blade.

'That's exactly what Marie keeps telling me.'

'We both agree that Finn's a jerk, but my gut tells me he didn't have anything to do with Jenny's overdose or Eliza's baby,' said Blade. 'We've got nothing placing him inside the hospital other than that one time he went to her party. The seven or eight people who were there that night would have noticed if Finn had been MIA for any length of time.'

'Let's see if we can get Finn's DNA, so we can rule him out,' said McQ.

As their car idled at a traffic light, both detective's phones vibrated simultaneously, each getting the same text message from the chief. Jenny O'Hearn had passed away ten minutes earlier.

When McQ arrived at his desk, a green sticky note was on his bulletin board. Frank Farwell's sample kit, was apparently stuck in U.S. Customs and Peter Parris had finally agreed to submit his DNA. McQ felt his ears get warm as he shared the update with his partner.

'Parris is giving it up?' said a surprised Blade. 'Wonder what changed his mind?'

'The note says his father begged him to clear himself, that he didn't want to lose another son. The old man already had one kid permanently in the hospital and didn't want another in jail.'

'If Parris has agreed to give it up, then it may not be him,' said Blade. 'And Frank Farwell is a real long shot. If we rule those two suspects out, we've got nothing.'

49

For three solid weeks, Tommy Devlin had spent most of his waking hours stalking hospital employees and promoting himself as the resident expert to international news syndicates and U.S. cable news networks. Public interest in the Eliza Stern case had continued to grow and *The Oceanside Bulletin* readers were clamoring for more. As each day passed, his editor was adamant that he devote a hundred percent of his time to the Stern investigation and do nothing else. That suited Devlin just fine. Eliza Stern was going to be his magic ticket out of Oceanside and on to the big time.

For the past several weeks, the reporter had been fed a lot of bogus leads—some went to dead ends and some to the ridiculous, like the 'dead baby found inside the wall' story. Thankfully, he had the experience and instinct not to run with loose talk before he checked a story out. Devlin's articles had been on the front page every day since the incident had been made public. His byline had been picked up by hundreds of newspapers around the country. He was starting to make a name for himself and he liked it.

As the leading local investigative journalist for the only Oceanside newspaper, Tommy had been invited to do pundit appearances on CNN, MSNBC, ABC and Fox News within the first ten days of his story breaking. Oceanside, once a relatively sleepy beach tourist town, was now a point of global fascination and Devlin was determined to milk it for all it was worth. Bizarre crimes like this didn't happen every day and might never happen for him again. He intended to use it to catapult himself into the cable news career that he believed was his destiny. He even got a call from the BBC and an Italian news agency asking for comments. If he played his cards right, he figured this coma baby story could make him a household name, just like Anderson Cooper.

After his numerous television appearances, when he walked into the *Bulletin* newsroom, he was razzed by the other reporters for being a 'big TV star.' That was all right by him. Eliza Stern's mystery baby had become his golden goose. A producer at NBC had even suggested they might want him to do a segment every night until the case was resolved. Sweet.

Today a guest news segment, tomorrow my own TV show. Maybe I'll get a Pulitzer Prize for this story? That would be the bomb. Thomas Devlin, Jr., Pulitzer Prize winner. I like the ring of that and I think there's a cash prize too. Nice.

Until he was 'discovered,' he still had his day job at the *Bulletin* and an obligation to grind out a daily story for his paper with very little new information to work with. This is where his creative writing skills came in handy.

Police Investigation Eliminates More Than 200
By Thomas Devlin, Jr.

The all-hands on investigation by the Oceanside Police Department into the rape of Eliza Stern and subsequent birth of a male child has consumed the resources of the Oceanside and Palm Beach County police organizations. DNA samples have been taken and processed from over 200 possible suspects. Because of the large numbers of people to vet, some of the kits were sent to the FBI for processing. Local authorities are working hand in hand with federal law enforcement to find a match.

According to the two lead detectives, Detective John McQuillan and Detective Anita Blalock, both with Oceanside PD, over 200 people have been ruled out but there are still more lab tests to complete. All male personnel have been asked to provide samples for testing. 'It may take some time,' said Detective McQuillan, 'but we will figure out who did this and bring them to justice.'

Dr. Angela Crawford, acting facility administrator at Oceanside Manor, said her entire staff and all records have been made completely available to the police. 'We are fully co-operating with law enforcement and hope to have a swift conclusion. The chaos that has ensued since this terrible incident has disrupted the lives of both staff and patients and their families,' said Dr. Crawford, who has been placed in charge of Oceanside Manor while Dr. Frank Farwell, chief facility administrator, has been on sabbatical in Ecuador. Dr. Farwell is expected to return to Oceanside sooner than originally planned, due to the severity of this situation.

Devlin added a few pictures of the detectives, one of Angela Crawford and a shot of the entrance of Oceanside Manor to his article and got ready to send it on to his editor. It didn't have much meat on it — the cops were playing this case close to the vest and it was all he had. As he pushed send, his phone rang. 'Devlin,' the reporter barked into the phone.

'Mr. Devlin, my name is Andrew Fein, I'm a producer on

Anderson Cooper's show at CNN. We were hoping you might be available to do a remote segment with Anderson from our Palm Beach studios tonight. Is that a possibility?'

Tommy Devlin smiled and looked up to the heavens. Eliza Stern and her baby were going to make him a star.

50

After Eli's mid-morning feeding, David put him in his crib and turned on the colorful musical mobile. The baby's bright eyes followed the swirling characters as they went around and around while 'Send in the Clowns' played softly.

'You like that song, don't you?' said a smiling David. 'You've got good taste, kid. Only the best for you.' Once he was sure Eli was settled, David straightened up the nursery and sat in a chair next to the crib and opened his laptop. The day before he had written ten glorious pages and he felt like today, he could do twice that much. He picked up where he had left off and was soon deep in the writing zone. He had finished about 2,000 words when he heard the chime of the front doorbell.

He opened the door. A short stocky woman of about forty dressed in black stood in front of him carrying an overstuffed tote bag and an umbrella. 'Mr. Crawford?' she said.

David nodded.

'I'm Ms. Esposito,' she said as she handed him her card. 'I work as a field agent for Palm Beach child services. My job is to check in on our foster families to see how everything is going and if there is anything we can do to help with the transition. May I come in?'

David stepped aside to let the lady enter. Once they were seated in the living room, Ms. Esposito pulled out her notebook. 'How would you say things are going, Mr. Crawford?' she said, poised to take notes.

'Very well, actually. He's a lovely little boy. My wife and I are quite taken with him. He only wakes once a night and usually a twenty-minute bottle does the trick and he's out like a light.'

'I'm so glad it has been smooth sailing for you. It's a wonderful thing that you and your wife have done for this little boy, especially after all the horrible publicity. If it weren't for people like you, he'd be in institutional care right now. Not all kids are so lucky.'

'We're glad we were able to do it. Truthfully, we've enjoyed every minute.'

'That's nice to hear. Not all of our foster parents feel that way.'

'He's an amazing baby. Would you like to see him?' said a proud David.

'That's one of the main reasons I'm here.'

David led the social worker up the wooden stairs to Eli's room. The mobile was still spinning slowly and the baby was awake and watching the moving animals dance in a circle. Ms. Esposito took out her phone and began to take pictures of the room, the baby and the crib. 'I need this for his file, to have a record of how he's being cared for. You don't mind, do you?'

'Do whatever you need to do,' said David, shrugging. 'As you can see, we've set up a nice nursery for him and he has everything he needs.'

After the social worker ticked through her litany of personal questions and seemed satisfied, she packed up her things and got ready to leave. 'I'll be back to check in on you and the baby every other week,' said Ms. Esposito.

'Will we set up a regular appointment?'

'No. We prefer to pop in so we get a realistic picture of what the home life is like,' said the social worker. 'We don't want families cleaning up or staging the visit.'

'How long will you continue to *visit* us?'

'Until we feel certain that everything is fine,' said the woman.

'Doesn't everything look fine to you?'

'Yes, Mr. Crawford, it does. Everything looks great. It's just the way we do things,' said the woman. 'We have to protect our smallest clients who can't speak for themselves.'

Later that evening, when Angela arrived home, she dropped her bags on the kitchen counter and headed directly upstairs to Eli's room.

'Don't wake him,' warned David who stopped his wife at the top of the stairs. 'I just got him to sleep.'

'I haven't seen him all day,' said Angela, pouting. 'I won't wake him, I just want to hold him.'

'Angie, if you pick him up, you'll wake him.'

Ignoring her husband, Angela brushed by and entered the baby's room with David right behind her. She leaned over the crib and gently lifted the infant. The baby remained asleep as Angela let out a grateful sigh, feeling the warmth of the child in her arms. Moving very slowly, she sat down in the rocking chair near the crib and gazed down at the tiny miracle.

'You are the most beautiful baby I've ever seen,' she whispered, touching the soft ginger fuzz on his head. 'Isn't he incredible? Can you believe it's only been six days since we've had him? It feels like he's been in our lives forever.'

'I know. I feel the same way,' David whispered, smiling from the doorway.

'Imagine how we're going to feel a year from now. Can you believe it? We finally have our perfect family,' Angela said, looking down at the sleeping child.

51

'You're practically glowing today,' said her therapist to Angela at their weekly session.

'Am I?' said Angela with a 'cat that swallowed the canary' smile on her face.

'I've been following everything that's going on at Oceanside Manor and the terrible Eliza Stern story on the nightly news. Sounds like the police are nowhere,' said Virginia. 'Given the stress you must be dealing with, you're remarkably serene. You look more at peace than I ever remember seeing you and I've been working with you a long time. What's going on?'

'Do I really look peaceful?'

'You're being gamey today, Angela,' said the therapist. 'That's not like you. You're usually so direct.'

'The most wonderful thing has happened,' said Angela, bursting with excitement as she related how she and her husband were fostering Eliza Stern's baby.

When Angela finished, Virginia wore an expression of total surprise. 'I sure didn't see that coming,' said Virginia. 'Do you think that's a good idea? Especially with the ongoing investigation and all that goes with it. How will you have time for a baby? Babies don't feed themselves.'

Angela smiled. 'Everything is all set. David is the primary caregiver and he's loving it. We named the baby Eli, as an homage to Eliza. The little boy has no other relatives. You know David and I always wanted kids but I kept having miscarriages and the *in vitro* didn't work. I thought becoming a mother wasn't on the cards for me. When we realized they were going to send that sweet little boy into the foster system, David and I discussed everything and made our decision. It felt like the right thing to do, like it was meant to be. And now we know it was. Everything is just perfect.'

'You're planning to adopt him, then?'

'Of course. My husband is a new man already,' said Angela. 'You know how we've talked about David having no purpose. Now, he's got his old swagger and that twinkle is in his eyes again. The old David is back. He's the same guy I fell in love with again and he's already proving to be a wonderful father.'

'You always said you'd never adopt. I suggested it to you many times, remember?'

'I never wanted to. I guess we just fell in love with this baby,' said Angela, smiling sheepishly. 'Can't a girl change her mind?'

'And David?'

'He's over the moon right now,' said Angela. 'Eli is just what we needed. David started writing again after not writing anything for years. Just this week he's completed three chapters and is so proud of himself. This baby is a miracle on so many levels.'

'So, it seems,' said Virginia.

52

DAY 25

From the moment she had raced down to 3 West and delivered Eli everything in her world had changed. For nearly four weeks Angela's life was no longer her own. Ocean-side Manor was swarming with cops, technicians, and reporters, day and night. Instead of running an extended-care facility, Angela spent all of her waking hours dealing with hospital lawyers, angry patients' families, police, and unending prying queries from news organizations. In short, she was exhausted. Despite all the chaos, the worst part of her job was her almost daily interactions with the hospital board. Vitriolic Bob Beckmann continued to be impossible to deal with and had Angela permanently in his crosshairs.

When she arrived at her office a little before eight, she heard the phone ringing on her desk as she unlocked her door. She looked at the caller ID and rolled her eyes. Taking in a deep breath, she picked up Bob Beckmann's call.

'Good morning, Bob.'

'There's nothing good about it. I'm calling for an update on this mess.'

'As you know—'

'I want this debacle over,' he shouted. 'Today.'

'You must have me confused with the chief of police,' said Angela, losing her composure. 'I don't get to weigh in on the police investigation timeline. They'll finish when they finish. It's out of my hands.'

'Shut it down,' said the board president as he terminated the call.

Angela put her head in her hands. To distract herself from what had just happened, she picked up her cellphone and scrolled to the pictures of Eli she had taken the night before. Looking at them calmed her and made her smile.

I have a baby now. David is happy and writing again. I'm not going to let that overbearing bully rain on my parade. All of this, has been worth it—even enduring Beckmann.

After a full morning of budget meetings, Angela took a couple of calls from the police before she ducked out at lunchtime to send a registered letter to her attorney. It contained more documentation required for the Crawfords to remain a foster family to Eli. As she walked out of the post office and down the street towards her car, she passed a store that sold baby and kid's clothing. Drawn inside, before she knew it, her cart was filled with baby clothes and toys.

'Wow,' said the young woman at the register, 'you sure got a lot of stuff. Is this for a baby shower or something?'

'It's for my new baby,' said Angela, beaming. 'My husband and I are adopting a little boy. Do you want to see a picture of him?'

The girl nodded and Angela proudly whipped out her phone and showed the cashier.

'He's so cute,' said the girl. 'Look at his little cheeks, and that red hair.'

'He's an amazing child,' said Angela proudly. 'My husband and I are very lucky.'

53

Two weeks later, the police received more disappointing news and results. Frank Farwell's DNA sample kit was still held up at U.S. Customs. No one could give McQ a straight answer on what the problem was and when it would be released.

'This is beyond ridiculous,' said McQ to no one in particular as he slammed the phone into the receiver after an unproductive conversation with a U.S. Customs agent. 'We're not talking about smuggled drugs or the crown jewels here, it's a lousy sample kit.'

Seven of the remaining ten DNA candidates were not a match to Eliza Stern's baby. There were still three men left who refused to provide their DNA.

'You think one of those three could be our father of the year?' asked Blade as she pushed her chair back from her desk. 'If they won't give us their spit, I say we check each of their alibis the old-fashioned way and dig into their personal history. Whoever is responsible for attacking Eliza probably has a history of unsavory behavior. Someone just doesn't start raping unconscious women if they've been leading an otherwise exemplary life. There has got to be some foreshadowing. We find that and we'll find our perp.'

'There's also a chance that our rapist has stayed completely under the radar and isn't on our list at all,' said an aggravated McQ, tossing a file into his drawer. 'What if it was just some random creep who walked into the building and didn't sign in. Most of the people who work at reception are just volunteers, not security professionals. Someone could have wandered in, passed Eliza's room, saw an opportunity and on the spur of the moment decided to whack one off.'

'I suppose that's possible,' said Blade. 'If that's the case, we're screwed. One thing I feel certain of, the perp didn't anticipate leaving behind a DNA trail in the form of a baby.'

'All we can do now is focus on the three remaining men and hope one of them is our father,' said McQ.

'Maybe a little gentle pressure from us would help loosen some tongues.'

'Why, Anita, I think you're itching to play a little old-fashioned game of good cop/bad cop,' said McQ with a wink.

'I'll play if you will.'

'Let's go pay a little visit to Dr. Horowitz,' said McQ. 'Now that I think about it, we never got to congratulate him or Mrs. Horowitz on the birth of their twin boys.'

'No, we didn't,' said Blade with a smile. 'And you know how much I love kids.'

'You love 'em like a rash.'

Twenty minutes later, the detectives pulled up in front of the Horowitz's large white colonial home accented with royal blue shutters. When the doctor opened the door and saw the police, he quickly stepped outside and shut the front door softly behind him.

'What are you doing here?' asked Horowitz, whispering nervously while glancing up at his second-floor windows.

'We had a few loose ends to tie up and we were in the neighborhood,' said Blade, smiling. 'We thought, wouldn't it be nice to drop by and talk to Dr. Horowitz and congratulate him and Mrs. Horowitz on the new babies. Twins, so exciting.'

Horowitz stared at the detectives, uncertain if they were putting him on. 'My wife and the twins are napping.'

'That's a shame,' said McQ. 'We'll have to come back another time.'

'Why are you really here, detectives?'

McQ and Blade told Horowitz that their investigation into the Eliza Stern case was bleeding over into the Jenny O'Hearn overdose.

'Unless we can rule you out by your DNA,' said Blade, 'your relationship with Ms. O'Hearn might leak. If we can eliminate you on Stern, we'd probably be able to keep your name and relationship out of the O'Hearn inquiry. Would be such a shame for Mrs. Horowitz to read about all that business in the *Bulletin*.'

With a sudden change of heart, Dr. Steven Horowitz agreed to submit to a swab the following day.

54

DAY 60

The Crawfords' time with the baby passed quickly. Angela could hardly believe it when David reminded her that Eli had been in their house for more than a month and a half. Despite things being in order at home, the police investigations at the hospital were still ongoing. Between the search for Eliza's rapist and the questions surrounding Jenny's overdose and subsequent death, there had been little time for Angela to focus on anything else. Families and staff now complained about everything and she longed for the day Frank Farwell returned and she could turn over the reins.

That night with David sleeping beside her, Angela tossed and turned. After trying a variety of mind games to trick herself into slumber with no success, she got out of bed and went to Eli's room. A small night-light cast a pale yellow glow onto the walls. She leaned over the crib and watched the child breathe easily in and out. She knew she might wake him but she couldn't help herself and picked up the sleeping baby gently and sat down on the white rocking chair.

Somehow, holding Eli in her arms made all the negative energy swirling around her disappear. She hugged him tight and looked down at his round pink face and hands while she examined his tiny fingernails.

'You're perfect,' she whispered. 'Any woman would be lucky to be your mother and I'm the one who gets to have you.' The sleeping baby scrunched up his face, but didn't wake as Angela continued her blissful rocking.

She closed her eyes and thought back to her own childhood. Her parents were in their mid-forties when they adopted one-year-old Angela, and her three-year-old brother, Michael. Angela couldn't remember much of anything before she was five and her brother seven. She could visualize herself and Michael playing together in their yard; hide-and-seek, puppet shows, lying in the backyard on the grass looking up at the moving clouds.

'That one looks like a horse,' said Michael, pointing to one of the clouds over their heads.

'Which one?' said Angela, squinting her eyes.

'That one, there.'

'That cloud looks like a cow, not a horse,' said Angela with complete confidence as they both giggled.

The two siblings shared secrets and jokes that only they understood.

As they grew older, Angela made her own friends and was invited to playdates and parties while her older brother stayed more to himself. For most of their early years, Michael looked out for his little sister and protected her. When he was eleven almost twelve, her parents started getting weekly reports from the middle school that their son was causing problems. Once, when Angela's school was closed for a half day of parent–teacher conferences, her mother dragged nine-year-old Angela with her to her brother's middle school. She made Angela sit in the waiting room while she talked to the school psychologist. The door to the office wasn't closed and Angela could hear everything they said, although much of it didn't make sense until years later.

'Mrs. Asmodeo, your son doesn't follow the school rules no matter how often he's redirected,' said the school psychologist. 'Michael picks fights with the other kids and won't listen to his teachers.'

'Maybe the rules don't make sense to him,' her mother had offered. 'My son is highly intelligent. He reads a lot and he's teaching himself how to play the guitar.'

'This isn't a conversation about Michael's intelligence or creativity,' said the psychologist. 'It's about Michael causing a disturbance at school every day. He's been known to use bad language and even shove a few kids from time to time in the halls. The other children keep their distance and some of them are genuinely afraid of him.'

'That's ridiculous,' said Angela's mother. 'My son wouldn't hurt a fly.'

'His isolation can't be good for him and it's probably exacerbating his moods. I've met with your son many times. Occasionally, he says things that don't make sense. Some of his teachers are concerned and have complained about his bursts of anger. The school administration feels we need to get him tested and evaluated.'

'I know my son,' said Angela's mother firmly. 'He's just highly creative and particular. Einstein didn't fit in either and look what he achieved. Ever hear of the theory of relativity?'

The school psychologist let out an exasperated sigh followed by five seconds of silence. 'Mrs. Asmodeo, some parents are very open to doing testing to help figure things out and make their kid's lives better. To deny Michael has a problem doesn't help him, and I believe he needs the support.'

Angela peeked into the psychologist's office and saw her mother fold her arms across her chest.

'Mrs. Asmodeo,' said the psychologist, trying again, 'we'd like to have an evaluation done on your son. The school will cover all the costs. Michael may have some learning disabilities that are frustrating him. If we can get to the bottom of it, we might be able to put some things in place so he can better adjust and cope.'

'I told you, there's nothing wrong with my son,' his mother insisted.

But there was something wrong with him, Mom, thought Angela, *you refused to see it.*

Angela's mother had always dismissed all the complaints, convinced that Michael was just spirited and more likely bored with the tedium of the classroom because of his high intellect.

By the time Michael was in high school, he was on a steady diet of heavy metal music and spent more and more time alone in his room. He barely spoke to Angela or her parents.

Eli sneezed, bringing Angela back to the present. She opened her eyes and looked down at his angelic face. He was still asleep and she closed her own eyes again.

The day she came home from school and found her brother was vividly etched in her brain. It was January 12, it was drizzling outside. She was fourteen and in the eighth grade and had stayed late after school for the science club. Her mother and father were both at work and that afternoon Angela didn't get home until 5:15pm. She opened the front door and the house was eerily quiet. Usually, when she got home she could hear the bass of Michael's music thumping from behind his always closed bedroom door. But this day, the house was silent. Sometimes, Angela had heard her brother talking to someone in his room when she knew no one was there. There was no phone in his room. She never told anyone but it scared her. When she asked him about it, he just laughed and told her it was *his secret* and she needed to get her own secrets.

That January 12th afternoon, Angela called out as she walked through her house. 'Michael, are you here? Mike?' At first, she didn't think anything of it and went into the kitchen to get something to eat. It was Wednesday and her father always picked up Kentucky Fried Chicken on Wednesdays, one of her favorites. Her parents usually got home around 6:30. Feeling a little hungry, she fixed herself a small snack and unpacked her books. By 5:30, it occurred to her that it was odd that Michael wasn't home. He was always in his room listening to music. Once in a while, he'd go outside to sneak a cigarette or something stronger. Angela knew about that, too, but she didn't tell.

You didn't know anything, Mom, because you didn't want to know. You never wanted to know about the bad stuff. I couldn't tell you because you couldn't handle it.

She remembered sitting at the kitchen table that day and starting her homework when something told her to look around the house for her brother. She walked upstairs to Michael's room, placed her hand on the knob and turned it. Slowly, she opened the door and flipped on the light. It was empty. She looked around her brother's room, a place where she had once been welcome. When they were little, they were in and out of each other's rooms constantly. About four years earlier, Michael had suddenly stopped playing with her. His walls were now covered in bizarre and dark posters and his blinds were always drawn. Not finding her brother and it being almost 6pm, Angela checked the other two bedrooms and still could find no sign of him.

She went back downstairs to the living room and that's when she noticed the basement door was slightly ajar. She opened the cellar door and called out. 'Mike, you down there?'

No answer. Something told her to go down anyway. She flipped on the light switch at the top of the stairs. The old wooden steps creaked as she slowly descended. All of her senses were heightened, her hearing and sense of smell on overdrive. The musty smell of mildew increased with each step she took. When she reached the bottom of the steps she turned and looked around the faux-wood-paneled playroom still containing the toy remnants of their childhood. Her brother was swinging by his neck from a pipe on the ceiling.

55

To take his mind off work and introduce some R & R into their lives, Marie dragged McQ on an overnight trip to Universal Studios in Orlando. For almost two months, McQ and Blade had been pulling six-and-seven-day work weeks logging twelve to fifteen hours a day. Marie thought her significant other needed some fun time.

'You have to let off a little steam or you're going to explode,' said Marie, clucking like a mother hen.

'I'm fine,' said McQ.

'We're going,' said a determined Marie when the detective protested. 'You need to think about something besides Eliza Stern for a change.'

'I don't feel like driving all the way to Orlando. Besides, it's going to be too crowded.'

'I'll drive. We're going,' said Marie emphatically. 'You can even have one of those enormous, disgusting, cardio-stopping turkey legs that you like so much and I won't say a thing.'

'Really?'

'Really.'

For two months, McQ and Blade had been squeezed from all

sides. The press had been relentless, practically mocking the investigation and the police who were running it. The hospital's administrators and lawyers along with the Oceanside Manor board were demanding an arrest and showed their dissatisfaction daily. The police brass and politicians including the governor of Florida were also breathing down McQ and Blade's necks and wanting answers—yesterday.

As the last of the lab results came in, all the remaining leads had dried up and there wasn't much left to investigate. They still got the odd tipster call from time to time, which they followed up on, but they never went anywhere. Much to the consternation of the mayor, the Oceanside PD was no closer to an arrest than they were two months earlier when the baby was born. The only thing they knew for sure now was—who *didn't* do it. They had succeeded in ruling out many but identifying the predator had remained elusive.

'Why do you think this crime is getting so much media attention?' McQ wondered out loud to Blade during the first week of the investigation.

'That's easy,' said Blade. 'It's the "ick factor." Some guy getting it on with an unconscious young woman is pretty darn icky. People love that kind of stuff. I hate to say it but *sick* sells.'

The investigation had been going on long enough that public interest had waned. The onsite media had thinned out and only a quarter of the news vehicles and reporters were still hanging around. Tommy Devlin's rising star was not as bright as it had been. For a few weeks, Devlin had been a nightly staple on a variety of cable news shows, but not anymore. When the Eliza Stern story first broke, the public couldn't get enough of it. Like everything else, news runs in cycles and there were always newer, shinier objects for the public to shift their attention to.

As months passed and the horror of what happened to Eliza Stern settled into the public's collective consciousness, people soon turned to a new debacle—a mass shooting in Indiana with thirty-seven fatalities. And with that, the media was off and running after the next salacious story.

As McQ and Marie drove up the Florida Turnpike towards Orlando, Marie reviewed Universal's rides and attractions on the app on her phone. 'I want to go to the new Harry Potter Diagon Alley first. That wasn't open the last time we went. How long has it been since we've been there?'

'We went about six years ago.'

'And the Simpsons, I love that one. Remember? It smells like baby powder.'

Marie reminded him of all the attractions at Universal and McQ started to look forward to a relaxing two days away from Oceanside. Even though thoughts of his case were never fully out of his mind, he pulled into the Universal Cabana Bay Hotel parking lot, and within thirty minutes they were checked in.

They boarded a free shuttle to the park entrance and along with hundreds of others walked en masse towards the gates. At some point, there was a slow-down in the movement of the crowd even though they were nowhere near the entrance.

'What's the hold up?' said an irritated McQ, trying to get a handle on why the foot traffic in front of them had stalled. As they inched closer, they saw what it was—a security checkpoint. Every single person entering the park was being fingerprinted and had to go through a metal detector. They soon learned your fingerprint became your ID to get you in and out of the park.

'Security has gotten incredibly sophisticated,' said McQ to his girlfriend. 'I guess that's what this world has come to. Now families have to be fingerprinted and scanned for metal before they can go on the Spiderman ride. It's sad.'

'If it keeps me safe,' said Marie, 'I'm good with it.'

'The fingerprinting isn't to protect you, Marie. They do it to prevent people from sharing tickets.'

'That's messed up,' said Marie, aghast. 'My privacy is compromised because they're afraid of people sharing tickets? What gives them the right to do that? There should be a law against that.'

'Do you not want to go in?'

'No,' said Marie, narrowing her eyes. 'I'll do it, but it's not right. Who knows what they do with that information.'

After getting their fingerprints scanned and going through the metal detectors, Marie and McQ headed to Diagon Alley but stopped for a turkey leg on the way, just as Marie had promised.

By six o'clock that night, they were both tired, having gotten up and out of Oceanside before seven that morning. They went for an early dinner to one of McQ's favorite places, Margaritaville.

As it always was, the place was Jimmy Buffett lively and even had a giant margarita volcano that erupted every ten or fifteen minutes in the middle of the dining room. Looking over the menu, McQ tested Marie to see if she would honor her commitment on no food restrictions or associated comments.

'I think I'll start with some of those volcano nachos,' said McQ, waiting for a reaction. Marie didn't flinch. 'Then I'll probably get the NY Sirloin with mashed potatoes and cheese.' Marie did not look up from her menu and kept reading.

'This isn't fun,' said McQ, pouting.

'What?'

'I was going to order nachos and steak and you didn't say a single word.'

'I promised you I wouldn't bug you.'

'You didn't say anything when I ate that entire turkey leg this morning.'

'Now, you want me to say something?'

'At least before, I knew you cared.'

Marie started to laugh. 'You're unbelievable. If you eat nachos and a sirloin steak with potatoes and cheese, you're going to keel over and die and I'll have to take you home in a box.'

McQ grinned and reached for her hand. As he looked lovingly into Marie's eyes he jerked his head back. 'Wait a second,' he said. 'Why didn't I think of that before?'

'Think of what?'

'There are a bunch of commercial organizations collecting fingerprint data beyond just law enforcement. Universal does it and so does Disney. I completely forgot about that. Stadiums, car rentals and even airlines are using biometric technology. All sorts of establishments that cater to large groups of people and crowd control are experimenting with this stuff.'

'That's terrible. Where are all of the privacy laws to protect us?'

'Don't you see, Marie? Maybe the man who assaulted Eliza Stern or attacked Jenny O'Hearn didn't have a criminal record,' said McQ. 'That might be why the unidentified set of prints we collected in Eliza's room didn't have a match from police or FBI databases. But maybe this joker enjoys theme parks or major league baseball or rented a car once or twice.'

'You're so smart.'

'I'm not that smart or I would have thought of this a while ago.'

'But, when we gave our fingerprints here at Universal, the guy at the booth said they dispose of all the records and prints once your ticket is no longer valid,' said Marie.

An incredulous McQ looked at his girlfriend. 'And you believed him because?' Marie was silent. 'Of course, that's what they tell you, Marie. Data is valuable. That's the currency everyone trades in now. I don't care what they told us, I promise you, nobody's throwing that data away. That's pure gold. Now

I'm thinking, maybe we can tap into it and match those unidentified prints we found in Eliza Stern's room.'

He pulled out his phone and did a few Google searches. 'There are several players in the Bio Metrics space but the big one is *Know U*. Tomorrow, I'm going to see if we can get into their database.'

The next day, the Oceanside police chief reached out to Mayor Tim Davidson, who in turn contacted the governor of Florida. Calls were placed to Universal Studios, Disney and a few other organizations that recorded fingerprints. With some gentle prodding from the governor, a few of the companies agreed to allow the police to crossmatch against their database of fingerprints. It was going to take some time because the companies weren't set up for that kind of vetting, but McQ would wait however long it took. If they were able to find a match from Eliza's room or the storage room where Jenny O'Hearn had overdosed, it could blow the whole case wide open.

56

The public's interest in Eliza Stern's baby had indeed peaked and the story was no longer headlining the news. People were still curious about what happened but without being fed continuous tidbits of information, the short attention span of the public had moved on.

Tommy Devlin, who only a few weeks before had been on every network's speed dial hadn't heard from anyone in over ten days. Talk radio hosts had clamored for interviews with him to get the inside track on the baby at Oceanside Manor. He could still taste the cinnamon flavored coffee and blueberry muffins in the CNN green room and now it was all slipping away. The last time he did a segment on CNN, one of the assistant producers casually mentioned he'd be a great fit at the network. The guy said the network brass thought he had a face for TV. Devlin knew he had to get the Stern story back on the front pages of America's newspapers and TV screens or he'd never get his shot. There would never be a story as big as Eliza Stern in Oceanside again, that he was sure of.

As he had every day for the past two months, Tommy positioned himself once again in the Oceanside Manor parking lot under a tree near the entrance, hoping to get a fresh lead. Only a handful of reporters were still camped out there and from what he could tell, they were all on the B team. Most of them were sitting alone in their cars or smoking cigarettes under the shade of a row of palms.

He checked his phone every five minutes to see if there were any new emails or texts from the cable shows. Nothing. He looked up from his phone and saw two women walking up to the brick building. They were the same chatty two who had given him the bogus tip about the baby in the wall. He sprinted over to them.

'Hey, ladies, remember me?' said Devlin, smiling.

'Yeah,' said the tall one. 'I've seen you on TV a lot. I saw you a few times on CNN and Fox News.'

'Oh yeah?' said Tommy, grinning. 'How do you think I did?'

'You were great,' said the short girl, smiling at him. 'I saw you on Anderson Cooper, too.'

'Anderson's a good guy. He and I, we're pretty tight,' said Tommy. 'We got a lot in common. I'll probably get together with him the next time I go up to New York to do a segment. We'll probably go out for a beer or something.'

'Really?' said both girls, duly impressed.

'So, ladies,' said Tommy, 'I might go back on the news shows soon but only if I dig up something important to tell them. This story has sort of stagnated. It's been two months and nothing new has happened. You hear about anything unusual going on inside?'

The two women looked at each other and wrinkled their noses.

'Well,' said the short one slowly and deliberately. 'I over-heard a couple of people talking in a break room. I had a headache and was lying down behind a partition and they didn't know I was there.'

'Who was talking?'

'They were cops,' said the short girl.

'You told me you didn't see them,' interrupted the tall girl.

'I *didn't* see them but I heard them and they sounded like cops and one of them had a police radio on and it kept going off,' said the short one. 'They were definitely cops.'

'Ladies, ladies...what did the police officers say?'

'They said that they did all these DNA tests and cleared just about every person who came in contact with this place between April and June of last year. They said there were still a few outstanding people who wouldn't give up their DNA and there was one person who they were especially interested in.'

'Really? Did they say who that person was?' asked Tommy, starting to pant.

The short woman looked at her tall friend while the tall one narrowed her eyes and shook her head, signaling they should both keep their mouths shut. The short woman, enjoying the limelight and the attention from the reporter who was a personal pal of Anderson Cooper, ignored her friend and turned back to Devlin.

'You can't tell anyone, but they said they are waiting for a DNA sample from Dr. Frank Farwell, our chief facility administrator,' said the short woman. 'They said the money was on Farwell.'

'You shouldn't have told him that,' said the tall one angrily.

'But hasn't Farwell been out of the country for over a year?' asked Tommy, writing furiously in his notepad. 'Isn't he the one who's been in South America the whole time?'

'Yes,' said the short woman, 'but according to what the doctors determined, Eliza Stern was assaulted between April and June and Dr. Farwell was here for a few days during that time period.'

'That seems like an awfully tiny window to pin all their

hopes on. A few days? After all this time, that's all they got?' asked Tommy.

'There's one more reason,' said the tall girl, now wanting to get in on the action with the reporter.

'What's that?' asked Tommy.

'Eliza Stern's baby, who is now two months old has red hair,' said the tall girl as if she had just shared the secrets of the universe.

'Why does that matter?' asked Tommy.

'You know who else has red hair?'

'Ronald McDonald?' said Devlin, laughing at his own joke.

'Dr. Frank Farwell,' said the tall girl, nodding with a satisfied smile.

Tommy's eyes lit up and he smiled from ear to ear as he jotted the information down.

'Are you going to report that on CNN?' asked the short girl. 'If you do, don't you dare use our names.'

Tommy assured them everything would be kept confidential and the two women turned and walked into the front door of Oceanside Manor. Career building wheels turned inside Devlin's head.

If I take this info to the news shows, they'd have a lead to run with and I'd be asked to comment on it. It's not been verified and it's really only a little gossip from the hospital parking lot, but the information did technically come from the cops. That short girl sounded pretty convinced. Besides, if Farwell didn't do anything, once they get his DNA, he'll be cleared. In the meantime, I'll be back on prime time.

57

McQ and Marie had been invited to Blade and Eve's for a Friday night dinner. McQ and his girlfriend had been looking forward to it all week because Eve, an occupational therapist by trade, was also a phenomenal hostess and cook. Though Eve cooked strictly vegetarian and McQ leaned more towards red meat and fried foods, even he had to admit the dishes Eve served up were nothing short of spectacular.

'I'll tell you what, Evie, if I could make stuff like this,' said McQ, helping himself to more, 'I might give up Chick Fil-A.'

'Yeah, right,' said Marie with a laugh. 'That'll be the day.'

'The dishes Eve made tonight aren't that hard to make,' said Blade.

'Look who's talking,' interrupted Eve, laughing as she pulled her long curly brown hair up into a ponytail. 'When have you ever cooked, hon? That would be—never.'

'I make our coffee in the morning. Besides, you do it so well. My cooking would only be a colossal disappointment for everyone concerned,' said Blade with a grin and a wink at McQ.

Everyone helped clear the table and the group moved into the living room.

'Hear anything more from the guys at the FBI?' Blade asked her partner.

'Oh no,' groaned Marie, 'we're not going to talk about Eliza Stern again?'

'I want to talk about it,' Eve said. 'Anita never tells me anything.'

'You want to change places with me?' said Marie. 'Eliza Stern is all McQ talks about but he doesn't tell me any of the interesting details. Everything's confidential. I have to listen to him rant but I can't know anything juicy. Does that seem fair to you?'

'My wife doesn't tell me anything,' Eve said good-naturedly, looking at Blade and scrunching up her face.

'Here we go,' said Blade, turning to McQ for some support. 'I'll tell you what, we'll talk about the investigation for ten minutes but after that we're done. Nothing we say leaves this room. Okay?'

McQ and Blade gave the two women an overview of the Stern investigation but said nothing terribly confidential. Eve was enthralled, Marie was bored—she'd heard it all before.

'It should be simple to figure out who did it,' Eve said. 'DNA doesn't lie, at least that's what they say on *Law & Order*.'

'That's correct,' said McQ, 'but you've got to have someone to match it to. So far, we've evaluated hundreds of people and not one of them was a match.'

'We had a few holdouts for a while who were at the top of our list,' said Blade. 'One was a doctor at the hospital with privacy issues, another was the brother of a patient. They've since both checked out negative.'

'There's one more DNA result we're waiting for but it's a long shot,' said McQ.

'Who?' chorused Marie and Eve.

'Dr. Frank Farwell. He's the Oceanside Manor administrator

who has been on sabbatical in South America. He left around the time Eliza would have become pregnant.'

'What makes you think it's him?' asked Eve.

'For one thing,' said McQ, 'the timing of his departure could have worked and...'

'It was his hair, or what was left of it that tipped us off,' Blade said, jumping in with a wicked smile. 'Eliza's got light blondish brown hair but the baby's hair is definitely red, just like what's left of Farwell's.'

'We've been waiting for his DNA to come from Ecuador for weeks. It's been held up at U.S. Customs for some unknown reason but,' said Blade with a relieved smile, 'today it cleared and we should have it in a day or two and then it's off to the lab.'

'And what if it's not him? What's next?' asked Eve, leaning forward in her chair.

'Back to the drawing board,' said McQ. 'We'll have to figure out another way to make an ID.'

'What about fingerprints?' asked Eve.

'There were loads of them in Eliza's room and in the supply room where we found Jenny O'Hearn,' said McQ. 'The additional reach that we got from the prints at the theme parks enabled us to identify a few more prints that weren't in the police database. We got matches on a couple of hospital aides, two nurses, and even Drs. Horowitz and Crawford. Guess they'd all been to Orlando at some point. But those people also had a legitimate reason for being in Eliza's room so while it had promise, the whole exercise was a bust. In the end, almost every fingerprint match that was suspect, was later cleared by DNA.'

58

After holding on to his uncorroborated information about Frank Farwell for a couple of days, Devlin sat in his six-year-old blue Honda Civic and called his contact at CNN to share the news. Sure, his first obligation was technically to *The Oceanside Bulletin* but Devlin had long ago decided that his real first responsibility was to himself. Loyalty to the *Bulletin* was not going to get him a TV job. He had an explosive little headline in his sweaty palms and he was taking it on the road straight to the cable news shows.

After he spilled the beans to his contact at CNN, he was put on hold for a couple of minutes. When the guy came back on the phone, he asked if Devlin could get on a plane to New York and be there for the 8pm news hour. That's exactly what Devlin had been hoping to hear. He agreed and dashed back to the *Bulletin* office to talk to his editor. This time, he was going to work it to his advantage, but he had to set it up just right. A year from now, he intended to be working in television in New York, but he had to protect himself in case things didn't work out the way he planned. He had bills to pay and if his plan backfired, he still needed to keep his job at the newspaper.

He told his editor what he had learned and how CNN now wanted him on the air that same night.

'That's pretty explosive stuff you dug up,' said the editor. 'Farwell, the chief administrator of Oceanside Manor? Oh boy, that's a going to go like wildfire. You feel confident about your sources?'

'One hundred percent,' said Tommy, grabbing his coat. 'It came straight from the cops but I can't say that yet. But it was an official source. I'll write the full story for tomorrow morning's paper on the plane and email it to you when I land in New York tonight. This is going to be huge.'

As he promised, when Devlin landed at LaGuardia Airport, he stopped in a lounge, connected to wifi and sent the morning article to his editor.

Explosive New Developments in the Eliza Stern Sexual Assault Case
By Thomas Devlin, Jr.

It's been over two months since the information was first made public regarding Eliza Stern and the birth of her baby while a patient at Oceanside Manor (an Oceanside Medical Center affiliate). Because Ms. Stern is in an unconscious state, it is believed that she had been sexually assaulted. The young woman has been in a coma for nearly twelve years after a terrible car accident on the Florida Turnpike where all members of her family were killed.

On January 13th of this year, Ms. Stern went into spontaneous labor and shortly thereafter a healthy baby boy was delivered. Police were immediately summoned and a massive investigation has been underway to identify who the perpetrator of this assault was. After reviewing hospital records of visitors and employees, hundreds were interrogated and subsequently provided DNA samples to the police.

As of this week, law enforcement had yet to find a match and had only a small handful of people still left to consider. Today, *The Oceanside Bulletin* was told through a confidential source that the police want to question the chief administrator of Oceanside Manor, Dr. Frank Farwell. Dr. Farwell has been on sabbatical in Ecuador since the middle of last year but police have determined that he was still in residence at Oceanside Manor for a few days during the time period that Ms. Stern was most likely assaulted. Over the past two months, the baby boy has developed red hair. Pictures of Dr. Farwell from last year's board of director's dinner show him to also be a redhead. According to geneticists, only about 1-2% of the population has red hair...

When Tommy arrived at the CNN studios, he was warmly greeted by the staff who rushed him into the green room. The hair and makeup people gave him a brush and a dusting and he was escorted onto the set to join the host. The interview went extremely well and Tommy provided enough information and innuendo to tantalize a news hungry audience while staying on the safe side of the law. Truth was, Devlin had no clue if the information was correct. He didn't care. He just wanted to get back on TV—and it worked.

That night, still at the police station, McQ and Blade were at their desks working a few angles when one of the deputy's came in and told them to turn on CNN. When McQ got to the channel the first thing he saw was Tommy Devlin with a self-satisfied look on his face.

'What the hell is that hack saying now?' said McQ. 'We haven't put out anything new in the last week. Why would he be up in New York now?'

McQ and Blade watched the entire interview and McQ felt his blood begin to boil. 'I can't believe that self-promoting jerk just did that. How did he find out about Farwell? That was all confidential. Nothing has been verified. What we saw Devlin just do was total speculation.'

'Unbelievable,' said Blade. 'Only a handful of people knew we were looking at Farwell. I know the three cops who were working on this line of questioning. I can vouch for all of them. None of them would have said a word.'

'Somebody said something,' said McQ. 'Wait until Farwell gets wind of it.'

'He still might be our daddy,' said Blade.

'From the way things are going, half the population of Florida might be the daddy.'

59

'Thanks for squeezing me in, Virginia,' said Angela as she breezed past her therapist and took her usual seat in the black leather chair. 'My life isn't my own these days between the absolute insanity at the hospital and having a new baby in the house. I barely have time to eat.'

'How are you feeling?'

'Mostly good.'

'Mostly?'

'A little overwhelmed,' said Angela. 'I'm trying to run a hospital that's had a continuous police and FBI presence. Everyone on my staff is looking at each other wondering if one of their co-workers is the one who did it. And now, after all the chaos, it looks like the police may have nothing.'

'Nothing?'

'We may never learn who Eli's father is,' said Angela, shaking her head.

'How do you feel about that?'

'Honestly, I don't care anymore,' said Angela. 'In three weeks, Frank Farwell will be back and he can deal with the nightmare that I've been living. Eli's father is of no importance whatsoever to me. What matters now is that he's my son and he's a beautiful, healthy baby who has brought enormous joy into David's and my life.'

'Aren't you concerned about the genetic blueprint that Eli may have inherited? Wasn't that always your issue with adoption? That you didn't know what kind of mental family tree you were going to get?'

Angela took a deep breath and let it out slowly. 'It was because of what happened with my brother that I felt that way. I loved Michael but he put my parents through hell. Eli isn't anything like my brother. I can tell, he has the sweetest, most gentle soul.'

'He's two months old,' said Virginia. 'Hitler was sweet and gentle when he was two months old.'

'You're comparing my baby to Hitler?' said Angela, starting to bristle.

'Of course not. I'm sure Eli is fine,' said Virginia. 'But given the circumstances and knowing that the father likely has a screw loose, don't you want to know what you're dealing with?'

'It doesn't matter to me or to my husband,' said Angela becoming agitated. 'We know Eli is all right.'

'That's quite a turnaround from the woman who for years refused to consider adoption despite the fact that she desperately wanted a baby,' said Virginia. 'Maybe we should explore that.'

'People change their minds all the time. Can we please talk about something else?'

'Absolutely, this is your session. What do you want to talk about?'

'In a few weeks, my old boss will be back and I will happily pass over the tiller of Oceanside Manor to him,' said Angela. 'Now that I have an infant at home, Eli's my priority and I want to create more of a work–life balance.'

'Aren't you and David just fostering?' asked Virginia carefully. 'You're talking like it's a forgone conclusion that Eli will be staying with you. There's a lot of steps that it takes to adopt a baby. You need to prepare yourself that anything can happen.'

Angela glared at her therapist, her brows knitted together, and she suddenly stood up.

'We still have a few more minutes left in our session,' said Virginia.

'I'm not going to sit here and have you fill my life with toxic energy,' said Angela, her voice rising. 'It's like you don't want me to have this baby. Just because you don't have any kids, you don't want anyone else to have them either.'

'I'm sorry. That's not what I—'

Virginia didn't finish her sentence because Angela had already walked out the door.

60

After taking a statement at a gas station on Federal Highway where a woman had pulled a knife on her boyfriend the night before, McQ turned the Camry to drive south along Ocean Highway. The tall palm fronds fluttered from the strong breeze as streams of excited tourists carried beach chairs and lunches for their much-anticipated day at the shore. The visitors were all in Oceanside for a holiday, oblivious to any crime that might be happening. That was the way it was supposed to be—a sun-drenched paradise, where you left your cares behind. It was McQ and Blade's job to keep Oceanside safe so the tourists continued to come and spend their money. Happy and safe kept the economy going, the restaurants full, and the boutiques selling bathing suits and beach bags.

The detectives drove through some of the neighborhoods on the barrier island by the beach. Everything was pristine and manicured and if it wasn't, it was being torn down to build something grander in the high-priced neighborhood. House prices ranged from as much as thirty million to the smallest of homes priced at a cool one million. Any way you sliced it, if you wanted to own real estate by the shore in Oceanside, you had better have a few dollars put away.

'You gotta admit, Anita, this is one beautiful place,' said McQ, looking out his window, admiring the ocean. 'It's lunchtime. How about we do a stop at Chick-fil-A?'

Twenty minutes later, after devouring his bacon chicken sandwich and a sweet tea in the car, McQ smiled. 'That was all I needed. I think better when I've had something to eat. You don't want anything?'

'I don't put poison in my body,' said Blade.

'It didn't taste like poison to me,' said McQ, wiping his mouth and starting the car. 'You don't know what you're missing.' They rode in silence for a minute listening to some of the calls coming in over the radio.

'You're awfully quiet today, Anita,' said McQ. 'Still glad you took my call when I asked you to come down here for the open detective job?'

'I'm feeling frustrated. I wish we could get some closure on the Stern case. It's driving me crazy that we're nowhere.'

'Let's try thinking about it from a completely different angle,' said McQ as he drove. 'We got the DNA on everyone who was in the building but no matches.'

'Right.'

'We matched all the fingerprints we found with hospital personnel with the exception of two full and one partial.'

'Correct.'

'We found out two of those prints were from the plant guy that we got off the database at the theme park but he had already been exonerated by his DNA sample, so it was a wash. Every lead we've chased down has gone nowhere. We can't catch a break on this one.'

'There's got to be another way to skin this,' said Blade.

They drove down the beach road silently, each in their own

thoughts.

'Wait a second,' said Blade. 'Obviously, we're missing some-one. Somebody didn't make it onto our master list. If they weren't on the master list, we wouldn't have checked their DNA. I've heard that some police departments have been using alter-native sources. In California, they found this serial killer because the guy's cousin wanted to know where their family roots were from. Why don't we see if we can get a hit from one of those genealogy sites?'

'How does it work?' asked McQ.

'Let's say I'm your sister,' said Blade, 'and you're a serial rapist.'

'Thanks.'

'Unbeknownst to you, I, your sister, decide I want to find out what percentage Norwegian I am.'

'I can tell you right now, you don't look Norwegian,' said McQ, winking.

'Just stay with me,' said Blade, on a roll. 'I want to find out my ancestry and I send my DNA sample into one of those sites. Six weeks later I get a printout that tells me I'm related to Genghis Khan and Napoleon.'

'Okay.'

'And that's it,' said Blade. 'Now, this genealogy company has my DNA. If we take Eliza Stern's baby's DNA and run it through that genealogy company, it won't find the exact match because I, your sister did it and not you, but it will give us a close match and we might be able to identify the real perpetrator.'

'I always thought you were a genius, Anita.'

'It's a gift.'

The next day the two detectives put together a list of the top three genealogy sites and made some phone calls. They would use a process similar to when they used someone's Facebook profile to see who might be in their social network. If the baby's

DNA was a close match to someone who had a brother, father or cousin who worked at the hospital, or even lived in or near Oceanside, they would be able to identify their man.

The first and largest company said their policy was to *not* share their data with anyone, including the police. Blade got the same reaction when she reached out to the second largest genealogy company—another dead-end. On the third call, they got a break. FamilyRoots DNA had worked extensively with the FBI and said they would allow police to look for family matches providing it was for a violent crime like rape or murder. The detectives' luck had changed.

While on the phone with FamilyRoots DNA, McQ threw a ball of paper at his partner and gave Blade a thumbs up. Since the arrest of some high-profile murderers and rapists, police had identified suspects in twenty-six cold cases. Prior to FamilyRoots agreeing to help law enforcement, the only resource was a public database called GEDMatch which wasn't nearly as rich or specific as the private companies. Police could now upload DNA data from a crime scene and search the company's database to find relatives of potential suspects if not the suspect themselves.

'The woman at FamilyRoots said that they got some push-back from privacy advocates who didn't want the police messing with people's private data,' said McQ, 'but they're going to allow it anyway, at least for now.'

'What a crazy world we live in,' said Blade. 'Nobody minds if Facebook or Google use and sell your data for a profit but for police to catch a murderer or rapist, that's where they draw the line?'

'I hear you. It makes no sense,' said McQ. 'We could still get a court order for the other genealogy companies, but let's chase this one down since they are willing to play with us and see what crawls out.'

61

DAY 80

When his plane from Ecuador landed on a Thursday afternoon in Fort Lauderdale, Frank Farwell was fuming. They had CNN in Ecuador and Farwell had seen all the coverage about him. Tommy Devlin had intimated on television and in local papers that the police were seriously looking at Farwell for the rape of Eliza Stern. The development in the story had been picked up by media outlets around the world. Even down in Ecuador, people had heard about the case. When Frank saw his name and picture on the front page of a Spanish language paper he cut his trip short to return to Oceanside and deal with all the insanity.

'To suggest that I had anything to do with it is ridiculous,' he had said to his Florida attorney during a contentious phone call from Ecuador. 'I never touched that girl. I'll sue Devlin, CNN and *The Oceanside Bulletin* for libel and slander. It's a disgrace that they can say something like that and get away with it. The media are a bunch of slimeballs. They'll say anything to sell more ads. They don't know who they are dealing with.'

'Let your DNA clear you first, Frank,' said his attorney, trying to soothe his client. 'You'll be back in four days. My understanding is that your kit is at the lab right now. After you're ruled out, we can go after the press with both barrels.'

Two days later, DNA reports cleared Frank Farwell, but he was still spitting mad and looking for blood. At the Fort Lauderdale airport, Frank picked up his luggage from the baggage carousel at the international terminal and ordered an Uber. It felt good to be back in the United States after being in South America for so long. In the morning, he would go into Oceanside Manor to see what condition things were in. The following Monday he'd be back in his old office to right the ship that had gone severely off course, hit some rocks and was about to sink.

The next morning when he pulled into the familiar Oceanside Manor parking lot, there was only a single news van from a Palm Beach affiliate station parked across the street. When he entered the building, he was greeted with a mixture of surprise and fear by the hospital staff, who were not expecting him. He went straight up to his old office where he found his assistant, Vera, at her desk. It took her a moment to realize it was her old boss standing in front of her. She too, hadn't been expecting him.

'Dr. Farwell,' said Vera, standing up and smoothing her hair. 'I didn't know you were back. Welcome home. I'm sure you've heard, it's been so chaotic since you left.'

'I've heard. I'm not officially starting until Monday. Where's Dr. Crawford?'

'She's in her...I mean, your office,' said the assistant, starting to walk towards the administrator's closed door.

'Sit,' said Farwell, smiling. 'Let me surprise her.'

He walked softly over to the door and gently pushed it open. Angela looked up from her desk.

'You're back,' she said. 'I didn't think you'd be here for a few more weeks.'

'I didn't have much choice. After Devlin plastered my name

all over the news, I had to get back here and contain things,' said Farwell. 'Enjoy your time running the place?'

'Shut up, Frank. You know it's been hell.'

'Where are we on the whole investigation, anyway?' said Farwell.

'I think the police have run down all their leads and there's nothing new. It's been quiet the last few days.'

'Quiet is good.'

Frank told Angela he intended to start managing Oceanside Manor that Monday and the two of them would work together for the first week as they transitioned the operations back to him. He asked her to arrange a meeting with the detectives on the case for Monday afternoon so he could get up to speed. He'd deal with the board on Tuesday, a little bit at a time.

'I heard,' said Farwell, 'that you and David are taking care of the baby.'

'Yes.'

'You think that's wise given everything that's happened?'

'I don't need a lecture from you, too,' said Angela, the hair on the back of her neck standing up. 'The baby was the innocent in all of this. They were going to send him into foster care. David and I tried for years to have a baby and it never worked for us. It just made sense. The baby has a home and now we have a son.'

'You're planning to keep him?'

'Right now, we're just fostering, but yes, adoption is our plan.'

'Will you be leaving us?' said Farwell, hoping she would.

'I'm going to continue to work and David is going to be at home to take care of Eli.'

'Eli?'

'He's named after Eliza.'

Farwell nodded. 'C'mon, walk me around the building, so I can get a look at the state of things,' said Frank.

Nurses, doctors and aides waved to him as he and Angela passed and welcomed their old boss home. It felt good being back on his home turf. After he finished his walk-through, he got in his car and drove directly to *The Oceanside Bulletin* and asked to speak to the editor in chief. A few minutes later, an assistant walked him back to the editor's office.

'What can I do for you, Dr. Farwell?' said the suspicious editor. 'You want to make a statement on the Stern case?'

'I've got a bone to pick with you. A bone named Devlin,' said Farwell. 'And, it's going to cost you some cash. A lot of cash.'

62

The Oceanside PD was humming on a Monday morning. Though it was the shoulder vacation season, there were a few massive festivals going on as well as an international tennis tournament. Hotels were at capacity and word around town was that condo rentals were booked solid. You couldn't get near a restaurant without a reservation and even the hot dog stands had a fifteen-minute wait. The influx of people kept the police extremely busy; more car accidents, brawls, thefts, mayhem and even—more murder.

McQ and Blalock were at their desks reviewing new data on several of their open cases when a FedEx envelope was placed in McQuillan's in-box.

'It has to be the results on that DNA sample we sent to FamilyRoots,' said McQ, grabbing the envelope, ripping it open and scanning the documents. 'Would you look at this!'

'Would I look at what?' asked Blade, not taking her eyes off the paper she was reading.

McQ leaned over, tapped his partner's shoulders with the envelope and placed the document in her hand.

She quickly scanned the page. 'In a million years, I never

would have guessed that,' said Blade making a clicking sound with her tongue. 'Not what I expected at all. Looks like we've been barking up the completely wrong tree, partner. But how the hell...'

'I'm still not clear on how it all fits together,' said McQ, scratching his head. 'I'm waiting for my brain to kick into gear and come up with an explanation.'

'You think this is right?' said Blade. 'It doesn't make any sense.'

An hour later, McQ and Blade assembled the Eliza Stern police team to update them on the new information they had just received.

'As most of you know, we co-ordinated with the FBI and the Family Roots genealogy company, and have been waiting a long time for the results. It was a long shot but the effort appears to have paid off. Family Roots sent us their results today and I'm happy to announce, we have a match.'

Applause and whistles erupted from the small crowd.

'They found a partial match to a woman named Bette Moreno who lives in New York City,' said McQ. There was a wave of surprised grumbling in the room.

While McQ continued to talk, a few of the police officers in the meeting pulled out their phones and googled Bette Moreno and looked her up on various social media channels. They found her on Facebook: she lived in Forrest Hills in Queens, NY. On further exploration of Moreno's online friends and connections they saw no link to Florida.

Blade placed a call to the NYPD to ask for some help. It reminded her of how she first met John McQuillan. He was working on the Quinn Roberts case in New York and he had called the Atlanta PD to ask for her help with his investigation. The rest was history. The perp in McQ's case was now serving a life sentence in a federal prison and she and McQ had since become partners.

The NYPD was a thousand times the size of the Oceanside PD but cops are cops and when a brother calls for some help with a case, help is given. Blade was quickly connected to a police captain who assigned the task to a couple of patrolmen. Later that same day, the two uniformed NYC police officers took a ride over to see Ms. Bette Moreno. Ms. Moreno was home alone and was rather surprised when the pair of cops showed up at her apartment door.

'Are you here about the guy next door who smacks his girlfriend around?' Ms. Moreno said through the partially open crack in her door, safety chain still on.

'No,' said one of the officers. 'Is there a problem with your neighbor?'

'I thought you were here about them,' she said. 'They make an awful racket. I've called the police a few times when they get really loud but when the cops show up, the girlfriend tells them everything's fine. What are you gonna do?'

'We can't do anything in those situations if people won't press charges,' said one officer. 'We're here because we have a few questions we'd like to ask you about a different matter.'

'About what?'

'Ms. Moreno,' said the other officer, 'we're helping on an out-of-state investigation and oddly, one of the pieces of evidence in that investigation led us to you. We're trying to figure out what the connection is.'

'Am I in trouble?'

'No, I don't think so,' said the first officer. 'Can you tell us what connection you might have with the state of Florida?'

'I like to go there on vacation sometimes, especially in January or February,' she said. 'These last few winters have been awful. It just snowed and snowed. I thought it would never end. I can't take the cold anymore.'

'Yeah, it was really bad last year,' said the first officer. 'When you go to Florida where do you visit?'

'My family went to the Florida Keys two years ago and last year we went to Disney in Orlando for Christmas,' said Bette Moreno. 'They do a really nice holiday show at Disney, you ever been?'

'I took my six-year-old last year,' said the first police officer. 'You go anywhere else in Florida?'

'I have a brother who lives in Oceanside. We try to get down every other year to see him,' she said. 'He's my only sibling.'

The two cops shot a look between them. 'When was the last time you visited your brother?'

'Let's see, that would have been last April on my son's spring break from college,' said Moreno. 'My husband and my son and I all went down for about a week.'

Another look was exchanged between the police officers. 'Ms. Moreno,' said the second police officer, taking out a notebook and pen. 'Can I get your brother's name, please?'

'David Crawford. He's a writer, a novelist. He's won all kinds of literary awards,' she said proudly. 'His wife, Angela, is a doctor. She runs that place where that woman in the coma had the baby. My brother and my sister-in-law are actually taking care of that baby for a while. The story was all over the news. You must have heard about it. Crazy story.'

The two cops nodded.

'Does this have something to do with that?' she asked, realizing they weren't at her door for a social visit. 'What does any of this have to do with me?'

'When you were in Oceanside, did you ever go to the Oceanside Manor building?'

'I've been there once or twice to pick my sister-in-law up, but

I don't remember if we were there on the last visit. I don't think so.' The woman had a puzzled look on her face as she tried to remember. 'Wait, I think there was one day that I was out shopping with my sister-in-law and my son, Mark. He's a junior at NYU. Angela got a call while we were out and said she needed to swing by her office on our way home to pick something up.'

'Did all of you go inside?' asked the first police officer.

'You think I'm going to sit out in a car in that Florida heat? You bet we went inside. Too hot to wait outside in the sun and Angela wasn't sure how long it would take her.'

'Do you remember if you signed in or showed any ID when you entered the hospital?' asked the second policeman.

'I don't remember,' said Bette, wrinkling her forehead. 'I don't think we did because we were with my sister-in-law and she runs the place. I think they just waved at us.'

'How long were you on the premises?'

'It was supposed to be a ten-minute stop but after we arrived,' said Bette, 'Angela got pulled into an emergency meeting for about twenty-five minutes. I used the time to check my messages from work.'

'And your son, was he with you the whole time?'

'We sat together for a few minutes until he said he was hungry and went to the cafeteria. Why are you asking me about my son?'

'How long was your son gone?' asked the police officer.

'I don't know, maybe twenty minutes. Why are you asking about my son?'

'Nothing in particular,' said the second police officer. 'Just gathering the facts.'

'Facts about what?' asked a surprised Mark Moreno who had just walked into the apartment and saw the police standing in his living room.

The officers explained they were doing some routine investigating because there had been a DNA match with Bette Moreno on the Eliza Stern case.

'How could that be?' gasped Bette. 'I don't know much about DNA other than what I see on cop shows but isn't DNA for each person totally unique? How could my DNA be a match?'

The two police officers looked at young Mark Moreno whose face went pale.

'I didn't have anything to do with that baby,' said Mark Moreno, finally understanding what the police officers were implying. 'That's disgusting. Besides, I have a girlfriend. I don't need to tap brain-dead women. I get enough action on my own.'

When the police left the Moreno apartment, they called McQ.

'I think it's time we make a house call,' said McQ to Blade after he hung up the phone. 'I still can't quite figure out exactly how this all comes together. It's like we've got jigsaw puzzle pieces from two different puzzles, you know what I mean?'

'I guess more will be revealed when we start pulling at this ball of yarn,' said Blade as they grabbed their bags and headed to their car.

63

When the NYPD reported back to McQ and Blade about Bette Moreno's connection to Oceanside and the fact that her brother was David Crawford, it opened up a whole new can of worms, including a few they didn't know existed. They now had several new suspects.

'Based on their shared DNA, either David Crawford or his nephew, Mark Moreno, could be the father of Eliza Stern's baby,' said McQ to his partner as they drove in the direction of the Crawford house. 'It's time we pay David Crawford a visit.'

David was home alone with his four-and-a-half-month-old son, putting the final touches on the first draft of his new manuscript. Happily jumping and squealing in his swing, Eli was the picture of a well-cared for baby. The phone rang. It was David's sister in New York and she was hysterical.

'Two cops were just in my apartment asking questions about you and my son and that woman from Angela's hospital who had the baby, the one you and Angela are fostering,' said Bette Moreno in a panic. 'What's going on? They practically accused Mark of raping that woman. My son didn't do anything. You know him, he's a good kid. He's just a college student for God's sake.'

'They think Mark had something to do with Eliza Stern?' said David. 'That's insane. They're grasping at straws because they've got nothing and they're trying to save face. Angela told me they haven't one solid lead and she's furious. Wait until she hears about this ridiculous harassment.'

'Are you positive everything is all right?' asked his frightened sister.

He calmed her down, got her off the phone, and started to call his wife when he was interrupted by the chime of the front doorbell. When McQ and Blade flashed their police IDs, David was caught off guard and let them in to the living room.

'What a coincidence,' said David, taking a defensive pose. 'I was just about to make an official complaint about the police.'

The two detectives explained that they were the team that had been working with his wife on the Stern investigation.

'Why are you bothering my family?' said David, getting angry. 'My sister in New York just called me, freaking out because a couple of NYPD cops had gone to her place and suggested that my twenty-year-old nephew was a suspect. Why are you harassing my family? You scared the shit out of him and my sister. Mark has never even been to Oceanside Manor.'

'Now, that's where you're wrong,' said Blade, looking down at her notes. 'According your sister, she and your nephew stopped by Oceanside Manor with your wife when they were down here during your nephew's spring break last year.'

'I didn't know that,' said a surprised David. 'That proves nothing. Besides, my nephew is a good kid. He wouldn't do something like that. He's an honor student at NYU.'

The baby squealed, interrupting the conversation.

'Cute kid,' said McQ, looking over David's shoulder at the smiling little boy in the swing. Out of habit, the detective quickly scanned every item in the living room. Family photos were scattered about. There was a large recent picture in a silver frame of David, Angela and Eli posing together.

'You didn't answer my question, detective,' said David, getting in McQ's face. 'Why are you bothering my nephew?'

While McQ systematically answered his questions, Blade examined other family photos in the far corner of the room and spotted Angela and David's wedding picture.

'That's a beautiful wedding portrait of you and Dr. Crawford,' said Blade, tilting her head towards the photo so McQ would take notice. Angela was wearing a long white beaded gown and veil. The creamy color of the dress perfectly offset her olive complexion and dark wavy hair. Next to her, a young smiling David, dressed in a black tuxedo, had his arm snugly around his new bride's waist. Time had been kind and neither looked much different from their twenty-year-old wedding picture—except for one thing. David's hair, now prematurely a silver white, used to be red. Blade and McQ noticed the hair color at the exact same moment and shared a subtle look.

'Mr. Crawford, the reason the police went to visit your nephew and why we're here today is because the DNA strand from that little boy there,' McQ said, pointing to the baby, 'had a partial match to your sister. Obviously, she can't be the father of that baby, so that leaves either you or your nephew.'

'Are you crazy?' said David, getting agitated. 'I've already told you, I've never been inside that building. Ask anyone who knows me. I hate hospitals. I haven't gone to a hospital since my father died fifteen years ago. I've never even laid eyes on Eliza Stern. What the hell do you want from me?'

'We want your DNA,' said Blade.

'Do I need a lawyer?' asked David, picking up Eli and holding him close as if to protect the baby from the police.

'Mr. Crawford,' said McQ, rubbing his face. 'If you had

nothing to do with this, give us your DNA and clear your name. It's that easy.'

Eli had a dirty diaper and started fussing. David excused himself for a minute and took the baby upstairs to change him.

'You think he's good for it?' said Blade whispering to her partner.

'Maybe, but I'm not a hundred percent there yet,' said McQ. 'You know my ears get all twitchy when I hear bullshit. They ain't twitching right now. Regardless, I still want his DNA.'

A moment later, David appeared with a clean and happy little ginger-haired boy.

'We'd like to send a technician over here to do a DNA swab,' said McQ.

David didn't respond.

Blade stepped towards him and spoke in a confidential whisper. 'I heard through the grapevine that you and your wife are planning to adopt this little boy,' she said.

'That's correct,' David replied without emotion.

'I don't work for social services but from what I understand, if there's the tiniest cloud of doubt about you because of this case, it could negatively affect the approval of an adoption,' said Blade in a most helpful tone, southern accent kicking in. 'I've been around this kind of thing for a long time and in my experience, if there is even the slightest hint of impropriety, the adoptions get turned down. Now, you wouldn't want to risk losing Eli, would you?'

David's heart melted as he hugged the little boy tighter in his arms. Between a rock and a hard place, he didn't think he should have to supply his DNA to anyone. On the other hand, he knew for sure he wasn't the baby's father and a genetic test would definitely clear him. He couldn't risk losing Eli by being uncooperative. He agreed.

'It's a big waste of time,' said David angrily, 'but if it puts an end to all this craziness, I'll do it. While you're jerking around with me, the real criminal is wandering free, maybe attacking other women.'

McQ made a call and a technician was dispatched to the Crawford residence. Thirty minutes later, they had David Crawford's DNA on route to the lab.

'Thanks for helping us out,' said McQ. 'You did the right thing. If it's like you said, this test will rule you out and we can focus our investigation on other people,' said McQ.

'Like my nephew?' asked David. 'My sister said you took his DNA, too.'

'The kid said he had nothing to hide and willingly gave it to us. We're just covering all our bases,' said McQ.

Outside, as the detectives got in their car, McQ scratched his head and stared off into space.

'Was it me,' he said to his partner, 'or did you notice that little Eli is a carbon copy of David Crawford.'

'They have the exact same face. It's hard not to miss.'

When Angela got home that night and found out the police had asked for her husband and nephew's DNA she was furious.

'Why did they want your DNA?' she demanded. 'Why was I not informed? They're trying anything because they've come up with nothing and now they're harassing me—us. I know what they're doing. They're getting back at me for being in their face every day, just for doing my job.'

'You're being paranoid. Forget about it,' said her husband. 'Everything will be fine. My DNA will clear me. We both know I've never been inside your building.'

64

'How are things going?' asked Angela's therapist. 'You and David adjusting to being parents?'

Angela looked at Virginia and smiled. 'Being a mom is the greatest thing I've ever done,' she said, digging into her bag and pulling out a few photos of Eli and handing them to Virginia.

'He's gorgeous,' said Virginia, examining the pictures. 'You know this is weird, and I've only met your husband once, but Eli kind of looks like him. Does anyone else think that?'

'I don't think so,' said Angela, 'at least no one's said that.'

'Definitely, Eli looks like David. Your husband's a handsome guy so that's not a bad thing,' said Virginia, laughing while handing the photos back to Angela.

'Okay, so tell me what's going on,' said Virginia, getting back to business. 'Have things simmered down at work now that your boss has come back from South America?'

'Yes and no,' said Angela, looking at the chipped red nail polish on her hands. 'I'm back in my old job as assistant admin. A lot of the responsibilities including dealing with the board are off my shoulders, so that's positive.'

'What's the "no" part?'

'The police investigation into Eliza Stern is ongoing and it affects everyone,' said Angela, wringing her hands. 'Staff are unnerved, people look at each other funny in the hallways wondering if the person they are talking to is "the one." Families of patients are suspicious and nervous and the building still has a persistent police presence.'

'How does all that make you feel?'

'Like I want to run away,' said Angela. 'I'd like to pack up the car with David and Eli and just move to California or Arizona and start afresh. I could start practicing medicine again, open one of those little walk-in clinics. I thought hospital administration would give me balance in my life, but it's been the furthest thing from that. It's been awful.'

'Running away doesn't solve anything,' said Virginia. 'Maybe you *should* go back to medicine but you don't need to move across the country to do that. We need good doctors here, too.'

'It feels like South Florida has become too toxic for me,' said Angela, getting upset. 'I don't know what I think anymore. I just want to enjoy my son. There's been all this weird stuff happening.'

'Like what?'

'I can't talk about it right now.'

'That's why we're here. To air things out and shine a light on them.'

'I'm not ready to do that yet.'

65

David prepared a special dinner for him and Angela that night. He bathed and fed Eli early and the baby was playing in his crib. He went downstairs to the kitchen to check on the meal that was simmering on the stove. He looked in each pot and pan and decided the Mexican mole chicken was simmering the way it was supposed to and went back upstairs to Eli's room. The five-month-old was still awake but blinking his eyes, a sure sign he was getting sleepy. David turned on one of the music boxes and soft twinkling sounds gently started to play. The air in the room smelled like baby lotion and David felt a sense of overwhelming joy and gratitude.

At fifty-three, he had never imagined he'd have a baby in his life or that being a parent could have added so much to his entire outlook. A door had been opened to his soul and sunshine was streaming in. The dark cloud that had hung over him for so long was gone and life was full of new and wonderful surprises. In the mornings, he practically jumped out of bed to pick up the baby. He relished the hours walking, feeding and reading to Eli. His relationship with his wife had returned to the way it had been when they first got married. They were playful and silly again and touched each other frequently, something they had rarely done over the past couple of years.

The biggest surprise of all was how parenting Eli had somehow ended his decade-long writer's block. He hadn't anticipated that. Words now poured out of him, almost too fast for his fingers to type and get them all down on the page. Though Eli had only been with them for five months, David had finished his new novel and reconnected with his old agent, Corbin Rotero. Everything was different for the better. David saw Eli's eyes close and tiptoed out of the room. He closed the door halfway and went downstairs to check his cooking dinner.

Ten minutes later, while still in the kitchen, David heard the front door open and close, followed by the familiar sound of Angela's keys being tossed with a thud onto the bookcase in the living room.

'I'm home,' she called from the front of the house.

'In the kitchen.'

A moment later, Angela stood in the kitchen doorway.

'Something smells good,' she said with a raised eyebrow, noticing the table was set with their good dishes and candles were burning. 'What's going on?' she asked with a curious half smile.

'We're having a party,' said David. 'Actually, it's technically a fiesta because I'm serving Mexican food. Olé.'

'What are we celebrating?' asked his wife, curious but puzzled.

David flashed a grin. 'I finished the third draft of my book. It's all done.'

A smile spread across Angela's face as she crossed the room and wrapped her arms around her husband, giving him a big hug and a kiss on his neck.

'I told you that you could do it,' she said, holding him tight. 'I'm so proud of you. No more writer's block.'

'Ever since Eli arrived, the words have been spilling out,' said David. 'It's the weirdest thing.'

'Don't you see?' said Angela. 'He was what was missing in our lives. We weren't a family before he got here. We were just a couple going through the motions. Eli made us whole. He's our miracle baby on so many levels.'

'You're right, he is our miracle. Who would have guessed that such a terrible beginning would bring so much joy?'

Angela smiled. 'Smells good in here. Let me change and look in on the baby before we eat.'

She went up the stairs directly to Eli's room. He was asleep and Angela gazed down at the softly snoring child and adjusted his blanket. She put her hand near his mouth and felt his warm breath with each exhale and thought that her heart would burst.

'You're exactly what I always dreamed of. I love you, my sweet baby,' she whispered as she leaned over and kissed the sleeping child on his head.

66

It had been more than four months since Jenny died and Danny Laffan had not been able to pack up her personal effects that still lay scattered around his apartment. Her notebooks, hairbrush and other items were sprinkled in every room and made him feel like she was still with him. The day before, his mother had been over and begged her son to box up Jenny's things and return them to her family.

'It's not healthy for you to keep all her stuff around. It's time to let Jenny go,' his mother had said. 'You can't have a relationship with a dead girl.'

Danny wasn't sure that it *was* time, but he had promised his worried mother that he would return Jenny's possessions to her parents, so he did. He got a cardboard box and systematically walked around his small apartment putting each of Jenny's belongings into it. Each time he found something he'd stop and stare at it, remembering the exact moment when Jenny was holding it.

He found her Batman Pez dispenser on a shelf, and remembered the day Jenny bought it and proudly offered him a piece of candy.

'You're the only adult I know who has one of those,' Danny had said, teasing her.

'When I was a little girl, I desperately wanted a Pez,' Jenny had replied. 'All the other kids at school had them and I asked my mother if I could get one, too. It was the cool thing to have in the fourth grade.'

'I had one.'

'Exactly my point. I begged my mother but for some reason, she wouldn't get me one,' said Jenny. 'I think it permanently scarred me. I promised myself when I grew up and had my own money, I was going to buy a new Pez dispenser every year. I have quite a collection now.'

Tears filled Danny's eyes as he remembered random moments with Jenny. He brushed the droplets away with his fingers and continued with his task. He found a half-eaten bag of skittles, a couple of hair clips and untold numbers of ponytail bands and wondered why there were so many of them. He picked them up and threw away most of the little things. He found a brown leather tote bag, it was the one Jenny used to take everywhere. Inside the satchel, was a small makeup pouch, a copy of a book Jenny had been reading, *34 Days* by Anita Waller, three blue pens, a water bottle, a Spiderman Pez dispenser and a notebook. The bag had been sitting untouched in the corner of his bedroom ever since Jenny died. Until this point, he couldn't bring himself to look in it—too painful.

He put the trash bag down and sat on his couch with the notebook and opened it. Pretty quickly, he realized the contents were not just notetaking from school but it was essentially Jenny's private journal. Shaking, he started to read from the first page which was started nearly a year earlier. Most of the entries were Jenny's simple musings on things in her daily life; what she ate for lunch, how a meeting went, how a patient was doing—

nothing major. Danny raced ahead to the dates that corresponded with the time that he and Jenny first got together.

August—I met this cute guy named Danny at a barbecue this past weekend. He was really nice. We talked the whole time and he asked me for my phone number. I hope he calls.

November—Danny and I went to his cousin's wedding in Miami together. It was the first time I met his whole family. I think everyone liked me, at least they acted like they did. I think I'm falling in love with him. Is that possible after only nine weeks?

Danny read all the pages of short little blurbs Jenny had written about their romance and before long he found himself sobbing. After allowing himself a good cry, he went back to the notebook.

February 15—Found some old strange records having something to do with E. S. Was going through the files and saw that someone had placed orders for E.S. to start getting special vitamins. There was also a change in the food order for her, starting in early May of last year bumping up her daily calorie intake and her nutrients cocktail. I googled the vitamins that were ordered and they're the same ones used in pregnancy, prenatal vitamins. Did someone know she was pregnant? Also, while I was in her room, I found a bottle of Pitocin. At first, I thought that maybe the person who sexually assaulted her was trying to abort the baby to get rid of the DNA evidence after they realized she was pregnant, but now I don't know. The vitamins shoot a hole in that theory.

Danny didn't understand what it all meant but thought Jenny might have been onto something important and he called Detective McQuillan.

67

DAY 153

After Danny Laffan showed McQ and Blade the entries in Jenny's journal, the detectives drove back to police headquarters in silence, each trying to work out the convoluted evidence. McQ made an unexpected left turn and Blade looked at him.

'That's not the way back to the office,' said Blade.

'No, it's not.'

'Where are we going?'

'Something is on the tip of my tongue. I need to think, Anita,' said the older detective. 'It feels like all the pieces of the puzzle are right in front of us but we're not putting them together right.'

'So, where are we going?'

'Taco Bell,' said McQ matter-of-factly. 'You know I think better when I'm eating a taco, it helps my neurons connect.'

McQ ordered the Crunchwrap Supreme with nachos. Blade had water.

'That looks disgusting,' said Blade, shaking her head as she watched her partner gleefully unwrap his meal.

'Have you ever tried a Crunchwrap Supreme?' said McQ after taking a big bite and smiling as he chewed.

'No, and I never will.'

'You don't know what you're missing,' he said, grinning and wiping red sauce from the corner of his mouth. 'Already I feel my brain starting to put the disparate pieces of this case into a better order.'

'Seriously?' said Blade with a raised eyebrow.

'Let's look at this whole thing from a different perspective. The way I see it, we've got conflicting data points,' said McQ. 'Someone changed Eliza Stern's food and vitamin regimen around the same time she got pregnant. That could mean that someone knew she was pregnant and was concerned about the health of the mother and baby so they added extra supplements.'

'Or, on the flip side,' said Blade jumping in, 'the person got Eliza pregnant, didn't want anyone to find out and was planning to abort the baby using Pitocin.'

'Correct,' said McQ, 'and this is where it doesn't add up. The Pitocin points to someone wanting to get rid of the baby but the vitamins indicate someone wanting to protect the baby.'

The two detectives stared out the window into the parking lot as McQ finished his meal. 'What if it isn't one person?' said McQ. 'What if there are two players, each with a different agenda?'

'And they don't know about the other one,' said Blade. 'Two people operating independently with completely distinct but opposing objectives.'

'Maybe a nurse or an aide realized Eliza was pregnant but didn't want to get involved in the drama or lose their job,' said McQ, 'but they still wanted to make sure the baby would be healthy so they surreptitiously changed the food and vitamin orders.'

'What if that person also knew who impregnated Eliza, but had a thing for the father and didn't want to get him in trouble,' said Blade.

'Now you're getting complicated,' said McQ, wrinkling his chin.

'And the baby daddy's plan was to go into Eliza's room, induce labor and abort the baby before anyone found out,' said Blade. 'That person would have to be a trained nurse or doctor.'

'You mean someone like...Steve Horowitz?' asked McQ.

'Horowitz fits the profile,' said Blade. 'All the girls at the hospital had crushes on him and he apparently regularly returned their admiration.'

'Except, Horowitz's DNA clears him,' said McQ. 'He's not our father.'

'Maybe another doctor?'

McQ took the last bite of his Crunchwrap and licked his lips. 'I've got a completely different thought,' he said. 'We screwed up. We missed something, Anita. There's one person's DNA we never checked.'

'Who?'

'Eliza Stern.'

68

An hour later, McQ requested a police technician accompany him to Oceanside Manor to get a DNA sample from Eliza Stern. When they got to the reception desk, McQ asked to see Frank Farwell and was told to go on up to the administrative offices.

Farwell was waiting outside of his office in the hall when the detective and the technician got off the elevator. McQ instructed the technician to sit in the waiting area while he met privately with Farwell.

'Are you here because you have good news for me?' asked Farwell. 'Did you find out who did it?'

'Not yet, but things are moving again,' said McQ. 'I'm here because we'd like to do a DNA swab on your patient, Eliza Stern, and I need your permission.'

'Why do you want her DNA?'

'It should have been checked from the beginning,' said McQ. 'We've taken samples from half the population of Oceanside. Ms. Stern's DNA should have been part of the original mix. It's just routine stuff.'

Farwell shook his head. 'When is this going to end, McQuillan? Hasn't the woman been violated enough? We need closure on this, until that happens, things are never going to go back to normal.'

'Ms. Stern's DNA?'

'Fine. You have my permission.'

Five minutes later, the police technician had the sample and sent it on to the lab.

69

Two weeks had passed and the results of Eliza Stern's DNA test arrived in a large tan envelope and was placed in the in-box that McQ and Blade shared. Both detectives saw it at the same time and reached for it.

'You want to do the honors, Anita?'

'I would love to,' said Blade with a snort as she pulled the oversized envelope from his fingers and quickly sliced it open with a rather large pocket knife.

'You carry a knife, too?' said McQ with a smile. 'A gun isn't enough for you?'

'You can never have too much firepower,' said Blade as she put her knife into her pocket and pulled the lab documents out of the envelope. Carefully she scanned the results on the page.

'Well?' said McQ leaning forward and scratching his ears.

'Would you look at that,' Blade said, eyes still on the report. 'What do you know?'

'I don't know anything,' said an impatient McQ. 'How about letting me in on it?'

Enjoying the drama of the moment, Blade took her time. She sat back in her seat and crossed her arms.

'Much to my surprise,' said Blade, 'it appears Eliza Stern's DNA is *not* a match with that baby.'

'Which means?' said McQ.

'Which means...' said Blade, pausing.

'Eliza Stern is not the mother of the baby,' the two detectives said in unison as they stared at each other.

'My ears are in full throttle right now,' said McQ.

'If Eliza isn't the mother...wait...I don't get it,' said Blade. 'How could the baby not have Eliza's DNA? A team of nurses and doctors saw the baby come out of Eliza's body.'

'The baby came out of Eliza,' said McQ, nodding his head. 'But the bigger question is, how did the baby get into Eliza to begin with?'

'The only DNA we do know that matches the baby is David Crawford and his nephew,' said McQ. 'Let's go see the famous novelist.'

When they walked out of the police station, a clap of thunder sounded and it began to drizzle. As they walked, several raindrops spotted the blacktop in the parking lot. 'Great,' said McQ, looking up at the gray sky, 'it wasn't supposed to rain until later tonight, we're supposed to get a wicked storm.' Speeding across town on the slick wet streets, they eventually pulled up in front of the Crawford's house. When David answered the front door holding six-month old Eli, he was once again surprised to see police officers.

'What do you want?' David asked suspiciously.

'Kid's getting big,' said McQ. 'Anyone ever tell you he looks just like you.'

'No.'

'Can we come in, Mr. Crawford?' said Blade.

'No.'

'We have a few questions we'd like to ask you,' said McQ. 'It would be better to do it inside than out here on the street. Baby might catch a cold.'

'I'm not going to answer any questions,' said David, bristling. 'Unless you're here to arrest me, I don't have to answer anything. Call my lawyer.'

'Mr. Crawford,' said Blade. 'We just got the results of Eliza Stern's DNA test and your tests. Turns out, she's not Eli's mother but it appears that you are indeed his father. You want to explain that to us?'

'I don't know what you're talking about,' said David, starting to close the front door. 'Talk to my attorney.'

McQ stuck his foot in the door. 'We'd like to talk to your wife as well. Is Dr. Crawford at home?'

'She's at work,' said David as he closed the front door and bolted it.

After the detective's car pulled away from the curb, David put Eli in his playpen and immediately called his wife.

'Those two detectives were just here again,' said David frantically. 'They said Eliza Stern's DNA shows she isn't Eli's mother. I don't understand any of this. How could Eliza not be Eli's mother? You delivered the baby. A whole roomful of people saw the birth. The detectives said they wanted to talk to you, too.'

'Did they say anything else?' said Angela, her voice elevating.

David didn't respond, as his brain tried to parse all the information.

'David,' said Angela, 'you need to focus.'

'They said I'm Eli's biological father,' shouted David. 'That's impossible. I've never even seen Eliza Stern. I don't understand any of this. What's happening?'

Angela looked out of her office window and stood up. She

put one hand on her desk to steady herself. Three police squad cars had just pulled into the front parking lot.

'I'll call you back,' she said as she hung up the phone, grabbed her bag and walked out of her office. Once in the hallway, she entered a back stairwell, her entire body shaking. Afraid she might slip, she gripped the railing tightly while sliding her hand down the metal as she walked down. The echo of her heels on the bare cement steps reverberated in the concrete stairwell. When she reached the bottom, she pushed the bar on the heavy metal door and opened it slightly and peered out to the rear parking lot. It had started raining, and there was no one hanging around outside smoking as they often did. Her car was ten seconds away from where she stood. She slipped out the door, briskly walked to her vehicle and got in. Twenty seconds later she was off the hospital grounds and driving down Oceanside's main street towards her house.

70

The rain grew stronger, making visibility difficult. Angela drove as fast as possible, but not enough to draw the attention of a traffic cop. She pulled quickly into her driveway sending the gravel flying in different directions and parked her car in the garage. David, who had been upstairs, came running down when he heard the garage door. When he got to the bottom step, he found Angela standing in the middle of the room staring at a framed photo of Eli that she held in her right hand.

'Angela?'

His wife didn't respond.

He grabbed her arm to get her attention. 'What's going on?' shouted David.

'It's over,' screamed Angela, tears mixed with black mascara running down her cheeks as she pulled away from him. She turned and went to the hall closet next to the front door and pulled a suitcase down from a high shelf. 'I've got to leave right now. The police will be here soon.'

'What are you talking about?' said David. 'What have you done?'

'I did it for us,' she yelled as she ran up the stairs, 'for our baby.'

David followed her up the stairs and grabbed her at the top step. 'What are you talking about?'

'Don't you get it yet?' she said, crying and hyperventilating. 'After the *in vitro* didn't work and I had my hysterectomy, there was no other way for us. Eliza was just lying there with this young, healthy uterus—a lifeless body attached to machines. I gave her a purpose.'

'I don't understand,' said David with a look of total confusion.

'No one was supposed to know,' said Angela, her voice catching on every third word while she stuffed random items of clothing into her bag. 'I got our frozen embryos in a nitrogen canister from when we did the *in vitro* program.'

David stared at his wife in disbelief.

'I monitored Eliza's menstrual cycle and picked the optimal day for conception. I scheduled the staff on skeleton crew that week so there wouldn't be anyone around during the night shift. The one person who was on, I made certain was called off the floor for a few hours. That gave me time to implant *our* embryo into Eliza.'

'Angela, the woman was in a coma. She was defenseless.'

'I didn't hurt her. You've got to believe me. I took every precaution. Eliza's fine and we have Eli. I did it for us, so we could have our own baby.'

'You did this for you,' shouted a horrified David. 'How were you going to deliver the baby before anyone found out? This is insane.'

'I was going to induce labor at night several weeks before the due date and make sure no one was around. After the baby was born, I was going to bring him home and tell people we adopted him.'

David's mouth dropped open.

'But Eliza went into labor early which ruined everything and caught me off guard. That's when everyone realized she was pregnant. Before that day, no one knew.'

'This can't be true,' said David, wringing his hands and running them through his hair. 'What lie were you going to tell me when you walked into our house with a baby?'

'I was going to tell you the truth.'

'Give me a break. You thought I'd be cool with this whole perverted thing?'

'I thought once you knew the baby was actually yours, you'd be happy about it and get used to the idea,' said Angela, pleading. 'Everything was going great until that stupid eager beaver nurse had to play detective,' said Angela. 'I didn't think she was that smart. I had to stop her.'

'Did you do something to Jenny O'Hearn?'

'She found out about the prenatal vitamins I'd been giving to Eliza and discovered the bottle of Pitocin that I accidently left in Eliza's room. She started putting two and two together. I had to protect our baby.'

David's face contorted into a mask of horror.

'We would have lost our son,' said Angela. 'Your son, Eli.'

'This is sick,' shouted David as Angela walked away from him towards the stairs.

'Don't you dare judge me,' said Angela, raising her voice. 'I was the one holding down the job, working twelve hours a day. We were drowning financially while you wallowed in your literary fantasy world.'

'Don't change the subject. I was making progress on my novel.'

'You hadn't written anything in twenty years,' screamed Angela. 'The last book you wrote tanked. We were up to our eyeballs in your gambling debts and half the bookies in South

Florida were after you for money. Everyone thinks because I'm a doctor we were rolling in the dough. Oceanside Manor is a small second-rate facility and I was only an acting director. You know what's happened to the healthcare system in this country. You knew how little money I made, yet you continued to piss it away!'

'Shut up,' David shouted. For a moment there was complete silence. David put a hand on each of Angela's shoulders and looked into her eyes. 'I asked you a question and I want the truth,' he said. 'What did you do to Jenny O'Hearn?'

Angela looked away and chewed on her lip. 'I was in a meeting in my office with the hospital legal people when my phone rang. My assistant was out so I excused myself and answered the call.'

'Cut to the chase, Angela.'

'It was Jenny, she had been hunting around in Eliza's room and had gone through some boxes of records. She said she found some of Eliza's old charts from last year and noticed an odd combination of supplements and vitamins had been added to Eliza's daily cocktail of food and liquids. She said she wanted me to come have a look at something she found.'

'Then, what happened?' said David, stone-faced.

'Of course, I knew what she found. I added prenatal vitamins and additional nutritional supplements to Eliza's daily regimen so that our baby would get everything he needed to grow,' said Angela. 'When Jenny started poking around, I knew it would only be a matter of time before she made the connections, if she hadn't already. She would have figured out that someone was monitoring a pregnancy. She had all the facts, she just hadn't put them together yet. You don't use those vitamins for any other reason besides pregnancy.'

'Did you do something to her?' asked David.

'Why would you say that?' said Angela. 'It was well documented in her employment files that Jenny used to have a substance abuse problem.'

'You expect me to believe that Jenny arbitrarily decided to use drugs again just as she was about to mess up your demented scheme,' said David with a look of disbelief. 'You think I'm that stupid?' He glared at his wife as his mind tried to make sense of the incredible story he had just heard. 'I don't even know you,' he shouted. 'What have you done?'

'It was for us, for Eli,' said Angela, 'our flesh and blood son.'

'You did it for you. Don't drag me into this.'

'Things are so much better for us now. You're writing again and we have Eli. We're finally a family.'

'You're a monster,' screamed David, running his hands through his silvery hair. 'You always wondered if you had inherited the same crazy as your brother and I always assured you that you and he were different. I was wrong. You're just as insane as Michael.'

David turned and walked out of the room into the den, slamming the door behind him, leaving Angela sobbing in the living room. He sat down on the couch and rubbed his temples. His head throbbed as he tried to make sense of everything he had just learned and figure out what to do next. He ran through every possible scenario but none of them ended well.

71

For nearly ten minutes David contemplated his next move, grappling with the realization that the baby he had been taking care of was really his son. *Eli is my real son. I'm his biological father. He's truly mine.*

Deep in thought, he heard the grinding of the garage door motor and jumped up and ran into the living room.

'Angela!' he shouted, looking around.

There was no answer. He ran up the stairs to Eli's room and saw both the baby and the diaper bag were gone. He ran back down the stairs and out into their front yard. He could see the faint glint of Angela's red tail lights in the distance. He got into his car to chase her, but by the time he backed out onto the street, she was out of sight.

Racing back into the house to get his phone, he tried to key his wife's number in. The adrenaline racing through his veins made him type too quickly and he kept dialing the wrong number. *Calm yourself. Take a deep breath. Maybe she just went to the store or the park or for a drive.* Deep down, he knew the truth. She wasn't coming back.

He took a deep breath and slowly punched in Angela's

number. It rang once, twice, three, four, five and six times and went to voicemail. He called again and again. Over and over it sent him to voicemail. He texted her.

Angela, please answer the phone. We need to talk.

He paced while he waited for five minutes with no answer and texted again.

Angie, call me.

Nothing. 'Goddammit, Angela,' said David, shouting as he called again. 'Pick up the goddamned phone.'

Again, it rang six times and went to voicemail. This time David left a message. 'Angela, maybe I'm overreacting and maybe you just took Eli out to the store. But I'm losing it. You laid all that stuff on me and you walked out of the house without saying anything. Please come home, we need to talk. Call me, okay?'

David Crawford repeatedly called and texted his wife until her voicemail was full and would take no additional messages. *Would she do anything to hurt Eli? Would she hurt our baby?* Nearly thirty minutes had passed. It was now dark and stormy and David was in a full panic. Not knowing what else to do, and fearing the worst, he reluctantly called the police.

He was connected right away to Detective McQuillan, who was waiting for sign-off by a judge on a search warrant for the Crawford home. When McQ picked up the call, David could barely get his words out. The detective had to stop him several times and make him repeat what he had just said.

'She said all these crazy things. She said Jenny O'Hearn was getting too close. We had a fight. Angela took the baby and it's raining.'

'Slow down, Mr. Crawford,' said McQ, while kicking Blade in the shin. Blade looked up and McQ mouthed *David Crawford* to his partner and nodded his head towards the exit and waved to her. Without asking questions, Blade obediently followed him out the door as he continued his phone conversation.

'We're on our way,' said McQ in a supportive tone. 'You and your wife had a fight. She probably just needed to let off a little steam. That's what my ex-wife used to do after we'd have an argument. We'll be there in a few minutes.'

'What's going on?' said Blade as she slid into the driver's seat.

'Looks like the hen flew the coop with the chick,' said McQ.

'We've been working together too long,' said Blade, 'I actually understood that.'

Back at the Crawford house, David dialed and redialed his wife. The rain was coming down harder and the wind had picked up. Not knowing what else to do while he waited for the police, he turned on the nightly news to distract himself. The weatherman was predicting heavy thunderstorms for eastern Palm Beach County that night. Oceanside was in the eye of the storm.

David punched Angela's number into the phone for what must have been the fiftieth time. It rang four times and Angela miraculously answered.

'David, I'm going away. I'm leaving with our son.'

'Come home. We need to talk.'

'There's nothing more to say. If I come back, I'm going to jail. You know that's what will happen. I can't do that. All I ever wanted was my own family. I have my son now and I'm not going to give him up.'

'Angela, this is crazy,' pleaded David. 'So, you're going to be a fugitive? Think about what you're saying.'

'I won't give up Eli. I've waited too long and worked too hard to get him. I'll go someplace where no one can find us and we'll start over—just the two of us. Don't look for us, David. I'm begging you. Give us a chance.'

'He's my son, too,' shouted David.

'Not anymore,' said his wife, crying. 'I'll be his mother and father. Eli and I are going far away where no one will ever find us and...'

David heard the earth-shattering sound of metal crashing, then only the blaring of the car alarm and the faint sound of a baby crying.

72

Less than a minute after David's phone call with Angela went dead, McQ and Blade pulled up in front of the Crawford house with their siren blaring. McQ immediately called the Palm Beach County police and they put out an APB on Angela's car and asked for reports of any car accidents in the last thirty minutes. The police figured Angela would have been driving north on the turnpike or I 95 since going south would have put her in the Florida Keys and that would have been a dead-end—she had to be going north. Gauging the time she had left, and the road conditions, the police quickly determined what part of the state Angela was most likely to be in.

'Make sure you let them know,' said McQ to the dispatcher, 'there's a baby in that car.'

Thirty-five minutes later, outside of greater Orlando during a torrential tropical storm, a rescue team found Angela's car wreck. A red pickup truck had T-boned the driver's side of her car after she had gotten off the turnpike to wait out the rain and ran a stop sign. The emergency rescue crew had to use the jaws of life to release her from the mangled metal heap that surrounded her body. When they finally got her out, she was unconscious and had lost a tremendous amount of blood. An EMS team did field triage and rushed Angela to the nearest hospital. Miraculously, Eli, still in his car seat in the back on the passenger side, didn't have a scratch on him. A police officer lifted the baby, intact in his seat, out of what was left of the vehicle and put the child in a squad car and called the station.

Angela was rushed into surgery with significant head and neck trauma, a broken pelvis and a shattered left arm and leg. The left side of her face had been crushed and broken glass caused numerous lacerations to one full side of her body. During the difficult and lengthy surgery, Angela's heart stopped twice but she survived and was moved into the ICU.

73

Tommy Devlin stood in the crowd in the parking lot behind the Oceanside PD looking up at the podium. Pen in hand, he was waiting for the police to begin their press conference wrapping up the Eliza Stern case. Devlin's shining star at CNN had fallen like a brick when the Stern case dragged on with no conclusion. It didn't help that Frank Farwell also threatened to sue the network because of Devlin's appearance reporting inaccurate information about him. Now that there were brand-new developments in the Stern case, national interest was renewed and Devlin hoped the cable news shows would again come a-calling. He missed those blueberry muffins in the CNN green room before his on-air appearances. He still wanted another bite from the cable news pie.

Oceanside was once again swarming with news vans from all the major networks, cable shows, local TV stations and newspapers. Devlin waved to the CNN guys like they were old college buddies and walked over to greet them. 'Hey, nice to see ya,' Devlin said to the CNN crew as he thrust out his hand. 'Can you believe all this stuff going on around here? I'm available if you need a quote or some local insight.'

A group of uniformed police officers in formal dress fanned across the makeshift stage. One man approached the microphone.

'Good Morning,' said Oceanside's chief of police. 'We're here today to report final findings on the Eliza Stern case. It's been a long and arduous investigation and the police officers and detectives who worked the case morning and night have been focused and determined to bring closure for this community. I'd like to invite the two lead detectives on the case, Detective John McQuillan and Detective Anita Blalock up to the microphone to provide you with the details.'

The police chief stepped back from the microphone and an uncomfortable McQ and Blade took center stage. 'Good Morning. Detective Blalock and I have been working on this case from day one,' McQ started. 'As you know, this crime attracted national and even international attention due to the unusual circumstances. Like everyone else, we made some initial assumptions that turned out to be incorrect. Through meticulous police research we used all the modern technology available and we were ultimately able to discover exactly what had happened.'

Tommy Devlin listened to McQ's entire explanation and couldn't get the words down in his notebook fast enough. When Detective McQuillan finished, Devlin looked around at the stunned and mainly silent crowd. Everyone's mouth hung open. Then all hell broke loose and the questions started flying.

'Holy shit,' said Devlin, smiling to his photographer. 'I'll tell ya one thing, this is one whacky hospital. Make sure you get pictures of those detectives and the mayor for the lead story. I'm going to have another front pager!'

74

The night after the police press conference, McQ and Marie drove over to Blade and Eve's condo for dinner to commemorate the end of the six-month long investigation.

'You're awfully quiet,' said Marie as their car turned onto Blade's street.

'I'm tired and glad it's over,' said McQ.

'You're glad? I'm ecstatic. You weren't exactly a peach these last few months.'

'I'll make it up to you.'

'I'm planning on it,' said Marie as she got out of the car. 'Another trip to Universal?'

McQ groaned as they went into Blade's apartment building.

Eve had prepared an incredible banquet for the four of them.

'You've done it again, Evie,' said McQ. 'The soup is delicious.'

'And healthy too,' said Blade, smiling at Eve.

'Don't go ruining it,' said McQ, wrinkling his nose.

'This is the kind of thing you should be eating,' said Marie, pursing her lips and rolling her eyes in lockstep with the two other women.

'It's carrot, ginger and coconut with a vegetable-based broth,' said Eve. 'Very low calorie.'

'Okay, message received. I need to drop ten,' said McQ.

A few minutes later, the foursome cleaned up the dinner dishes and settled down in the living room.

'Now that the case is over, can you explain to us exactly what happened?' asked Eve. 'Anita never tells me anything. I have to learn about everything from the news. I watched your press conference yesterday and you both looked very nice, by the way,' Eve said, squeezing Blade's hand. 'But now I'd like to understand how it all went down.'

'Me too,' said Marie.

McQ looked at Blade who gestured with a wave of her hand and a smile that he could do the honors. He nodded his head and leaned forward.

'Apparently, Dr. Crawford and her husband had been in an *in vitro* fertilization program for several years at Oceanside Medical Center,' said McQ. 'Angela had embryos implanted on five separate occasions but she miscarried all of them and the couple gave up. They still had eleven frozen embryos in storage at the hospital. According to her husband, his wife had hoped that maybe one day, as technology and treatments improved, there still might be a chance. But later, she had to have a hysterectomy, the window closed and that's when she must have come up with her plan.'

Blade jumped in. 'Dr. Crawford realized that at Oceanside Manor, she was surrounded by plenty of people who could easily gestate her baby,' said Blade. 'She chose Eliza Stern because she was young with no friends or relatives and it would be less likely that anyone would notice anything. Being that Dr. Crawford was a trained gynecologist, she was more than familiar with how to transport, handle and administer the delicate embryos and she eventually transferred them into Eliza.'

'Why didn't they just get a surrogate?' asked Marie.

'She and her husband had discussed it, but apparently, Angela maintained for years that she wanted no part of it,' said McQ. 'She was concerned about monitoring the nutrition, drug and alcohol practices of a surrogate, afraid that somehow her baby would be compromised. Also, finding a healthy and co-operative surrogate isn't easy and can be extremely expensive. David Crawford told us they didn't have the money for it. Turns out he frequented the casinos a little too often and owed money to a lot of people, a lot of the wrong people. We found out he had been banned from a number of the casinos in South Florida.'

'The plot thickens' said Marie, eyes wide. 'So, then what happened?'

'Once her boss, Frank Farwell, left for Ecuador and she was running the show, Angela figured that was her window of opportunity and she went for it,' said Blade.

'Wow,' said Eve, letting out a sigh. 'That's so incredibly demented, but at the same time, weirdly brilliant.'

'Once she knew Eliza was pregnant,' Blade continued, 'she adjusted the feeding plan on Eliza's charts to include everything a pregnant woman needed to grow a healthy baby.'

'Wasn't she afraid one of the doctors or nurses would see the girl's stomach getting bigger?' asked Marie.

'One would think so,' said McQ, shaking his head. 'But when we talked to a few other OB-GYNs they said that with minimal calories and because the patient was on her back the baby bump might not be very noticeable.'

Marie and Eve looked at each other in amazement.

'Angela's orders provided the precise number of calories needed to sustain a baby but to minimize the weight gain,' said Blade. 'It must have worked because no alarm bells went off with the staff.'

'She had it all figured out, only she didn't anticipate one thing,' said Blade.

'What was that?' said Eve in a whisper.

'Eliza went into labor early, way ahead of schedule,' said Blade. 'Angela had already hidden a bottle of Pitocin, a synthetic form of oxytocin used to induce labor, in Eliza's room and planned to deliver the baby at an opportune time by using the drug. When Eliza went into labor on her own, it caught Angela completely off guard. She was the only doctor around when the nurses realized Eliza was in labor, they called Angela and she wound up delivering her own baby.'

'Oh my God, she must have been freaking out when she got that phone call,' said Marie, mouth open.

'When the investigation began, everyone in the world assumed the perpetrator was a man,' said McQ. 'Me included.'

'It was a reasonable assumption,' said Blade defensively.

'Hey, everyone thought it was a man,' said McQ. 'We missed that one. Since Eliza Stern had no family, the baby was headed into foster care. That's when Angela stepped forward, like a fairy godmother, pulled a few strings and offered to foster the baby. She also recruited the same young nurse who had been there for the delivery to help her.'

'Jenny O'Hearn,' said Marie while chewing on her thumb. 'The girl who overdosed?'

'Bingo,' said McQ. 'Angela put Jenny in charge of compiling all the research. Everything was going great from Angela's perspective until Jenny stumbled across Eliza Stern's old feeding, medication and exam schedule. While going through the records, Jenny noticed that Eliza started receiving prenatal vitamins around the time we now know Eliza got pregnant.'

'Oh snap!' said Marie.

'We didn't know anything about the vitamins until Jenny's boyfriend turned over her journal,' said McQ. 'That's when the pieces started to come together. As Jenny continued to dig around, she called Angela to tell her what she had discovered. A few hours later, Jenny was found unconscious in a supply room from a drug overdose.'

'Angela Crawford did something to the nurse, too?' asked Eve.

'Based on the last conversation David Crawford had with his wife, he suspected Angela had attacked Jenny,' said McQ. 'It was noted in the hospital records that Jenny had a history with drugs. Angela was one of the few people who had access to that information. It was easy enough to make people believe Jenny had a relapse. We believe Angela gave Jenny an overdose of Dilaudid, an opioid pain medication. That poor girl was just collateral damage in Angela's quest to be a mother.'

It was touch and go for a while and Angela remained in intensive care at the Orlando hospital for a very long time. Almost every part of her body had been injured and she required numerous surgeries. In time, her body started to mend and her broken limbs appeared to be healing to her surgeon's satisfaction though she still had a long way to go. After twelve weeks, her doctors determined she was stable enough to be moved closer to home and signed orders to have her moved back to Oceanside. She was sent by transport to Oceanside Manor where she would receive additional care and be closer to her husband and son.

Six months later, on his last day of work at *The Oceanside Bulletin*, Tommy Devlin strutted into his editor's office with great fanfare and turned in his final column about a student brawl on the south side of town. The older newspaper man shook Tommy's hand and thanked the reporter for all his hard work. Out in the bullpen, expectant staffers gathered around a cake that had been placed on an empty desk.

'Looks like your co-workers are throwing you a little going away party,' said the editor, eyeing the commotion going on outside his door. 'I guess it's not every day one of our own gets the nod from CNN.'

'Cool, right?' said Tommy, grinning proudly. 'Soon, I'll be doing some serious journalism.'

His boss threw him an indignant look.

'I mean, I was doing that here, too,' said Tommy, 'but CNN is international TV, it's a whole different ballgame.'

Tired of the conversation and not entirely sorry to see the career climbing, hard to manage Devlin move on, the editor waved to the waiting crowd outside his door. 'You'd better get to your party,' he said. 'Good luck.'

Tommy gave a wave and turned to leave when his editor asked him one last question.

'By the way, Devlin, where's your new job?'

Tommy spun around with a big smile. 'They haven't told me yet. I guess they're still trying to figure out where to best use my talents. HR asked me if I'd relocate, so I assume I'll be going to either Atlanta—CNN's headquarters or better yet, New York. That would be sweet. Hanging in New York with Anderson Cooper, like old times,' said Devlin. 'He and I were pretty tight. Watch me take a bite out of the Big Apple.'

'They're waiting for you to cut the cake,' said the weary editor. Tommy saluted and walked out of his editor's office for the last time and greeted his co-workers. After a few speeches and more high-fives than he could count—Tommy Devlin left the building.

A month later, he was a week into his new post as a correspondent for CNN. It had come as a shock when he got the call from HR that he was being assigned to the CNN field office in Juneau, Alaska.

'You'll be covering local Alaskan politics, the oil pipeline, and do some nice feel-good stories on whale watching and migrating herds of moose,' said the HR woman over the phone. 'Our viewers just love stories about moose.'

'But I thought I'd be going to Atlanta or New York,' said Tommy.

'The managing directors of the news division felt your skill set and on-camera persona would be best used in Alaska. Better get a warm coat and some mittens.'

75

FOUR YEARS LATER

Holding Eli's hand, David Crawford marched across the parking lot and through the front doors of Oceanside Manor and showed his ID as he signed in at the front desk. He waved to the familiar security guard who waved back as he and Eli passed through the lobby and walked to the elevator. As always, Eli asked if he could push the elevator buttons and fidgeted as they went up. When they got to the third floor, the father and son went to the 3 West wing to Eliza Stern's room.

Once inside the room, David pulled two chairs next to the side of Eliza's bed and father and son each took a seat.

'Why do we always come here, Daddy?' the four-year-old asked his father.

'You ask that every time we come, Eli,' said David gently. 'We come here to visit your mommy.'

'Okay.'

'Remember what I told you? This nice lady right here,' he said, pointing to Eliza, 'is the mommy who carried you in her tummy for so many months so that you could grow big and strong and be born and become my son.'

Eli nodded. After ten minutes of mainly silence, David said it was time to go.

'Say goodbye to Mommy Eliza,' the boy's father said.

'Bye, Mommy Eliza,' said the little redheaded boy who had grown into the spitting image of his father.

David took Eli's hand. They walked into the hallway and went directly into the room across from Eliza's. David pulled two empty chairs next to the bed and the father and son sat down.

'And this is your Mommy Angela,' said David with tears in his eyes, looking at the unconscious woman in the bed as the respirator made another long hissing sound. 'She's the one who created you.'

THE END

ACKNOWLEDGEMENTS

Thank you to my wonderful early readers for their time and insightful feedback. First, Peter Black, Diane McGarvey and Marlene Pedersen who read the earlier more painful, disjointed version and gave much needed constructive feedback. For the second rounds, a big thank you to Jill Chaifetz, Charles "Chuck" Kanganis, Jamie Holt, Lolly Arkin, Virginia Arronson, Regina and Bob Turkington and Lisa Goodman. You can't write in a vacuum and each bit of helpful criticism made the book better. Couldn't do it without you.

I'd also like to thank Sharon Anderson for her help verifying some of the medical information.

Many thanks to my editor at Bloodhound Books, Clare Law, who identified sections, characters and story arcs that needed fleshing out and pointed me in the right direction. You were right! Finally, thank you to the stellar Bloodhound Books team for all their support.

BOOK CLUB QUESTIONS

1. Oceanside, Florida seems like a quintessential vacation town and is practically a character in itself, do you think holiday towns like this one provide a normal environment or is living in one of these places different because of all the tourism?

2. Angela was a highly competent hospital administrator surrounded by men who often tried to cut her down and undermine her. How often do you think that happens to women in positions of power in real life? Do you think she held her own?

3. David and Angela had a complicated relationship. Do you think they really loved each other? Why did Angela allow her husband to stay home and do nothing? Was his inertia partly her fault? Was it her way of controlling him? Can a marriage sustain itself based on memories?

4. Detectives McQuillan and Blalock hit a lot of dead ends during the investigation. How realistic do you think that is — do

police solve crimes by diligent digging or is it through dramatic Ah-Ha moments?

5. The person who got Eliza Stern pregnant had their reasons. How do you feel about what that person did? Were they totally in the wrong? Did that person deserve the ending they got?

6. Reporter Tommy Devlin, supplies some comedic relief in the story. Do you think his invasiveness and self-promoting personality is representative of media today?

7. Sadly, cases of elderly, disabled or incapacitated patients being sexually or physically abused is not a one-time event. Incidents of sexual assault like this have been reported all over the world. Why do you think someone would do something like this and why haven't systems been put in place to prevent this?

8. Do you think David and Eli will be able to move on and lead a normal life after what happened?

Printed in Great Britain
by Amazon

58972590R00187